ISBN: 9781717769404

Cover Photo from Shutter stoc¹

Designed by Victoria Davies

D1605860

First Site is a work of fiction. Names, characters,
places, and incidents are either the product of the
author's imagination or are used fictitiously, and any
resemblance to actual persons, living or dead, business
establishments, events or locales is entirely
coincidental.

FIRST SITE

Rose Fresquez

ACKNOWLEDGEMENTS

I want to express my profound gratitude to each one of the wonderful people who helped me get this book ready.

To Candace Wright, Kathy Miskie, Melissa Rice, and Kari Murphy, for their help in reviewing my book from its early stages and for your prayers. Thanks for cheering me on through the writing process.

To Sara Huffman, for going through the entire manuscript and the advice along the way.

To my Father and Mother in law Philip and Barbara Fresquez for taking the time to watch the kids so that I could have extra time to research and study at the library.

To Deb Hall, for your support and for your tireless work in making my book stronger and presentable.

To Elizabeth Proske, you are God sent. Thank you for re-reading my manuscript with detail and making the suggestions to help me add the finishing touches.

Thank you to the firefighters in our community, who keep us safe. Also, the knowledge I learned from what a firehouse looks like when we took a tour with the boy scouts.

To my four kids, who remind me of God's love. Also, to my wonderful husband, Joel, who is my knight in shining armor. Most of all, to my Lord and Savior, who continues to strengthen me and takes me to greater lengths in every aspect of life.

CHAPTER 1

EZRA BUCHANAN leaned back in his chair at Fort Rock Fire Station #15 and rubbed his eyes. As acting lieutenant of Shift C, it had been his job for the past six weeks to record the crew's accomplished training, and he'd been updating reports from the last six hours of their 24-hour shift. It was a temporary position until Ty Williams, the shift's lieutenant, returned to his duties.

He yawned and glanced at the clock, realizing it was way past lunchtime. The rumbling in his stomach reminded him of the much-needed break he was about to take. He pulled out from his seat to check on how lunch was progressing downstairs. As he entered the kitchen, his nose delighted in the smell of barbecue coming from the Crock-Pot that was being monitored by Jake Larson, another firefighter.

"I was about to send a text that lunch is ready," Jake said to Ezra.

Even though all the guys in Shift C were a tight-knit group, Jake had become Ezra's closest friend. He was temporarily living at Ezra's house ever since his divorce nine months ago. If they weren't working, they were usually meeting up at a sporting event or going for a jog.

The station was staffed twenty-four hours with three rotating shifts, with the paramedics working a twelve-hour shift. There were three refrigerators to accommodate the three shifts. Ezra swung open Shift C's refrigerator and pulled out a can of coke.

"Thank goodness, because I am starving," he said and, then moved to their utility- sized kitchen to take a peek inside the Crock-Pot. "Smells great, by the way."

Jake grabbed his phone from the kitchen counter. "Thanks, man!" he said and started typing on his phone.

Miguel Ramirez, another firefighter in Shift C, walked in the kitchen with a grocery bag in his hand

and a frown on his face. He pulled out several packages of bread from the bag and placed them on the marble kitchen counter. He then pulled out a chocolate bar from the bag and shook his head. "Can you believe, this tiny piece of candy cost me three bucks?" Miguel lifted the candy bar in Jake's face before he ripped it open. "That store will not be getting any more business from me." He shoved the bar in his mouth.

Jake smiled "It's a convenient store, how else are they supposed to make their profit?"

Ezra helped with the drinks while Dalton, the probationary firefighter, pulled out plates from the cabinet.

Within a few minutes, seven out of the eight shift members were seated at the large table in the dining area with barbecue beef sandwiches. The eighth member was their chief, Marvin Speers, who'd been called to another emergency. They laughed and teased each other as they ate.

"Larson, have you heard from Aniya?" Angie, one of the part-time paramedic employee, asked.

Jake's jaw tightened as he moved the fork around his salad."Nothing yet." he said under gritted teeth.

"If it's of any comfort, my first marriage only lasted for six months," Miguel commented and then dabbed a napkin to his lips. "At least you had two years."

"That's why I am going to stay single to avoid all that nonsense," Dalton said with a mouth full of food.

"Jeez, swallow your food before you talk, kid," Julian Curie, the station's captain, shot out curling his lip in disgust, reminding Dalton he was still the new guy, then averted his eyes back to his plate.

Noticing Jakes tension, Ezra decided to shift the conversation. "Captain," he addressed Curie, who sat silently at the opposite side of the table. Curie was in his mid-forties and married with three kids. "Any update on Williams?"

Ty Williams was the lieutenant on leave whom Ezra was filling in for. They had all managed to visit him and his family a few times but not on a regular basis. Curie seemed to see him more often since they were best buddies.

"About that"—Curie paused in between bites—"I've meant to update you. Let's talk before the end of the shift."

They all continued to eat as they spoke over each other until the sound of the alarm caught their attention as dispatch announced;

"Fire at the Fort Rock Mall."

In an instant, the members were on their feet, some were reluctantly setting aside their meal, and a few groans from others, as they rushed from the dining area and stormed into the bay, where they hastily grabbed their gear."

Each firefighter was assigned a specific job, but that job shifted with each rotation. Sometimes Ezra was on the Ladder truck and sometimes at the Engine truck. Sometimes he drove, and sometimes he didn't. Jake did the driving most of the time. And he was Ezra's partner when they entered into the burning building. The schedule had been different since Dalton had to shadow Ezra.

Ezra took the shotgun position next to Jake, in the ladder truck, and Dalton sat in the back. Both the captain and Miguel rode the Engine Truck since both Trucks had been called for the emergency.

They exited, with the button pressed, the siren blaring as the bay door closed behind them. The Engine truck followed Angie and Cole in the ambulance, and the ladder truck came from behind.

The mall was on the east side of town. It was a two-story building, where the residents of Fort Rock shopped.

There were already two other engines from different stations by the time Station 15 pulled in, and they wasted no time in getting to work. Several firefighters had managed to make their way into the two-story building to help the rest of the people exit through the emergency doors and windows, while others started putting out the fire.

There were people from the community, awed by the flames. Several of them were taking pictures and videos on their phones, while the police officers were standing guard. Yellow police tape stretched around the parking lot, holding the crowd back.

Ordered to find a woman who was reportedly still inside, Ezra and Dalton pushed toward the building. Jake and Miguel held the water hoses on the fire, while Curie remained outside to control commands.

"This is so cool!" Dalton's eyes widened in amazement at the sight of the flames. "Let's go! can you—"

Ezra caught him up by the back of his gear. Dalton was still in training, and being his first fire, Ezra could see how his excitement could put him in danger. "You need to follow my lead, kid," Ezra said. "Stay focused." He led the probie to the designated search for their victim.

"I'm ready, LT," Dalton said, although he stopped short at the flames flicking towards their path. Dalton's eyes portrayed terror as he stared at the opposite side of the crumbling building.

"Just follow me," Ezra said.

"Fire Department, anybody here?" Ezra called as they searched in the dark space, only guided by their flashlights.

"Do I hear somebody coughing?" Dalton said. Ezra stilled to listen and heard a faint cough. "Hold on," Ezra said when he spotted a hysterical woman crouched in between shelves. Her foot was stuck under one of the heavy metal shelves.

Ezra placed his hands on the shelf. "Dalton, when I lift, I want you to pull her out."

The probie nodded, and after several grunts from Ezra, he'd managed to move the shelf, and the middle-aged woman was pulled out of the debris.

The building was darkened with a thick cloud of smoke, which made their visibility a challenge. The fire crackled as it devoured the building, chasing them from behind. They were all panting and hoping that their only exit would stay clear.

Relief swept over Ezra when he saw water hosed in their path. They'd finally made it safe until the woman in Ezra's arms coughed and spoke in a frail voice. "My grandson is still in there."

That was all it took for Ezra's adrenaline to spike.

"What's his name? "

"Kai"

"Do you know where he is?" Ezra asked. He needed to know the exact location to start the search; otherwise, at the rate, the fire was consuming the structure, the boy's life was at stake.

After confirmation, of the boy's location, Ezra handed the woman over to Dalton for him to take to the paramedics. Jake and Miguel were spraying and seemed to have their side of the building somewhat under control.

An announcement came through the radio. "All companies, evacuate the building." Ezra knew that there was not enough time for him to make it on the second level and back in time with the child, but he had to try; otherwise, he would never leave with himself if he left the child behind.

"Buchanan!" Jake called out frantically, but Ezra ignored him and kept going in the dark shadows and flames that awaited him on the other side.

***

Ezra skidded and leaped as he dodged the falling debris, his heart pounding a non controlled rhythm. A wall crumbled from behind.

"The explosion blocked my rear exit," Ezra spoke on the radio. "But I'm still searching for the victim on the lower level."

Ezra didn't hear any response; instead, he heard overlapping dispatch voices.

"Anyone here?" he called. "Kai!" Ezra called for the third time, and then he heard something like a child's cough and then saw movement between clothing racks. He smiled triumphantly as he gave an update on the radio. "Found the victim." He pushed the pile of clothing to the side, and there was a frantic child hunched with both hands in his face.

The boy looked pale and weak when Ezra picked him up. "I got you, Kai."

"How are you doing Kai?"

Except for a cough, the boy didn't respond. Ezra guessed him to be about six or seven years old. "I'm going to get you out of here."

"I have the victim," Ezra announced.

"Good, now you need to evacuate the building now," Curie said.

"We're moving toward the west side," Ezra spoke through the radio the moment he saw an exit. Another wall crumbled, creating a curtain of darkness. It was now darker than it'd been earlier.

With the left hand holding Kai, Ezra used his other hand to turn on his light. The boy was not in great shape, smoke and falling debris were reducing any chances of survival for both of them. When the boy gave a choking gasp, and then stuck his tongue out to his dry lips, Ezra was forced to break a rule.

Ezra set Kai aside and took off his mask, sealing it on the boy's face for a few minutes, and then put it back on himself. He took turns with the mask until the crackling sound through the radio came in.

Ezra knew better than anyone that he shouldn't have taken off his mask, because if he were not in good shape, he wouldn't be able to save the boy. He listened to the chatter on the radio and could hear things happening outside.

He gave a status report to everybody on the receiving end of the radio. At Least they'd moved to a safer side of the building, Although not for so long.

"Ezra, it's Curie, do you copy?"

"Yes, Captain."

"We're making arrangements to find a way out for you soon," Curie promised. I will see about getting a team to cut through the wall to create an exit."

Ezra held the child tight. Thankfully he did, because when the wood creaked, the floor collapsed, pushing them to the first floor.

Ezra groaned at the painful landing, but the little guy clung to him as they rolled to avoid being buried under the falling debris. Ezra gathered the boy and placed his coat over him like a mother hen protecting it's young. Ezra granted as he struggled to get up. His pass alarm went off, which was expected since he'd been still for more than eighteen seconds.

"One of my guys is still in the building," Curie announced, while outside just as another explosion hit. Curie's face contorted with worry, brows furrowing, as he watched the raging fire moving toward the west side of the building. The air was dark with smoke and Curie could only hope for his colleague's safety.

Now that Ezra's pass alarm was beeping, God only knew if he was buried under the structure and Curie could only hold to the faith that Ezra was still alive. The smoke was coming up quickly, and Curie knew they didn't have much time to get Ezra out. He paced back and forth, his jaw tightened as he thought of relaxing his shoulders so not to express panic to the rest of his colleagues.

As more fire engines joined the scene, Curie retreated the men from Station 15 back to their trucks. He contacted Ezra one more time as he made his way toward the building. By this time the beeping from Ezra's alarm had stopped— an indication that he was not buried under the structure as he'd assumed. Curie was about to make the command for Ezra's search when Ezra's voice crackled from the radio.

"Found the exit!" Ezra's announcement was greeted with cheers from the crew.

The building continued to crumble as the group waited for their fellow firefighter and friend to emerge. "There he is!" Miguel said, breathing a sigh of relief as he pointed in Ezra's direction.

Ezra held the boy in his arms, and headed for the ambulance, passing him over to the team of paramedics, and watched as they performed CPR on him. He smiled and blew out a deep breath when they found the boy's pulse.

The parking lot was crowded with fire trucks, police cars and media trucks filming the entire event.

Jake trudged in Ezra's direction, taking in a deep sigh of relief when he approached him.

He slapped his shoulder "You okay, man?"

Ezra took off his self-contained breathing helmet and coat and dropped them to the ground. Dripping with sweat, he coughed as he inhaled the outside smoky air. He could feel his heart pounding as if it was about to rip out of his chest.

"I'm fine, Larson. Thanks."

"Man!" Jake shook his head. "I am glad you made it in one piece."

"Me too." Ezra couldn't be more relieved that the boy was going to be okay too.

Curie soon joined the men and handed a water bottle to Ezra, he gulped it down and poured the rest of it over his head.

"Hey," Angie gave Ezra a once over. "That was too close, she said. "I'm glad you're safe." she squeezed his shoulder.

Ezra sighed. "Yeah, me too."

"I need to check you, just to make sure you're okay," Angie said

"I don't need to a check-up." He said dismissively as if his whole body didn't ache. What he needed was a long warm shower.

Almost an hour later, the flames were out. The building had lost the roof and half the structure.

Leaving the other engines to finish with clean-up, Station 15 returned to their house.

***

After a long shower at the station, Ezra moved to one of the two brown leather couches in their designated living room. He needed to rest his head for a moment as he reflected on the near-death experience that had happened only a few hours ago.

He'd had to dodge a few walls and leap before some heavy debris came crashing down on him. Thankfully the boy had been light enough for him to make his leaps. Otherwise, they very well might have been buried under it all.

He closed his eyes to thank God for the safety of all the people who had escaped the building, including all the firefighters who'd responded to that call. He was relieved that no one was hurt. Except for a few people who needed slight medical attention, everyone was alive and well.

A hand tapping on his shoulder jolted him out of his thoughts. "You're sleeping?" Curie said as he sat on the chair across from him.

"Not anymore," Ezra said playfully as he slowly pushed up to sit, "I wasn't sleeping."

"You shouldn't be anyway," Curie teased. "Great job out there, by the way." Curie cleared his throat.

"You broke a rule today, you shouldn't have gone back inside the building, but I will let that go. I know that you're committed not only to the job but all your colleagues. You spend time knowing people on a deeper level, and you're not afraid to dive into risk when needed."

Ezra moved his hand to rub his face. "We worked as a team out there. We all did our best."

Curie cleared his throat. "Now about Williams, he's not coming back," Curie said. "He's recovering well, but he wants to spend time with his family, and is perhaps considering to switch to a different career."

Williams, the former lieutenant in his mid-thirties, had a heart attack and took a leave of absence from the fire department. He was expected to return if he recovered properly, but having come close to losing his life, well, that changed things.

Ezra's eyes flew open in shock. He had known it might take a while for Williams to recover and that he may struggle upon coming back—but the fire department coursed through that man's blood. It was everything to him.

"He's not coming back?" he asked. He looked up to him and all the guys he'd become acquainted with in the department. Losing Williams meant losing part of his family. He would see him, but not as often as he did on the job. Still, Ezra understood. Coming so close to death changed things for a man— or anyone, for that matter.

Curie nodded and added, "Marvin and I feel you're the right man for this position. That is if you wish to take it."

Still digesting the fact that Williams wouldn't be returning, he couldn't even begin to process the job offer. "Looks like I am getting the hang of all the paperwork," Ezra said.

"I know, you will still do your firefighter duties as well."

Ezra nodded, allowing a long silence, before he muttered, "Thanks. I will let you know if I decide to accept that offer." It was a huge responsibility with a lot of paperwork, and Ezra was afraid he was not yet ready.

"Great, then!" Curie rose."Take the first two weeks in June off; You deserve a break." Ezra raised his brows; Curie continued, "We'll get people to cover for you, and since you do that for everybody, I am sure it will not be a problem."

Ezra didn't know what to do with that kind of news, but he knew that he could use a break. He couldn't remember the last time he had more than two days off. The captain was right— Ezra was always covering for the others and working extra hours. He never once thought about taking time off, though he desperately needed to get away for a bit and spend time with his loved ones.

"Well," he said, "thanks, Captain!"

Curie slapped him on the shoulder and left.

***

An hour before their shift was over, they did a final cleanup of the kitchen and dishes. They also refilled the air tanks. Ezra made sure to go through the inventory with his colleagues and made a list of things needed for their next shift. By the time it was seven thirty in the morning, everyone seemed exhausted and ready to head home.

Ezra hopped in his Jeep and started the engine. The drive was short but full of weariness. Before he exited his vehicle, his phone rang, and he pulled it out of his duffle bag.

His mom's name appeared on the screen. She probably wanted an update on the big fire. He'd seen her missed calls earlier but hadn't managed to call her back.

He let out a weary sigh; it wouldn't help if he ignored her. She'd keep calling. She was always the first person who called before each shift, between his shifts, and after each shift. If he knew of the prayers he could count on consistently, it was his mother's. That was the one woman who cared deeply for him, and it was no wonder Curie teased him that his noncommittal situation only existed because he compared each woman to his mom. With such a comparison, he knew he might never find the perfect woman in this lifetime.

"Hi, Mom."

"Honey, are you okay?" Her voice was shaky. "We saw the fire on the news."

"Yeah." His response wasn't too convincing, but he didn't want to explain the details of how the building almost buried him alive.

Crystal Buchanan worried about Ezra and his brother, even if they were rescuing a cat from a tree. He was not about to give her a real reason to worry. "I am good, Mom," he assured her. I'm just tired."

"I thank God you're safe, and the little boy you rescued."

His mother rambled on for a few minutes, telling him how her day went and how she wished he had an easier job but was so grateful he saved people. "I'm so proud of you," she said.

"Thanks, Mom."

After insisting he join her and his dad for dinner, she ended the conversation. "Get some rest, honey. I love you."

After a night like he'd just had, there was no way he was getting any rest, no matter how tired he was. He had adrenaline coursing through him and needed to do something –Perhaps a run if his body could take it, or rock climbing. But he didn't have to let his mom know that resting was far from his to-do list at the moment.

"I love you too, Mom."

Hearing from his mom, especially on days like this, warmed something inside him, even though days like today also caused him to wish he had a wife to get home to, someone to love and be loved back. He should have thought twice, before letting his previous relationship go into flames. He closed his phone and made his way to the house.

CHAPTER 2

THE SUN PEEKED through the clouds, heralding a morning that was cool, but not overly so. It was a perfect day for Ezra to enjoy a run at Rock Park, Colorado. Few other people were walking or riding bikes at the park.

Running was one of the many exercises Ezra did on a regular basis, not only because his job required him to stay in shape, but because he enjoyed it.

"Dude, you're going camping for a whole week?" Jake asked between gasps as they took a break. They had been running for quite a while and were almost back to the house. "Thought it was only for one or two nights or something like that." With the palm of his hand, Jake wiped sweat from his dark brown forehead.

The sky was clear and blue, which was fine with Ezra after the spring snow they'd had in May. He was thankful to be starting June with plenty of sunshine.

"Ten days, just a little over a week," Ezra responded as he stretched his legs under a tree. The calm breeze swept over his body, chilling his hot skin and drying out the sweat that threatened to flood his face.

Ezra was always ready for the next adventure anytime, even when he only had a few hours to spare. Being outdoors was a perfect avenue for him to think and reason, but he hadn't had an overnight trip in a while. That's why he was looking forward to the two weeks off, especially after all the changes at work.

Being an acting lieutenant had added an extra dose of responsibility—making sure that his unit was up to date with their training, educating civilians on fire safety—on top of paperwork and the spontaneous tasks that were assigned to him by his Chief and Captain.

And now he was being considered to take over the role permanently. Perhaps a promotion would be a good thing. He couldn't complain in that regard, but vacation was even better. It had been three years since he'd gone camping with his family, something they used to do twice every summer before everyone got busy.

Being the middle child, he was the glue between his siblings, and he still felt the need to arrange these trips whenever he could. For that reason, he'd invited his siblings.

His brother, Andrew, owned a truck and would be driving their parents' fifth wheel with his sister Renee. Ezra's contribution for the trip was to make reservations.

"Come join us on your days off," Ezra leaned against the tree. "Since you're currently single, it'll give you time to think of other things besides your wife."

"Ex-wife," Jake corrected in a strained voice.

Not everybody was cut out for the full camping experience, but Jake had been struggling ever since his wife divorced him six months ago without an explanation, ending a two-year marriage and shattering him.

Ezra tried reaching out to him, getting him to work with the pain and learn to let it go, but Jake could hardly speak his ex-wife's name. Jake had left the house to his wife and had been looking for an affordable place to rent when Ezra offered him to stay in one of the extra bedrooms at his townhouse until he got back to his feet.

They both worked the same shift at the fire station—Jake had another job as a trainer and Ezra had a temporary rock climbing job at the same parkour gym. It was nice that on Ezra's days off, he still had someone to run with him, and do workouts, too. Both men had lean, athletic bodies that visibly displayed the results of their rigorous exercise, both at work and outside of work.

Besides encouraging and praying for Jake, Ezra was at a loss as to how to help his friend. He figured a night in the mountains would be an excellent distraction for Jake to clear his mind. It didn't escape Ezra that his friend had a deep dislike for camping, and he knew it might take some convincing, but he was sure it would be worth it.

Still, Ezra recalled the time he had taken Jake four-wheeling once in his Jeep without the roof up, and Jake had been annoyed by all the bugs and mud.

Living with Jake had been an experience, though—just like with any roommate. Despite a few pet peeves, the duo got along well. However, Ezra had to admit it pained him to witness Jake's heartache.

Watching his friend cope with a painful divorce allowed Ezra to feel grateful for his single lifestyle. Sometimes it bothered him that he hadn't yet found someone to settle down with, but he kept busy enough with work, church, and family, which left no room for attachment, and most importantly there was no room for heartache.

Jake's gaze was distant, with a water bottle paused to his mouth, processing the right response to put an end to Ezra's outrageous request. Ezra had been there for him these last nine months, and he hated letting him down. He figured this was a pity offer, but he didn't know what to say. He shook his head and broke the silence. "Camping is not for me, man," he said, lifting one of his hands in mock surrender.

Even though Jake had tried to set the issue of his divorce aside, he still felt something was missing. He wanted what Ezra had, something that made Ezra happy, and excited about day-to-day life.

The man was full of life yet humble; he loved and cared for everyone. Jake was thankful to be a part of Ezra's crew and happy for his friend's promotion at work. Of all the things he would do for Ezra, camping was way out of his comfort zone. Jake still needed to take baby steps. He was confident that spending a night in the woods would only make him even more miserable.

"Good luck, though, bro." He moved a hand over his wet, short black hair. His gaze moved to the girl who was riding towards them at such an intense speed. Before he could think, Ezra dove to yank the girl off the bike that was out of control. "You're okay? " Ezra asked.

The girl nodded, panting with a frantic face. Jake guessed her to be twelve years old.

They watched her bike forcefully bounce off one of the trees by the open field. After helping adjust the girl's brakes to her bike, Ezra patted her on the shoulder and told her to be careful.

Ezra took a deep breath, "Come and bike with us on Saturday when you're off. It's not too far; you can even get back home and sleep in your bed,"

Jake nodded and teased his friend. "For a few minutes, I'd forgotten that you don't take no for an answer."

"Glad you remembered!" Ezra spoke in triumph and slapped Jake's shoulder. "I will race you to the finish!"

Ezra set himself in motion to run and quickly flew past Jake.

"Hey!" Jake called out as he followed and eventually passed Ezra.

Running was the one activity Jake could do in his sleep, his long legs guiding him to his destination.

***

Leila huffed down the stairs for the fifth time from her third-floor apartment, carrying a sleeping bag in one hand and a pillow in the other. Taking a quick moment to catch her breath, she glanced at the view of Pikes Peak that was still covered with a dusting of snow.

However, a breeze stirred to remind her of the warm June air. It was a beautiful sunny day, and for that she was grateful. She was ready for what the upcoming summer days had to offer.

A smile tugged at her lips as she approached her five-passenger SUV to load her items. Her thoughts went to the one person making this trip a reality. Bianca Perez Clarke.

Bianca had been Leila's best friend since high school. From the moment Bianca found out about Leila's summer bucket list, she was supportive as ever, and offered to join her on the ten-day camping trip as a twenty-fifth birthday present.

A month ago, Leila had made a summer bucket list with her students, and upon realizing she'd never been camping, they'd challenged her to add camping to her list.

She was nervous at first, partly because the closest she'd been to the outdoors were city parks and the Inflatable 5K run she did every summer.

Knowing that her friend Bianca used to camp, Leila approached her for suggestions for the best place to experience camping for first-timers. Bianca offered to join her instead; she said she knew of a scenic place to camp. Bianca was paying for the camp fees as Leila's twenty-fifth birthday present. So she could join Leila and make it a girls' getaway. She'd arranged to take a little over a week off work, and for her mother to watch her four-year-old daughter.

With one more load to go, Leila returned to her one-bedroom apartment. Experiencing a slight sense of panic that she could be forgetting something, she double-checked her packing list, then turned to her mirror to apply another coat of mint lip balm before grabbing her last bag and closing the door behind her.

As she created room for her bag in the car, she was starting to realize that going camping felt like carrying your whole house with you. She'd managed to compact everything with just enough room left for the cooler that she would be picking up from her parents' house.

"Leila," said a voice in a heavy accent from the side of the building. Leila lifted her head and noticed the cheerful gentleman walking toward her.

She greeted with a smile to match his. "Hi, Eduardo!"

Eduardo was Leila's apartment manager, who Leila guessed to be in his early forties and would qualify to be the best property manager.

"Where are you off to?"

"I'm going camping."

She didn't think much of camping when the students had suggested it, but later when she was alone, she realized it was a perfect idea. It fit with the changes she wanted to make in her life. The kids knew about Leila's fear of spiders, so they were surprised their somewhat fearful teacher would dare set foot in the great outdoors.

Eduardo's response was no different. He laughed loudly and shook his head in amusement. He probably remembered the last time he'd had to help Leila get rid of a spider from her apartment, but couldn't find the spider. Unless he assured Leila he'd found it; she was determined to stay the night to her parents' house or a hotel until the spider was found.

"You don't seem to me like the camping type." He said soberly, barely concealing his amusement when Leila glared at him.

"Why would you say that?" she asked as she shut the back of her car.

"Well, you are freaky of bugs." She knew he meant to say freaked out by bugs.

Without even flinching, she shook her head. "Not all bugs." She paused. "Just the spiders."

She knew it was pathetic, but the mere thought sent chills down the rest of her body. Someone had once suggested that she go to therapy because it had become such an intense fear. Despite her annoyance, she was grateful for Eduardo. Not all property managers would show up every time a Spider Emergency—as Leila dubbed it—arose.

"Hmm." He gave her a doubtful look.

"I have bug spray," she declared, waving her finds.

Eduardo simply nodded, biting back another roar of laughter.

Leila shook her head in amusement. "Tell Martha that I will watch the kids so that you can go on a date when I return."

That's something she did for them often, her way of saying thank you for being the Spider 911.

"She will like that."

Once in the car, she squeezed in beside all of her camping gear and drove off to make one final stop at her parents' house to get her food.

***

Ezra hopped from his navy-blue Jeep Wrangler with the elevated tires, decked out in his brown outdoor pants, a Colorado State T-shirt, and brown hiking shoes. He ran a hand through his brown hair before inhaling the fresh mountain air he'd missed over the last couple of weeks. He often came four-wheeling or mountain biking when he had some free time between his firefighting and rock climbing jobs if he was not with his small group from Church.

Ezra surveyed the campground's property as his shoes crunched the pine needles that carpeted the ground. When he had pulled in to map out the bike trails they would be taking with his group for the next two days at the Colorado Trail, he'd wandered farther and stumbled upon a campground tucked deep in the woods.

Of all the times he'd camped with his family, he was surprised they hadn't camped here before.

As he moved to look at the various trails within the campground's property, he saw that they were connected to the Colorado Trail. He also noticed a self-pay station next to the plastered map. That might come in handy since he never made reservations online due to his spontaneity. That was why he camped midweek, to avoid competing with other campers.

He continued his tour around the campground, admiring the breathtaking view of the mountains, the mature pine trees, and the gentle sound of water streaming near Site One.

First Site

It was peaceful and quiet away from the main road, except for the sound of the woodland creatures that bounced around.

With no tent or trailer in sight, Ezra was pleased that he was the first camper to arrive. He looked at his phone, noting that it was quarter past noon. With only five sites available, he decided to go with the best view and scenery at the first site.

It was set aside away from all the other sites and also the most prominent site, perfect for their fifth wheel trailer.

Since his job was to book the campsite, and his siblings to drive the trailer, he dialed his phone to let them know the campground's name and location, but then he realized the lack of signal in the area.

Despite the failed network, he liked this campground. Perfect to disconnect from electronics. He would still have to call his siblings when he drove to the next town on his way to his parents' event center, where he was the fill-in singer for the night.

Robert and Crystal Buchanan lived in Parker, Colorado. They owned the Silent Cove Retreat Center in Buena Vista and a couple of others in the mountains. Even though they had camp hosts every summer managing their facilities, the next two weeks they'd had to step in at the Silent Cove due to the host's family emergency.

The band they'd initially hired wouldn't arrive until Friday. That's why they'd turned to their three children to save the day. Ezra had agreed to help since they were camping within ten miles from the retreat center. At least all the music lessons and instruments they'd taken as kids paid off at times like this.

After searching for the camp host without much luck, Ezra returned to the self-pay station, where he pulled out an envelope, filled in his information, and slid the money inside. He licked the envelope to seal it, then dropped it in the heavy metal safe provided.

The only proof that he'd reserved the site was the small tab of a receipt that he'd ripped from the envelope, to go on the car dashboard. Even as he doubted there was a camp host, he wasn't sure how to place his name on the small wooden post on Site One.

He had no intention of leaving his bike or any of his belongings at the site as proof to other campers that the site had already been booked. With no certainty as to what time his siblings would arrive, he had to leave matters in God's hands.

With an exasperated sigh, he walked back to the site one more time. It had a fire ring and a picnic table just like all the other sites, but he didn't see a water source, which wouldn't be much of a hindrance since they had a trailer. He decided to take advantage of the quietness to practice a few songs on his guitar before heading to the retreat center.

***

There was no denying Leila's coffee intake had had an impact on her with the sudden bathroom breaks. Waking up at five a.m. due to the trip anxiety had left her no choice but to overdose with caffeine.

The stop at her parents' house had been brief but long enough for her dad to show her his current carpentry projects. It was great to see her dad excited about the work of his hands again. He'd lost interest in carpentry during the five years his wife had deserted him, but with her return, he seemed to resume his skills.

Amelia Morgan was from Jamaica and a type A personality, the very opposite of Chris Morgan. The different personalities could complement each other if done wisely. But Amelia was a planner and had to be in places twenty minutes earlier than the actual appointment; her strong personality conflicted with Chris's at some points.

Leila could say she inherited the best of both worlds. She had some of her mom's planning ability and her dad's laid-back personality.

After both her parents had helped load the car with a cooler full of frozen meals that Leila had made with her mom a week ago, the three of them had prayed together before her departure.

As Leila glanced at her phone, the map showed her to be an hour away from her destination. If asked, she wouldn't be able to describe the feeling she was experiencing.

Was it anxiety or excitement and a sense of adventure? Unsure of how to classify it, she decided to settle for excitement over her upcoming adventure, although she was sure there was some level of anxiety plaguing her mind.

Her heartbeat was faster, and she kept tapping her fingers while driving. Ten days of camping was going to be interesting. It may be a simple outing for most, but Leila was a homebody.

She felt like she'd stepped into her unforgettable movie. Fears about camping started to consume her, even though canceling was not an option. She'd promised to show her students pictures of her trip.

Although they were moving to third grade next year, she still did an end-of-summer potluck at the park, where all her students came with their families to have a final farewell in August before the new school year started.

What if she forgot something? What if she got stranded? Or came across a spider—or worse, a poisonous snake? Based on her knowledge of reptiles, snakes avoided the high country; she hoped that was true. Or—her heart pounded—a bear?

Knowing that her thoughts were getting out of hand, she decided to look at the brighter side of camping. She was going to be spending time with her best friend, connecting and sharing stories. They would both be disconnected from all electronics, giving them time to enjoy their surroundings.

As Leila neared Buena Vista, the car started making a funny sound. She had been sure to have it thoroughly serviced due to fear that something might go wrong. Leila was always afraid something might go wrong and took precautions to avoid it.

Her anxiety sometimes got the best of her, whether it was with planning a trip or facing a spider in her living room. Just as she was about to scream at her vehicle for acting up, it was as if she could hear a whisper in her ear. It was Proverbs 16:9 that rang in the back of her mind. "We can make our plans, but the Lord determines our steps." She whispered the words, and a smile appeared on her face.

She knew everything would be okay. Besides, she reminded herself, God had not given her a spirit of fear. She knew she must calm down and walk along the path set before her.

The first step was to find a place to stop. Her stomach growled in agreement. Besides, she also needed to take a bathroom break anyway. Maybe it was just a weird noise, and everything was okay.

Perhaps she'd have to cancel the whole camping trip, and for a moment she felt relief at the thought, but then a sense of sadness crept into her mind, gently reminding her that she needed to do this.

It was almost one thirty when Leila parked her car at the gas station. The sun hit her dark skin as she exited her vehicle. She'd filled her car's tank with gas and decided to park it to the side. Even though she wasn't very knowledgeable about diagnostics, she'd managed to recognize the flat tire immediately.

She decided to use the facilities and eat lunch before dealing with her car. If she let the stress consume her now, she knew she would end up canceling the trip, and she didn't want to do that. Instead, she went about her business as if everything was all right. Still, calling AAA for roadside assistance would be her priority after she got some food in her stomach. After all, she knew hunger tended to make her emotional.

With a Coke and a few items in her hand, Leila grabbed a pizza slice from the small toaster oven and joined the two people in line. Lifting her head, she noticed the strained look of the cashier; Perhaps it was time for her break, or she had something different on her mind. Leila did not miss the days of working as a cashier. She recalled as a teenager she had gotten a part-time job at a place similar to this. It had been miserable.

"Next," the cashier called.

"Hello!" Leila said and dropped her items on the counter.

"That will be $15.23, please."

She pulled a credit card from her wallet and offered it to the cashier.

"I am sorry," the cashier said, shaking her head. "The credit machine is temporarily out of order; we're taking cash only."

Did people still carry cash these days? She thought to herself before letting out a sigh of exasperation. "I don't carry cash. I guess I will just—"

"I got it." Her sentence was cut off by a male voice from behind.

She turned, and her gaze went to the man offering to pay her bill. He towered over her in height, his light skin a striking contrast to Leila's dark skin. It took her a moment to remember why she'd looked at him in the first place. "I'm fine, thanks for offering, though."

Just then her stomach growled, and she hoped neither the attractive man before her nor the cashier could hear. The man shook his head and began placing his items next to hers. "I insist," he said with a heartwarming smile.

He gave the cashier a curt nod and immediately pulled out his wallet, leaving Leila no room to object any further while the cashier scanned the items.

She'd thought of arguing further, and driving through the little town in search of fast food where they accepted credit cards, but she knew she had a call to make to AAA. She also wasn't sure how long the tire would hold up.

She returned his smile and reached for her items from the counter. "Thanks."

"You're welcome," the man said as he pulled out bills from his wallet and Leila made her exit.

Leila sat at the umbrella-covered picnic table outside the store, pouring her Coke in an ice-filled disposable cup. She inhaled the soft breeze that brushed her straight black hair across her face. She'd already made the call to AAA, but it would be another three to four hours before they'd show up.

Being in a small town, they had more customers than the technicians on staff, and the few technicians they had were already engaged somewhere else.

She tried to assess her options as she devoured her pizza. She could change the tire herself— not that she'd done that before, except for having watched her dad do it once —or she could stay and wait for another three hours. She also considered pulling up a YouTube video to guide her through the process.

Now would be a more logical time for her to panic, but instead, she felt relaxed. It had to be her parents' prayer before she left this morning, and if the girl who panicked over being late to places could remain calm in such an unfamiliar situation, then she had to remember that God was in control of the situation.

"Mind if I join you?" a voice in front of her asked, bringing her out of her daze. Her mind had been so busy that it had blocked out her sight.

CHAPTER 3

THE FACT THAT Leila didn't hear footsteps approach her was a bit alarming, but when she looked up, she saw the handsome man who had just paid for her lunch. Tilting her head, she took in his appearance.

She guessed him to be at least six feet two, which was quite tall compared to her five feet four inches. His T-shirt hugged his upper body, showing his lean, all-muscle build. More than that, Leila stared at his face—his sharp cheekbones and the broad smile it held, the kind that was instantly contagious. She smiled but then realized she should also say something instead of just staring at him like some creep.

"No" she tapped her forehead, "I mean yes, please." motioning for him to sit at the opposite side of the table. The place had one picnic table, which made sense, given the fact that most people grabbed their food and left. Not many people stuck around a gas station to eat their food, but Leila never ate in her car— she didn't want a single crumb in it.

As the man slid into the seat, Leila felt obligated to explain her delayed response. "I'm sorry, I was just thinking." She steadied herself by placing her arms on the table. Why her brain was having a hard time saying a simple yes, she had no idea. Sure, the man was attractive, but it wasn't as if she'd never spoken to a handsome man before.

"I think it's okay to think." He smiled, "That's how you conquer the world."

He sat waiting with a Coke in one hand and a foil-wrapped meal in the other. Leila tried to think of a witty response, but she was at a loss for words. The man said, "I also respect solitude, I don't mind—"

"No, please, stay!" A hand went to her forehead again, as if snapping herself out of it. "We can eat here together."

Placing his food at the table, he held out his hand. "I am Ezra Buchanan, by the way."

Leila was hesitant to shake his hand since her hand was smeared with grease from her pizza. "Sorry, my hands are . . . ," she trailed off, embarrassed.

Ezra kept his hand out despite her partial objection. She wiped her hand with a napkin and reached out to offer him a firm handshake. "Leila Morgan."

He stared at Leila's drink, and then his own. "Looks like we're both Coke fans, I see." Leila nodded. "Looks like it."

When Ezra excused himself to voice a prayer before eating, Leila watched and admired his confidence about praying in front of a stranger.

Ezra unwrapped his sandwich. "So, in your thoughts that I interrupted, who is the villain?"

Leila looked at him tilting her head in confusion. She noticed the gray in his eyes that held a slight hint of blue in them.

"Thoughts are like stories," Ezra explained, "and every story has a villain."

She glanced at him, and his face portrayed a teasing smile.

"The tire," she said finally. She'd been unsure of her response but was relieved when Ezra responded with a chuckle.

He grinned "Tell me more about the tire villain." He bit into his sandwich as Leila told him of the flat tire and her options to solve the problem.

His eyes widened as if in shock upon Leila's mention of changing a tire by herself. Probably because she was hardly dressed for the job in her bright-colored tank top and clean, dark hair.

"No kidding, I believe you got this villain down. Perhaps I can join you— we could be partners in crime."

Leila leaned forward, with both arms placed to the table, as she listened to Ezra talk freely. He didn't seem shy at all, which made it easier for Leila to talk to him.

"By the way, I could change a tire in my sleep," Ezra smiled. "Thought I'd add that to my resume."

Leila chuckled.

"Do I qualify to be your partner? " Ezra leaned back.

Leila lifted a questioning brow.

"No...no, that's not what I meant, I mean— you know what?" he shook his head and grinned when he looked at Leila's amused face. "Okay, either way is fine with me."

For a second, Leila's mind wandered, imagining what it would be like to be this guy's partner. She immediately snapped out of the silly thought.

She pointed the finger at him. "You're hired. I guess two is always better than one." Leila assumed him to be a mechanic if he changed tires in his sleep.

"I would have to pay you though." She sipped her soda. "But I don't have cash, as you noticed, so I would have to mail you a check or payment via PayPal."

"We'll discuss that later." Changing the subject, he asked, "So where are you headed? If you don't mind me asking." He took a sip of his drink. "I can tell you're just passing through since you're having lunch at a gas station."

Leila took the fact that he'd changed the subject to mean he would not be accepting any money from her. And yes, this was her summer of passing through with new experiences on her list. Being flustered by a guy, that was something new, but it was not on her summer bucket list.

"Camping." She poured soda into her iced cup. "It's a long story, but camping is the short version of it."

Ezra's face lit up at the mention of camping, "I love camping!" he said with a spark of excitement in his gray eyes. His shoulders relaxed when he told Leila about his favorite things about camping. He spoke about the outdoors in general.

"Even though it's your first time," looking her directly in the eyes, he said you would love it."

Given the appearance of the gentleman in front of her, Leila guessed him to be the outdoors type. His skin was slightly darker than what she'd suspect it to be during the winter, due to more days spent in the sun and perhaps neglected sunscreen.

Once she realized she was speaking to a camping expert, she managed to throw out some of her pressing questions about the activity.

"What do you do when camping?" She had to know since she and Bianca were staying for ten days. The more things to do, the better.

"Depending on where you camp, you could go swimming— there's a couple of lakes in the area. Biking is an option if you like to mountain bike, archery, kayaking, four-wheeling. " His eyes wide as he said, "Although I wouldn't recommend that on a spare tire." He went on to name other outdoor activities.

"Oh, and don't forget to feed the bears!" Ezra's gaze became more serious.

Leila gasped, "bears?" her eyes darted to Ezra, his face revealing a playful grin.

Ezra talked about using the safety metal food storage containers or keeping food in the car. He took notice of how intent Leila was to the subject of bears, and he placed his hand over hers. "I didn't mean to scare you," he said, then swiftly moved his hand back to his drink.

Leila smiled. "I've already read all that about bears. However, hearing you say it, made it more real."

By the end of the hour, they'd discussed where they lived, their reasons for being in Buena Vista, and several random topics.

When Ezra mentioned his hometown, Leila perked up with interest. "That's where my best friend lives," she said, leaning forward. "Where exactly in Fort Rock do you live?"

Ezra smiled, licking his fingers to get rid of the sauce from his sandwich. He was intrigued by how comfortable she was to talk to, which is why he found himself teasing her more than he usually would tease a stranger.

It had been a while since he'd had a normal conversation with a woman except for his mom and sister. Come to think of it; he'd never had a normal conversation with a woman except for the women in his family.

"Are you ready to take my social security number now?" he asked, arching his brow, accompanied by a chuckle.

Leila laughed too; she seemed to be picking up on his humor and enjoying his company. His teasing tone must have broken the awkwardness that first encounters with a stranger often held. His witty banter and gentle teasing seemed to have put Leila at ease around him.

The girl had such a melodic laugh. His eyes locked with hers as her laughter died down. Even as though he wished their visit to be longer, he knew he needed to get to the retreat center if he wanted to have some time to visit with his parents before the evening worship began.

The black girl across the table from him didn't seem to be his type at all, but there was something about her which caused Ezra to want to sit across from her again. It wasn't just her soft black velvet skin, nor the simplicity in her beauty, but there was something he couldn't place a finger on. Realizing that he was wasting more time daydreaming, he snapped his attention back to reality.

"We better change that tire of yours, so that you can get to camping."

Leila seemed as reluctant as he was to end their visit, but they both had someplace else to be.

Leila rose from the picnic table to clear the trash. Ezra reached to grab it out of her hand and added it to his, then moved to toss it in the trash can.

***

It took about twenty minutes for Leila's tire to be changed. After Ezra had cleaned his hands, he returned to say goodbye to Leila.

"Thank you," Leila said as she opened the door to her car. "You're very good at changing tires."

"Let's just say, we are great partners in crime." Ezra placed his hand on her shoulder. "We nailed the villain," he said, then pulled his hand back.

Leila took a deep breath to steady herself. Something in her longed to be able to stay and talk with this stranger, but she quickly reminded herself he probably didn't feel the same way, and besides, she needed to hurry up if she was to meet her friend on time.

After they'd said their goodbyes, Ezra made the broad steps in the direction of his car. Keeping her gaze on him, Leila hollered, "Happy singing!"

"Happy camping!" Ezra responded as he walked backward a few steps.

Leila sat silently in her car and pretended not to watch Ezra climb into his Jeep with the big tires. He quickly slid into the driver's seat, and she wondered how hard it would be for her to climb a vehicle that high. There was a bike attached to the rack behind the Jeep, and several things strapped to the roof rack. Leila had no doubt Ezra was a real outdoorsman.

Briefly, she wondered if she could ever be with a man like that. He was very outgoing, though Leila was the opposite of that, More reserved around adults, she could get her point across when necessary. Her personality was linked to the many times she'd moved. By the time she was ten, they'd moved five times, due to the nature of her father's job. One military base to another every two years, which made it difficult for Leila and her younger brother to make long-term friendships. It was not until she was in junior high, did they settle down in Colorado Springs, that Leila finally made a long-term friend.

Somehow she hadn't felt uneasy with Ezra. It probably had to do with his sense of humor. Ezra seemed daring and enjoyed the outdoors. Leila was not his type. She was thankful he was just a stranger she would never see again. She knew it would be a while before she forgot the guy, especially his eyes, and his sense of humor.

***

The drive through Fairplay was peaceful. The sight of ranches spread apart from each other, with cows and horses grazing in the fields, had a calming effect on Leila. A largely painted signpost indicated HIDDEN VALLEY. She could see the mountains pulse with life.

She rolled down the window at the driver's side to inhale the fresh mountain air as she approached the town's main street. The temperature had dropped another twenty degrees.

Leila could make out several awnings and signposts of different businesses on the main street; there was a Hidden Valley country store, Laundromat, outdoor equipment rental shop, and a few others she couldn't read quite clearly. She reluctantly diverted her attention back to her driving.

She turned down a rocky dirt road, which made the mountains seem closer as the road narrowed to a single lane. She could see a signpost shaped in the form of an arrow pointing straight ahead with the words HIDDEN VALLEY CAMPGROUND fully inscribed on it with faded black paint. She heaved a sigh of relief when she finally arrived.

Bianca's minivan was directly within Leila's view. She pulled up next to the vehicle and cut the engine.

Bianca got out of the car and waited for her.

Leila let out a squeal of excitement at the sight of her friend and went around the car to hug her.

"Leila!" Bianca said cheerfully.

Bianca was quite a beauty with flowing dark hair which fell behind her back in smooth curls.

"Bianca!" Leila returned the smile, and she tugged on a lock of Bianca's hair. "I like it longer."

"Thanks, I thought it was time for a change."

Bianca had always kept her hair short ever since her husband died.

They linked arms as they walked over the ground carpeted by pine needles toward the picnic table. There were several tall lodge pines, making the campground very shaded. The trees were trimmed, and there were a few fallen logs, which Leila thought would make good seats eventually. The beaming ecosystem rang with the echoes of about a million creatures, creating the perfect sound of nature as it hummed across the woods. Their feet crushed tiny twigs and thin branches as they moved across the landscape.

Leila's eyes darted to the large site "This is such a beautiful site, Bianca!" she sat at the picnic table.

"Wait till you see the other side of it," Bianca responded.

"Sorry I was running late." Leila apologized.

"Speaking of late, is your car all right?"

Leila had texted Bianca explaining her reason for being late. Even though that had been only twenty minutes ago, she hadn't mentioned her lunch with the stranger who'd paid for her lunch and helped change her tire. She nodded.

"Yes, just the tire." Her face creased into a smile as she thought of how it had been changed.

"You seem relaxed for having had a flat tire." Bianca raised her eyebrows curiously. "You're usually so anxious when things don't go as planned, and you're obsessed with being prompt. Bianca narrowed her gaze. "Why do I sense you're not telling me everything?"

Leila had to admit to herself that she often panicked over minor things, yet a flat tire hadn't seemed to arouse her anxiety? She still wasn't sure why, but she wasn't oblivious to the butterflies floating in her stomach.

"Well, I guess God has given me peace." Leila crossed one leg over the other.

Bianca gave her a knowing look. "Uh-huh."

Leila's thoughts were spinning around the stranger she'd met and how he had not only changed her tire but had walked her through the steps, preparing her if it should ever happen again. She hadn't gone underneath the car—Ezra had said he'd spare her from getting her hair messy—but he'd explained each step so she could understand.

"It's a long story." She sighed, "but a stranger helped— "

"Long story? Please!" Bianca put her arms on her lap."You will have to spill the details sooner or later; you might as well tell me now."

Leila brushed a bug from her toes and inhaled deeply. "Well, this guy I met at the gas station..." She gave her the details of her encounter with Ezra, and the lunch which ultimately led to a one-hour chat before the tire got changed.

Bianca's eyes were alive with interest, encouraging Leila to continue to talk.

"He was easygoing and fun to talk to," Leila spoke with excitement.

"Did you say he prayed in front of you?" Bianca's eyes gleamed. "Was he handsome?"

Leila could see why Bianca was intrigued by this conversation. Bianca and Leila had been through several ups and downs since high school. Bianca being two years older, she'd graduated before Leila and married her high school sweetheart, and even though death tore them apart, Bianca still had a daughter who reminded her of the love of her life.

As for Leila, she'd spent her high school years being a second mother to her younger brother when her mom left her dad. Leila had turned down a couple of possible dates due to commitments she had going on at home. She'd often had to help drive her brother to sporting events, play dates or stay home with him until their dad returned from work.

Now that Leila was old enough, suitable dates were scarce, since she had such a high standard for potential suitors. She didn't bother going out with a guy who wasn't a Christian. Bianca agreed with her on that, but Leila wasn't yet actively involved in her church, and the majority of the congregation were middle-aged or seniors. Given her insistence on having chemistry to the mix, it was going to be a long time before she found the right guy.

"Yes, he prayed, and he was handsome," she said under her breath. She had to admit his faith intrigued her even more. She didn't tell Bianca she felt a slight spark for Ezra. It would have sounded too clichéd. She hoped there was such a thing as love at first sight.

"Did you get his number?" Bianca asked.

Leila was ready to be done with this conversation.

"Do I look like someone who will take a guys number?"

"Hello? " Bianca's eyebrows lifted. "Because you haven't been on a date in forever."

For that Bianca was right, but again, Leila knew that her encounter with Ezra had been brief, for them to become friends.

"Anyway," Leila said with a grin, waving her friend's interest away. "Let's leave that behind us." She doubted she and Ezra would see each other again, and if they did, what were the chances he would fall for a woman from a different racial background?

***

In the next hour and a half, the girls talked about work, with Bianca telling some of her fun moments with her clients at the vet clinic. They laughed, then took in every bit of the quasi-Jurassic scenery which would be their temporary home for the next ten days.

Bianca rose from her seat, "We better get this tent set up."

After the tent was set up, Leila decided to add her personal touches, by setting up her battery-operated diffuser and adding essential oils to it. She placed it in the tent. At least she could enjoy a sweet aroma of peppermint and lavender while keeping mosquitoes at bay.

While Leila was happy setting up camp to be a comfortable environment, she couldn't help but notice her friend was moving slowly. Bianca's eyes were downcast, and she seemed to be somewhere else, deep in thought.

Maybe she was thinking about her husband — Leila knew Bianca still missed him terribly. Being out in the woods probably reminded Bianca of how she used to go camping with her husband before he died. Leila suddenly realized how hard this trip must be for her friend. Bianca had only camped once with her daughter, Daisy, and her mom since her husband had passed.

Concerned Leila asked. "Are you okay?"

"Just thinking of John, that's all," Bianca responded and exited the tent, leaving no room for further discussion.

After unloading their sleeping bags, pads, and all their belongings, they took a stroll to the rest of the campground's territory. They walked past four other campsites, which were smaller than Site One.

Site One was the only campsite on the east side of the campground, leaving it with an extended amount of space. The other four sites were located on the west side of the campground, with a variety of trailheads.

The sound of a stream caused Leila to pause. "Is that water?" Leila asked.

Bianca nodded as they continued their stroll ahead.

Across from the creek was an opening in the midst of pines with vibrant green grass and colorful wildflowers.

They sat down at the wooden bench next to the stream, soaking their feet in the bitterly cold water that moved in rippling, undulating symmetry of small waves.

As they made plans for the next few days, Leila mentioned some of the activities that Ezra had suggested over their meeting at the gas station.

Pulling out their feet from the cold water, they took in the fresh mountain air and enjoyed listening to all the different kinds of birds hovering above them, clattering in soothing twitters. Leila couldn't ask for a more peaceful and quiet place to relax.

By the time they returned to their campsite, the rest of the sites had been occupied by other campers, a couple of tents, and two pop-up trailers. Most of the campers were either making a fire or starting dinner. As the cool breeze swept, the smell of gasoline and campfire filled the evening air.

Based on the YouTube knowledge Leila had gained the previous week, she started the campfire using starter twigs, paper, and gasoline and then added the medium and big logs. Within minutes, the fire consumed the pit. They added extra layers of clothing and gathered around the campfire to warm up their thawed dinner.

The loud hissing noise of a truck hauling a fifth wheel trailer captured Bianca and Leila's attention as the vehicle shuddered to a stop at their campsite.

CHAPTER 4

A SLENDER LADY about their age stepped out of the truck and headed their way. As she approached, the dim firelight illuminated her profile. Both girls rose up from their camp chairs, curious about the stranger in front of them.

She waved a buzzing bug off her face."I apologize for the inconvenience, we're either lost, or there might be a conflict with the campsite."

Bianca and Leila listened intently.

"My brother texted and said he'd reserved Site One." The lady's eyes darted to the tent and then back to its occupants standing in front of her. "What's the name of this campground?" She must have missed the metal board sign by the entrance. Leila left Bianca to do the talking since she was the camping expert.

"Hidden Valley Campground," Bianca answered.

The lady pulled out her phone and frowned at the screen. "Yes, that's what he'd texted." She handed the phone to Bianca, who took it reluctantly.

Leila listened as she battled the buzzing bugs from her face.

Bianca handed back the lady's phone after giving it a cursory glance.

The lady let out a sigh, her hand rubbing her eyes. She looked like she had been drained of every bit of energy left in her. Stress was evident in her eyes.

"If he was here at noon," Bianca said, "It could very well be that he got here before we did, but besides putting your tent as proof of your reservation, there would be no way of knowing. "

Bianca told Leila and the stranger about the last time she'd come to the same campground with her deceased husband, and how they didn't have to place a reservation card on their site. Once they'd paid and set up the tent, they never saw a camp host the entire time. "With a campground as primitive as this is, and no

running water, I doubt there's a host on the premises."
Leila assumed, they'd probably double-booked the site.

"It's just the two of us with our small tent, if
you don't mind staying with us, you're more than
welcome to set up your trailer. It looks like we both
paid for the same site."Leila spoke up.

The site was big enough to fit a school group or
more. The only problem would be sharing the fire pit
that they would need for the morning and evening fires
when the temperatures drop.

"That's if you don't mind sharing the fire pit
with us," Leila added.

"A fire pit is the least of our worries right now."
The lady let out a sigh of relief. "Thanks for being so
flexible, I appreciate it. The last thing we need is more
of a drive."

The lady stretched out her hand. "I'm Renee, by
the way." Bianca and Leila introduced themselves.

"And my brother Andrew is the driver." She motioned toward the truck. It was hard to see the driver since it was dark except for the distant fires from each campsite. His face was silhouetted in the semi-darkness.

***

An hour after the neighbors had set up their trailer, Leila and Bianca invited them to dinner, to which they readily agreed. With four camp chairs around the fire pit, they each sat with a disposable bowl of the Jamaican chicken stew that Leila had brought from home.

"This is good," Andrew said before he scooped another spoon to his mouth. The fire had illuminated his face, and Leila could make out a few of his features; he had a long scruff jaw and a slight resemblance to Renee.

Renee nodded in agreement. "This soup is to die for."

Leila scooped her last spoon of soup from her bowl. "I'm glad you like it."

"My mom and I made it." Either everybody was just hungry, or the stew really tasted good, because Andrew had seconds and the girls polished off their full bowls.

After dinner, Renee offered to provide s'mores in return for the dinner. Andrew resigned to call it a night as he trudged back to the trailer.

"I cannot believe a graham cracker could taste this good, adding melted chocolate next to a marshmallow and sandwiching them between crackers. Mmm!" Leila nodded her head in satisfaction as she took another bite. "I must say I will be having s'mores every night this week."

"I could not agree more with you," Renee held a marshmallow on her metal stick. "Is this your first time to have s'mores?"

"Yes, it is."

"S'mores each night, Renee and Bianca declared in unison as they lifted their cracker sandwiches in a toast.

For the next thirty minutes, the three girls chatted.

Renee talked about her job as an interior designer and how she wasn't so fond of camping. "I only do it to spend quality time with my family."

"Couldn't you camp in cabins or somewhere they cook food for you?" Bianca asked.

"My brothers would think a cabin ridiculous since we have a fancy fifth wheel. One of them would rather do tent camping if given a choice."

"Maybe we could trade our tent for your fifth wheel then?" Leila teased.

They talked about all sorts of things, including fashion and favorite things to do. They were buried in conversation and laughter and getting along really well.

It was almost eleven by the time they called it a night. The two girls seemed glad to have made a new friend, and Renee said she was also looking forward to spending the rest of the ten days with them. "If my brothers opt for the strenuous activities, like rock climbing, you girls will be my backup plan."

Renee started walking, but then returned. "Can I take an extra bowl of soup? I want to save it for my other brother, who will be joining us later, in case he comes back hungry."

Leila handed Renee the rest of the leftover stew.

After safely putting out the fire, Leila and Bianca hauled the cooler back to the car and got rid of all the trash. They thanked God for a beautiful day and wished each other good night.

In the silence of the night, Leila lay still on the mattress pad wrapped in a warm sleeping bag, thinking of what she had done—and how it wasn't as scary and hard as she'd imagined.

She'd chosen to do something new and go camping with the bugs, rocks, and spiders. She had never slept outdoors in her life. It was her first time, but she felt renewed in some way— she was ticking an item off her bucket list. She drifted off to sleep with a slight smile of contentment creasing her lips.

***

The next afternoon, Leila and Bianca sat by the creek, admiring the way the dazzling sunset was reflected in the gentle stream of water bouncing off the rocks. There were a few mosquitoes, but the view surpassed everything. It made Leila forget every inconvenience. A few deer wandered in the open space, birthing a picture-perfect moment.

Relieved that they'd finished their first day, Leila was excited to mark off another thing on her bucket list. Earlier in the day, they'd taken a hike and had lunch at a cafe in Hidden Valley; they'd also found a place with public showers and cleaned up.

Their day had ended with horseback riding. Renee had joined them for the afternoon since both her brothers were gone. One brother had joined another camper for rock climbing, and the other had gone backpacking.

Bianca pulled a strand of hair from her face. "What do you think of camping?"

"I like it so far," Leila said with a slight nod, "but this is only Thursday. Ask me again on Monday, and I might have a different response then."

Bianca chuckled. "I think you're tougher than you give yourself credit for." She paused to clear her throat. "For someone who dislikes spiders—"

"Can't stand spiders," Leila corrected dramatically.

"Whatever," Bianca said, throwing her hand in the air. "I mean, you knew coming outdoors is where they live, but you still came anyway."

Bianca was always positive and gave people a reason to believe in themselves, even if they didn't. "I pay you to say that," Leila said as she pulled out her homemade bug spray from her sling backpack that she'd been carrying with her. "I'm your best friend, what else would you say?" She arched an eyebrow and then sprayed herself and gave her friend the bottle to do the same. The mosquitoes seemed to enjoy gathering around the creek tonight.

"What's up, girls?"

Renee greeted cheerfully, joining them on the wooden bench, which was thankfully long enough to fit the three ladies. They all needed a moment to rest.

"Hey," both Leila and Bianca greeted in unison.

"Sorry I had to look at the home magazines I'd downloaded to my Kindle."

Bianca and Leila listened as Renee told them on how she was getting some ideas for her upcoming client, who needed Victorian decor for a new house.

They talked a while longer until the temperatures dropped to a chilly mountain coldness; then they decided to walk back to the campsite to start the fire.

Since Renee's brothers hadn't returned yet and Renee had mentioned cooking wasn't a gift she possessed, Leila insisted she join them for their sloppy Joes dinner. Another meal Leila had prepared from home and brought frozen. "There's enough beef to feed a small army. You can take the rest back to the trailer for your brothers." Leila said.

By the time they put out the fire, Renee's brothers still hadn't returned, but the girls were all ready to call it a night.

The two friends made their way to the tent, and Leila crawled into her sleeping bag. Too exhausted to differentiate a real mattress from a pad, she closed her eyes.

The next morning, she woke to the golden beam of sun rays streaming into the tent through a thin opening. She glanced on the opposite side where Bianca lay, sound asleep. In an attempt not to wake her, Leila reached for her devotional book on the ground and her eyes widened. Leila let loose a piercing scream that shattered the quiet morning as it boomed through the woods, cutting across the thick density of early morning fog. She quickly unzipped the tent and stumbled out in frenzied madness.

The sight of a crawling insect with creepy long legs on her book had created instant heat in Leila's body. Even though it was cold, her heart raced faster as she tried to plan her escape.

CHAPTER 5

LEILA'S SHRIEK HAD jolted Bianca out of her sleep. Her panic was mixed with confusion, making her heave in a breath as she pushed herself groggily upright, clutching at the sleeping bag and sprinting toward the tent flap with no time to locate her shoes or jacket.

As she made her exit, she could think of only one thing that could have caused Leila to let out such a terrifying scream.

"Outside, she saw Andrew frozen with a piece of wood in one hand and a coffee mug in the other.

Andrew un-froze by dropping the wood and headed toward Leila. Bianca caught up and joined him and three other campers who had surrounded her friend to assess the situation.

"What's going on, Leila?" Bianca asked, standing on tiptoe to avoid the sharp pine needles that blanketed the ground.

"A spi- . . . ," Leila gasped, shivering, tightening her arms around her body. "It was huge, hairy and . . ."

With a disgusted frown, she pointed toward the tent. She wore no shoes or coat, just her cozy flannel pajamas. She still had to be freezing, but that was probably the least of her worries.

"A spider," Bianca said loud enough for the others to hear. They were standing a few feet away from their tent. She considered them the search-and-rescue team in this case.

"Where exactly did you see it?" Bianca asked gently, aware of her friend's severe arachnophobia.

There had been so many incidents when Leila was in high school and had called Bianca to get rid of spiders. It was usually when she was home alone, and her dad didn't plan on returning until later.

The most memorable day was when Leila had locked herself in her bedroom and called Bianca to come over to their house and remove the spider from the shower. She was supposed to pick up her brother from a play date and couldn't remain locked up in her room forever.

Bianca had dropped everything to go help for the sake of Leila's sanity—and her little brother. Upon arriving, Bianca had asked her why she didn't just close the bathroom door, but Leila thought the spider would escape to hunt her through the other areas of the house.

Why she was afraid of spiders, Bianca would never know, but she still helped her friend no matter the reason. She didn't have to understand the details. That's just what friends did for each other.

One of the guys had immediately left after Bianca's declaration of a spider, leaving three others behind, including Andrew.

"How can we help?" asked another gentleman.

"I think I got it," Bianca said and thanked them for their concern, then sent them off.

Except for Andrew, Bianca gave a cursory glance at his gaze and saw the determination in his blue eyes.

"I'm coming with you."

It wasn't a request, and Bianca couldn't argue with that. Andrew was right behind her. He spotted the spider immediately and coaxed it to crawl onto a rolled up newspaper, then exited the tent and sent it off into the woods.

"That was a fast search." Bianca shyly raked her messy hair with her hand. "Thank you for helping!"

"You're welcome," Andrew said and moved to give an update to Leila.

"How come I didn't see you with the spider?" Leila asked, her voice frantic.

After Andrew gave her details on how he'd caught and released the spider off to the woods, Leila let out a sigh of relief.

"Thank you!" she said breathlessly.

"Anytime," he responded and returned to his coffee, which was probably cold by now.

Bianca noticed Andrew seemed happier today than the first day they'd arrived. Maybe because of Leila's epic show. She shook off the thoughts and handed the jacket and shoes to Leila, who moved to embrace her in appreciation. Bianca had never once tried to make Leila feel bad about her fears, even though it was rough dealing with her little episodes.

"I am not touching that book again," Leila said adamantly.

Bianca nodded. "I know!" There was no need to argue since Leila always gave up anything for a few weeks that she'd seen a spider crawl onto.

After all the excitement, the girls decided it was time to relax and eat breakfast.

***

Leila sat with Bianca in Renee's trailer as they enjoyed oatmeal for breakfast. Renee had invited them over to calm Leila down after her spider incident. They talked and ate at the dining table which had enough seating for four.

"We used to camp with all my family in this trailer," Renee told them about some of the memories of camping and how her mom used to be afraid of spiders but overcame her phobia. "If you get tired of the tent too, the trailer sleeps eight to ten people. Renee said nonchalantly. "At least you won't have spiders crawling on you," she teased, glancing at Leila

Leila chuckled softly. "Thanks!" She wanted to take Renee's offer to bunk in their trailer, but she had to face her fears one way or another. She admired the interior that resembled another version of a house. "It looks nice in here." She didn't know why, but she'd imagined the trailer to be more cramped inside, with fewer amenities.

Bianca nodded. "Yes, it's very nice."

"It belongs to our parents, but it's almost ours since we can use it any time we need it," Renee said. "With both my brothers off to their morning excursions, would you like a tour of the rest of the trailer?"

"Yes please!" Bianca responded, and Leila nodded since she still had a mouth full of oatmeal.

There was a big couch that turned into a queen sleeper, and a room with two queen bunk beds. They looked at the medium-sized bathroom, not too spacious but nicely furnished with exquisite designs. They looked at another room with a king bed, before they were back again to the dining table that turned into a queen bed.

"What are you girls doing today?" Renee asked when they'd finished the tour.

"We are going to town to take showers, then make calls and get some more wood and ice," Leila responded.

"What are your plans?" Bianca asked Renee.

"Andrew and I are going canoeing, then visiting our parents this evening." She adjusted her earring that was about to fall off her ear. Renee told them she would be returning late. "If you need anything, my other brother should be back by then. I'm not so sure what time, but don't be afraid to ask for help. He's the easiest one to approach out of the three of us. Also, I know we owe you dinner," she added with a teasing smile geared to Leila. "You've fed us all your food!"

"I'm glad the food is not wasted."

After exchanging farewell hugs with their new friend, Bianca and Leila returned to their tent to prepare for their day, leaving Renee to do the same.

CHAPTER 6

THE SUN ROLLED out of the horizon, casting touches of golden rays on the steaming mountains that smoked with heavy fog towering up to the bright blue sky. It was almost ten when Bianca and Leila walked along Hidden Valley's downtown area. After Leila and Bianca had taken their morning showers, Leila made a brief call to her parents.

Even though she'd kept her phone off at the campground, the battery was running low, and Leila didn't have a charger.

When she met Bianca back at the car, her friend looked frazzled.

Leila's brows furrowed, "Is everything okay?"

"I'm afraid that my camping trip has come to an end."

Leila waited for her friend to explain further, and the brief silence stretched the moments in between, making each second seem longer than what it was. Bianca's eyebrows locked in place, and her forehead folded into wrinkled lines of worry.

"My mother had to take Daisy to urgent care last night because her temperature wouldn't go below 103 degrees. They said she has strep throat." Bianca blinked back tears. "I need to go home to be with her. I'll just ruin your trip if I stay behind and worry the entire time!"

"I'm coming with you, then," Leila offered.

"No, Leila," Bianca patted her friend's shoulder. "There's no need for you to miss out on your first camping trip. What kind of bucket list would it be if you only camped for one night? Plus, we all don't need to get strep throat."

Leila knew Bianca was right. She needed to stay healthy in case she had to help take care of Bianca and her family.

"You already know how to make a fire, the tent is set for you, and you have good neighbors who have offered to help should there be an emergency. That Andrew guy . . ." Bianca was silent for a second, then smiled. "He's good-looking and knows his way around a spider search. Perhaps you can get to know him better."

Leila gave her friend a mischievous smile,

"So you think he's good-looking?" Leila chuckled. And yes Andrew was handsome, but he didn't affect Leila in any way, but maybe, he affected Bianca somehow. She seemed to study the guy with more interest. "Perhaps I can put in a word for you."

"Keep your heart and eyes open," Bianca said, completely ignoring Leila's comment.

"You, too."

Bianca was still too young to shut out any potential relationships. Something told Leila that her friend hadn't gotten past her loss just yet. There was something about her that she couldn't place; maybe it was the weight of her loss that pulled down the edges of her shoulders, or perhaps she only imagined that.

"If you have another spider encounter, call Andrew," Bianca said assuredly. "Or this is your opportunity to overcome your phobia."

"That's very funny, Bianca."

At the mere mention of a spider, Leila considered for a moment to return home and call it a trip. But then she remembered why she made this trip and was excited to explore the new territory, and she had plans to spider-proof her tent, inside and out with her essential oils. Each spider that sniffed the sweet fragrance would have to find a different victim.

"Well, I will give it a try," Leila said with a smile.

"It's only ten thirty; if we get back to the campground, I can pack my luggage and perhaps we can hike before I leave."

"That's a plan I can work with." Leila nodded, pleased, and drove them back to their campground.

***

The late afternoon was hot considering the mountain temperatures, but the gentle breeze made the heat bearable enough for an afternoon hike. After saying goodbye to Bianca at two-thirty, Leila took a stroll on the same trail where they'd hiked earlier. She hadn't had time to take pictures then since Bianca was in a hurry to get back home, so she returned to take some afternoon shots.

She snapped pictures of the scenery along the way as she walked. The wildflowers stood out with their beauty. Among the several other flowers familiar to Leila were the red fairy trumpets that sent blossoms across the trail path, the copper mallow, and the yellow paintbrush.

The vibrant colors were picture-perfect. She was so buried in the beauty around her that she didn't pay attention to the group of cyclists heading down the trail from the opposite side.

Seeing them at the last moment, she jerked out of the way but misplaced her step as she turned and tilted awkwardly. She gasped at the sudden sharp pain in her ankle, then hopped on one foot to hobble out of the way. "Ouch," she muttered and sat on the wild grass to the side, wanting to whimper a little bit, and let the tears fall.

While still reeling from the pain, she heard a voice call out,

"You okay?"

The sonorous aura of the voice reeked of daunting familiarity. It caught her by the heart, and she couldn't help but look up. She lifted her eyes from her foot to the familiar face. Standing in front of her was the handsome Ezra Buchanan, with another nice-looking, athletically built dark-brown man standing behind him.

"Leila!" Wasting no time, Ezra dropped his bike to the side of the trail. He pulled off his helmet and placed it next to the bike. He crouched next to where Leila was seated and reached for her foot. His milky gray eyes drilled into her, and his concern was evident.

Surprised that he remembered her name, Leila scanned his face. He had two days worth of scruff on his long jaw, compared to the nicely shaven face she'd seen when they'd met at the gas station. He looked more handsome than she remembered, his skin more olive than the last time.

Who was this man? The man who paid for lunches for strangers he'd just met in the store changed strangers' tires, and now was a doctor on the trail taking care of clumsy strangers. She tried to hide her pain. There was absolutely no way the guy was going to consider her a wimp.

"Hi again," Leila greeted shyly.

He smiled at her, and the oddest thing happened: something buzzed low in her belly. She didn't like it. She didn't think she would ever see Ezra again. Meeting him for the second time, that was quite the charm, but she had to put her tricky mind aside.

The dark brown gentleman cast a glance toward Ezra, then to Leila, as if he sensed something in the air.

"You two know each other?" he asked, studying Leila with interest.

"Yes, we met two days ago," Ezra responded. "This is Leila. "

Ezra introduced the man as Jake, explaining that the two of them had been riding more slowly than everybody else since Jake was still new to mountain biking. Then to Jake, he said, "Looks like the group is almost at the bottom, where we're supposed to meet the others. I will meet you down the trail."

Jake nodded his response.

"Would you tell Alex to dismiss everybody?" Ezra said, his gaze never leaving Leila's leg.

"Meet you down, bro," Jake said as he readied his bike to take off.

"Jake's never ridden with my church group before, but he knows some of the guys since he'd gone rock-climbing with them before." If Ezra meant for his light conversation to relax Leila, it was working.

"Are you hurt?" Ezra asked.

"I think I twisted my ankle just a little, but I'm good." She didn't want him to assume she was in much pain and end up sending an ambulance, ruining her camping trip. She knew it was an extreme measure to take, but she figured Ezra was the concerned type. If he thought she was injured, she was sure he'd be the kind of guy who would call 911 or at least insist on taking her to the nearest emergency room.

He slid off her flip-flop, "let me look at it. Try to wiggle your foot and let me know if your ankle hurts."

She carefully wiggled her foot and winced when she felt a dull ache. She immediately replaced the wince with a soft smile for Ezra's sake. "I can wiggle fine."

Despite her response, Ezra didn't seem to believe her, the fact that his hands closed around her ankle. She pressed her lips together. Ezra pressed gently with his thumbs and took a deep breath.

"No swelling, he said, and massaged her ankle. "Let me know if I'm hurting you."

Her heart was pounding harder than average, and she felt a sudden rise in her body temperature.

"I'm fine." She forced herself to say.

Ezra's hands were damp with sweat, but they felt reassuring.

His kind eyes observed her, and he gave her an assuring smile that carried the heaviness of unspoken words.

"It's a mild sprain," Ezra concluded as he pushed himself up. "Do you need help walking back? I believe you're done with your hike." He held out his hand to help her up.

"Thank you!" She said in a choked voice. I can walk myself back, it's not that far anyway." She brushed grass off her leggings.

"Try to put some ice on it, or soak it in cold water, if possible," he suggested.

His gaze went to her feet as if assessing her choice in footwear.

He wiped a few drops of sweat from his face with the palm of his hand "Why didn't you hike with your friend?" he asked. "It's always good to have a walking partner."

Leila gave him a perplexed look. She had forgotten she'd told Ezra she was meeting a friend. She was impressed that he remembered and he'd been listening when they talked two days ago.

"She's . . . ," she started to answer, but her mind went blank. "Hmm, what did you just ask?"

Either her mind was groggy from her mild accident, or there was something in the air.

"Your friend? You were camping with a friend, right?" His eyebrow arched with a direct gaze at her.

"Oh yeah, she's not here, I mean not here with me . . ."

Since when did she start being tongue-tied? Perhaps it was the ankle.

Without her realizing it, her eyes drifted to his left hand. She didn't see a ring and continued to stutter for a few seconds. She was surprised at the sense of relief she felt that Ezra wasn't married. Why her brain was being overly active, she had no idea, and she decided to refocus.

Perhaps Ezra noticed her frazzled look.

"Are you sure you don't need me to carry you?" He looked as if he was ready to scoop her up and carry her right then and there, but he waited patiently for her response.

"I'm sure."

Ezra nodded. "I would have insisted if the sprain was more severe, but I really should check on the group. I want to be sure the group is dismissed."

Ezra slid his helmet over his tousled brown hair before picking up his bike again.

"It was nice to see you again," Ezra said.

"Me too," Leila responded, then tucked an escaped strand of hair behind her ear. "You better catch up with your group."

"Don't worry about that," he said. "I want to make sure you make it off the trail before another biker runs you over," he smiled as Leila stepped aside to let him pass.

Before he climbed onto his bike, Ezra twisted his neck to look back, just in time to see Leila stumble, catching herself to avoid a fall. Dropping his bike, Ezra flew right back to the rocky trail to help her. "I will just have to carry you," Ezra said as he returned to do what he seemed to do best.

Leila opened her mouth to object but knew there was no sense in doing so since Ezra had already swept her off the ground and started down the trail.

Leila must not have hidden her discomfort very well, because Ezra smiled. "This is what I would do for anybody he said. "At least I will feel better leaving you down the trail knowing you're safe." He marched down the trail while Leila continued to study him. He seemed to be the kind who was not used to taking no for an answer.

As if reading her mind, "I bet you think I'm bossy, huh?" he asked with a smile.

If Ezra could see her thoughts so clearly, she figured he was the type of man to be avoided at all costs. There were some thoughts meant to be secret.

"How did you know what I was thinking?" she asked.

"By looking at you." His lips creased into a half smile.

What was he . . . a detective? First, she thought he was a mechanic for swiftly changing her tire, then now, was he a doctor too? She had several questions for him and found the man to be intriguing, but there was no use in finding out. What were the chances they would run into each other again?

"You just look at people, and you know exactly what they're thinking?"

Ezra shrugged."Not always, I guess it depends on who." He gently put her down."You're now safe."

After Ezra had seen to Leila's safety off the trail, he returned for his bike, climbed on, and started the ride back to catch up with the rest of his group.

Leila stood for a moment as the fresh mountain air filled her lungs. She turned to smile at Ezra as he passed by her on his bike, then waved and opened her lips to motion her thanks.

Ezra acknowledged her gratitude with a nod. "Take it easy!" he said and rode off.

Leila shook her head in amusement and took a peek at him as he rode down the trail, his muscles contorting as he made his way. She wouldn't forget his genuine concern and kindness. The ankle didn't feel as painful after it had the right nurturing. A smile swept her face when she remembered Ezra's elevated Jeep from almost two days ago and the view she had of him while he climbed inside. She knew there wasn't much chance of them meeting again, but she couldn't deny he had intrigued her. She wanted to get to know more about him.

Giving up her photo snapping for the day, she strolled along on the rocky dirt road back to the campground to nurse her wound as the trail doctor had instructed.

Leila had not expected to see Ezra after the gas station encounter, but instead, she'd had another encounter with him today. Even though she wished to see him again, she doubted that would be the case. If that happened, then she'd know God was up to something.

***

As Ezra rode over the rocky hill, his thoughts drifted back to Leila. He'd been sure, that he would never see her again. Since his encounter with her at the gas station, oddly he'd found himself thinking about her. Something that was unusual for him, given his busy lifestyle. And today she'd stumbled across his path, literally.

What kind of hiker was she, to be wearing flip-flops on a trail like that? Not that he'd minded helping her. He smiled as the image of her paint free toenails played in his mind.

Not only was Leila light to carry, but she also smelled of a fresh scent of spring. Something floral, a smell that Ezra knew would linger on his own body—a scent that was going to linger on him for a while. He could have carried her another three miles just to smell her scent. And the girl looked as good as she smelled, her black skin silky and smooth. He now longed to take a quick, cold shower.

The sound of an animal snorting in pain jolted him from his daydreaming. He was close to a property that was surrounded by barbed wire. The area was open enough for him to scan his surroundings. Another sound came, and his eyes caught sight of a buck twisting around the barbed wire.

He walked close and sure enough, its antlers were held captive by the loose part of the wire. He pulled out his pocket knife from his pocket and crouched, although careful not to get kicked by the frantic animal.

"Okay boy, I'm here to help you." He spoke to the animal as if it could understand his language. And then he grabbed one of its antlers, and the buck struggled harder, sending Ezra tumbling onto his back.

Panting, Ezra figured he could either leave the poor animal alone, which would haunt him, not knowing its fate, or he could die trying to save it.

"Okay, God, this is one of your special creations, and I know you've placed me in its path so that I can free it. Please let the animal stay calm."

He sighed deeply and crouched close. This time the buck was panting, almost giving up the fight. Finding the right angle, Ezra clipped the wire and the animal galloped away without looking back.

By the time Ezra met with Jake, the group had been dismissed. Ezra was panting and covered with fresh perspiration.

Jake gave him a once over. "What happened to you?"

"Long story." He gave Jake details of his escapade with the deer.

Jake told him his plans to stay the night at a cabin.

Jake had enjoyed the mountain biking so much that he'd decided to stay the night at a cabin in Hidden Valley so he could go biking again tomorrow morning.

"Why don't you come and stay at camp with us? " Ezra asked.

"No way, I'm I staying in a typical man cave."

Ezra hoped this trip was taking Jake's mind off his ex-wife. Perhaps giving him the opportunity to think clearly, with few to no distractions, was what his friend needed. He'd been having spiritual conversations with Jake and praying with him since he'd been open to sharing parts of his heart lately

They then rode another trail and shared dinner together before Jake left for the cabin in Hidden Valley and Ezra returned to the campground.

CHAPTER 7

IT WAS BECOMING a habit for Leila to sit by the creek in the afternoon to watch the sunset. She'd done this daily since the first day at camp. Leila couldn't believe how much the fresh mountain air overtook her.

As she sat on the wooden bench, she listened to the gentle stream washing away in rhythm while she watched the beautiful meadow in its utmost serenity. After she'd nursed her ankle with lots of ice, she could tell it was much better.

She snapped a few pictures of her surroundings, with deer and the wildflowers in the background, as the sun rolled out of sight. The scenery enthralled her so much that all her cares and worries fell away, allowing Psalm 19 to fill her mind. "The heavens declare the glory of God; the skies proclaim the work of his hands." She spent the remaining hours of the afternoon meditating on God.

First Site

She returned to her tent site at six thirty and decided to start a campfire using lint. She'd seen it done on a YouTube video in preparation for her camping trip. It had only taken the person in the video a few seconds to get the fire started, but Leila quickly realized it was more work than it had appeared. Several attempts later, flames finally engulfed the fire pit.

As much as Leila enjoyed solitude, tonight seemed painfully quiet around the site. She glanced at the trailer, and there was no movement. She watched a few campsites from a distance. There had been a family two sites down that she'd noticed from time to time when the kids would let out screams of excitement. The rest of the sites were hidden from sight by the shade trees, giving the campers more privacy.

The silence that stretched across the mountains now seemed odd since Leila had company for the first two nights. The evening was a darker gray with a gloomy sky, not the usual colorful sunset, and temperatures seemed cooler all of a sudden.

After her plantain chips and apple dinner, she put out the campfire before going to bed. Without Bianca to talk to, all she could hear were the cricket noises and the gentle babbling of the creek. She dove into the silence and drifted off to sleep immediately.

***

A thunderstorm knocked Leila out of her sleep. An ear-splitting peal of thunder cracked the night as the sky flickered with endless streaks of lightning.

The thunder steadily boomed across the mountains, and the fierce wind reminded Leila of God's natural controlled force and His presence. She lay still, praying that her tent wouldn't blow over.

At that moment, she wished Bianca was still around to keep her company. When she glanced at her lit watch, it was two o'clock in the morning. The thunder roared violently as the rain began in massive torrents that noisily pounded her shuddering tent.

It amazed Leila how quickly the weather had shifted. Yesterday had been sunny with a clear sky. Even having looked at the forecast two days ago, she had seen no indication of rain for the entire week. But then again, forecast or no forecast, God controlled the weather.

Leila looked up and noticed her tent sinking in toward her, and the fear of her shelter failing was confirmed. Before she knew it, she was swimming in water. While Leila enjoyed swimming more than most, she didn't want to do so in her sleeping bag at such an awful hour.

The wind was howling and thrashing, threatening to tip the tent over, especially with the added weight. Leila wondered what would happen if her tent blew over. Pulling herself out of her sleeping bag, she began to think of her options. Fear threatened to take over, as a sense of uneasiness rose in her chest, and she once again wished her friend was here. Bianca would know what to do.

It was the bright flash followed by loud, roaring thunder that compelled her to think fast. She'd read in a tent camping booklet on what precautions to take against lightning. She knew her vehicle would be safe, but that would mean having it running all night to stay warm.

Her wet sleeping bag was of no use now. Either way, she was going to be cold. Alternatively, she could escape to the public bathroom, but that seemed worse than the first option.

Her desire to pack up and go home was overwhelming until she realized she'd have to disassemble the tent in the rain. After weighing all her options, she ended up with a more practical plan.

***

Ezra was sound asleep when the booming thunderstorm jerked him awake. He could hear the rain pelting the trailer roof. He sighed heavily. He'd been looking forward to a good night's sleep after having had a long day on the trail.

Despite his desperate pleas for the storm to stop so he could sleep, the thunder continued. He covered his head with a pillow to muffle the loud noise from the storm, but that didn't seem to help. The thunder got louder and louder until he threw the pillow to the floor and jolted from his bed.

What kind of storm was this? It wasn't until he headed out toward the living area of the trailer that he realized it was more than thunder after all.

Someone was pounding on the door. Even though he wasn't sure exactly what time it was, he knew it was very late and rainy. He could only assume it was his siblings returning late from their parents' cabin.

When he groggily walked to turn on the lights and opened the door, he was taken aback by what he saw.

He wasn't at all prepared for what stood before him in the form of a slender woman, soaked and dripping. Her arms wrapped around herself, she stood there shivering. He recognized her easily even with the dim light of the trailer on her face.

He had thought the woman he'd briefly seen from her back during the spider incident reminded him of Leila, but now he knew it had been her.

"I'm sorry to wake you," Leila said before the man she assumed was Andrew could utter a word.

She was so frazzled and didn't pay attention to the face at the entrance. "Water got into my tent," she said, shaking.

"Why don't you come inside first?" the man said as he motioned for her to enter. She wasted no time accepting the invitation. She closed the door behind her, then turned and ran into him. The man reached out to steady her, then took a step back.

When she shifted her gaze to his face to apologize for her wet flannels, her jaw dropped at the sight of Ezra. Him again? Why she kept running into this man everywhere she went was yet to be revealed. He could not be related to Andrew and Renee. What were the odds?

"Hey," he said with a warm smile, and somehow even with Leila's jittery lips, she found herself smiling at him.

"You're—"

"Andrew and Renee's brother," he answered with a wider grin.

Why hadn't she put two and two together? Ezra had mentioned going to sing at his parents' retreat center, and Renee had said the same thing. Now that he mentioned it, Leila realized he did resemble his siblings. Except for his own unique gray eyes— both Andrew and Renee had the light blue eyes.

"Sorry again for w-w-waking you," she said as her teeth tattered.

Rose Fresquez

Even with his mussed hair, Leila couldn't fail to notice how handsome he looked. For a brief moment, she forgot there was a thunderstorm and that she had been beaten ruthlessly by the massive torrents. Their presence seemed to fill up every bit of space until Ezra spoke up.

"You just interrupted my snoring, that's all," he said in a groggy voice.

"You have come to my rescue, like, three times. It's just—" she started to say before Ezra cut her off.

"Don't worry about it; I get rescued more times than you know."

Leila doubted the guy ever needed rescuing at any point. She would love to be there when that happened.

"You're shaking," he pointed out before disappearing in one of the rooms, returning with a dry towel, then pointed her toward the shower, which his sister had already pointed out when she gave Leila a tour.

Her eyes went to the duffle bag on the doormat, "All my clothes are in this bag, and I'm not sure any of them are still dry."

Ezra looked at the dripping bag. "I'll bring you some clean clothes to change into. You and Renee are almost the same size."

Even though she dreaded borrowing his sister's clothes, she didn't have much of a choice. She hoped to go to Hidden Valley and do laundry first thing in the morning. She assumed Andrew and Renee had to be back from their parents' place by now.

"Hopefully I didn't wake your siblings too." She listened for any snoring or heavy breathing from the other rooms, but it was hard to make out the sounds with the rain pattering on the roof.

"They didn't come back tonight, but they will be here tomorrow." He paused and corrected himself, "Or today. I bet it's past midnight."

Leila knew Ezra was happy to help, and she didn't have much of a choice in the matter, but she still managed to feel guilty for barging in on him so late. However, she was also oddly grateful to have run into him once more.

This would generally be where she would walk back to her wet tent or drive back home in the rain if her options were between staying in the trailer with a stranger or go freeze in her car.

After the last two encounters with Ezra, who had been her knight in shining armor and a gentleman who prayed in front of a stranger, she trusted God's instinct on this. He had to have a hand on this.

She could feel the stirrings in her heart confirming so. Besides, she had met his wonderful siblings, and she was sure she was safe. Ezra was a lot like his sister, down to earth and kind, and he radiated the same confidence as his more reserved brother.

Ezra narrowed his gaze on her as if reading her mind once again. "Don't worry; my siblings will be here tomorrow." He continued to clarify, "I will be sleeping on the opposite side of the trailer.

"You can sleep in the king bed, at the other end." He pointed her to one of the rooms. "Feel free to lock your door, too."

Her lips creased into an unrestrained smile, and she wondered how he had read her so clearly.

"Thanks, Ezra . . . for the clothes!" It was all she could manage to say before Ezra left the room. Her gaze followed his shadow as he walked away.

This was one of those days her organizational skills paid off: she'd managed to keep her lingerie, electronics, and Bible in the plastic container. Otherwise, they would have experienced the same fate as the rest of her luggage—wet.

Ezra knocked on the bathroom door just as she moved to the shower. She stuck her hand out, and he placed some dry clothes into it. "Thanks!"

Ezra hummed his response.

***

Now dressed in gray sweats and a tight-fitting purple tee, Leila felt refreshed after a warm shower. She felt her feet could use more layers. While still standing, she explored the fifth wheel's interior and understood why people choose to consider them as their homes to retire and travel.

She glanced at the mounted TV, then stared at the kitchen, which was bigger for camping. Not that she would enjoy being on the go without a permanent home, she'd already done that growing up and wanted a place where she could grow a garden, enjoy a yard, and return to at the end of the day. Somewhere called Home.

"Excuse me, Ezra," she called as he emerged from the bedroom.

He raked a hand through his tousled hair. "Yes, how can I help you?"

"Do you think Renee has a sweater and socks I could borrow?" She glanced down at her toes, her hands crossed over her chest. She hated to keep bothering him, but he'd already proven himself helpful.

Pleased at how his name rolled off her tongue, Ezra liked how she felt comfortable enough to ask for help. He knew for a fact that he wasn't gifted in the area of being a host, and he preferred it when people communicated their needs. It was a lot easier than guessing, and the last thing he wanted was for Leila to be uncomfortable. "Let me see what I can do," he sent her a reassuring smile.

In a matter of seconds, he returned with a pair of warm, colored socks, an Avengers throw, and a sweatshirt. "I couldn't find a sweater in Renee's luggage. I hope you don't mind using mine." He said. "It's clean."

Leila studied the throw with interest. She was probably wondering what he was doing with a superhero blanket.

"If you're wondering about the throw, it's mine." His grin wide, he explained, "I wore out my childhood blanket and had to buy another one. I'm an Avengers fan." He winced while expecting to be met by Leila's questioning gaze but instead he was met by a warm smile. Feeling extremely self-conscious, he managed to smile back.

"I think it's adorable that you have something to remind you of your childhood. I like things with a sentiment to them."

Did she call him cute? He'd never had to share a blanket with a girl before and hadn't expected to share a trailer with any woman besides his mom and sister.

As if sensing his inner battle, Leila told him about her blanket that she'd sewed, having added all the fabrics cut from her baby blankets and outfits. "I can look at them instead of having them tucked away."

"Now, that's sentiment," Ezra said in a low voice.

In a way, Ezra's shy smile made him look even cuter than before. A sentimental guy too, Leila thought and wondered what kind of childhood he'd had.

Leila put on the sweatshirt that smelled of earth and detergent.

"I made you hot chocolate." He steered her to the table. "I figured you might want to go back to sleep. Otherwise, I would have offered you coffee, instead."

"Thank you!" She moved to the seat, no doubt that God had sent an angel in the form of Ezra to lead her through this camping trip—even though she was still considering her departure in the morning, as soon as she got laundry done and returned Renee's clothes.

Ezra pulled out the steaming cup from the microwave. "Here you go, milady!"

Leila couldn't help but wonder at how confident he was, yet charming at the same time. She smiled as a thought crossed her mind—I wish I were his lady. Pushing the thought away, she turned her attention back to Ezra. She liked the way he spoke to her as if they had known each other for a very long time. There wasn't the level of awkwardness she would have expected in this situation with any other person.

"Thank you."

"You are welcome." He said, taking a seat across from her.

"After all you've done for me, I owe you and your siblings' meals for the rest of the week." She intended to leave them her prepared meals that still sat in her cooler. Especially since Bianca had gone, she needed to get rid of all that food somehow. There would be no use in taking it back.

"You don't have to do that. You've been feeding us, my sister, the most. That soup with chicken . . ." Ezra's shoulders relaxed in his seat. "It was mouthwatering." He smiled, and she noticed how his smile created a twist inside her.

She moved a wet strand of hair from her forehead."It's the Jamaican stew."

"I take it you're from Jamaica then?"

"My mom was born and raised, and her family is still there." Leila thought of her mom and dad, now back together. "When Mom moved from Jamaica, her first job was a waitress in a local ethnic cuisine in New York, where they met. My dad had just graduated from West Point at the time. It was funny how their relationship began." Her face creased into a smile as she recalled her mom's story. "My mom was the waitress serving my dad, and she got so nervous while serving him his curried stew, that she accidentally spilled it on his clothes and all over the table." Leila laughed, and Ezra joined in. The sound of their voices laughter mingling was another language they had in common.

Interesting, Ezra thought. Now he wanted to know more about this girl, even if there was no future in it.

He breathed in the sweet fragrance of her shampoo as it took over his nostrils. He could get used to that natural scent, similar to the earthy outdoors. Not that it mattered what Leila smelled like, but it seemed to trigger a peaceful sensation in him. He wondered what it'd be like to touch her dark tresses, inhaling her fragrance. He also wondered if her hair was as soft as it looked.

"I would love to go to Jamaica someday," he mused.

"I think you would like it." Leila took a sip of her drink. "You should go."

Ezra's mind drifted to a Jamaican vacation accompanied by Leila. He had no idea what Jamaica looked like, except for the beaches he'd seen in travel magazines. Whether he would like Jamaica or not, the thought of going there with Leila seemed appealing. Heck, he would want to go any place with Leila.

CHAPTER 8

LEILA PUT HER cup back to the table. "This hot chocolate is delicious."

"Glad you like it." Ezra smiled. "It's just the packaged stuff; I added a bit of vanilla and cinnamon."

"Aren't you going to have some?"

He waved off the suggestion. "Nah, I'm good. You needed a hot drink more than I do."

"Well," she said, clearing her throat, "I might choke if I am drinking alone while you stare at me."

He chuckled softly. "I would rather not perform CPR on you tonight . . . however, if I must, I'm prepared."

She giggled, and the sound of it penetrated Ezra's heart. Hearing the sweet melody of her laugh made him want to rethink his priorities, but he merely shook it off. It was a foolish thought. What were the chances? No, he couldn't let his mind continue to wander in such a way. Whatever his heart—no, his mind—was doing, he needed to ignore it. He had too much going on to start up what would surely be a fling—and he wasn't the fling type. Plus, he wasn't ready for a long-term relationship either. Not after what happened with Paige. He'd known right from their first date, that he didn't want to be in that relationship, but he'd ignored the warning signs thus wasting two years of his life.

However, Leila wasn't initiating anything, a matter of fact, Ezra seemed to be the one doing all the flirting. Although he could tell that Leila was enjoying his company as much as he was enjoying hers.

Rising from his seat, he shook his head in amusement at both Leila and himself. The thought of taking a beverage at three in the morning might nauseate him, but he figured it best to be polite and allow Leila to feel more comfortable.

"The group of bikers you were with today . . . are you in some bike club?"

"Something like that. I'm part of the outdoor ministry at our church. Someone else leads it, but he was out of town, and I offered to lead the biking this week. I had invited a couple of my buddies from work as well."

Since Ezra was camping with his siblings, he figured he could incorporate cycling into his schedule. Ezra talked about his small group.

"It's nice that you're so involved in your church," Leila said.

They talked about their faith, and finding out they were both on a similar ground spiritually was comforting.

"Do you attend a small group, Leila?"

"I wish I did, but I'm not as involved as you are just yet. I've been a Christian for one year."

Ezra had grown up in a Christian home and came to Christ at an early age, unlike Leila, who was still new to the faith.

Ezra told Leila what his small group meant to him and how it'd helped him connect with his church family. "With my odd hours at work, I would always feel like a guest at church if I didn't belong to a small group."

"My parents have a small group," Leila said. "No wonder they decided to host a weekly Sunday brunch with the people from their group."

"What motivated you to take a camping trip?" Ezra asked as he leaned into his chair.

Leila bit her lips. "I have a bucket list."

"Bucket list? Hmm." His smile faded. "You're not dying, are you?"

Leila chuckled softly. "My students, and for adventure's sake." She told him about how she'd made a list with her students.

"My family not being into the outdoors much, I've had some curiosity about exploring the mountains someday. I've read several books about the outdoors, though I didn't think I would be camping this soon."

"A teacher . . ." he nodded. She did look like a teacher now that she mentioned it. "What grade?"

"Second," she replied cheerfully and shared a few stories about her class. Ezra didn't miss the spark in her eyes as she talked about her students.

"Those young stars are blessed to have you! The world needs more kind and passionate teachers like you."

"How do you know that I'm kind?" She peered into his eyes, awaiting his response.

139

"I am a good judge of character." He rubbed the back of his head with his hand. "Your smile, your warm eyes, and the excitement in your eyes when you talk about your students."

The fact that he'd read her mind at more than one occasion made sense now. He seemed to notice all the little things about her, including her little body language habits. Things that no one else seemed to pick up on.

Although flattered, Leila wasn't too sure what to do with the compliment. She decided to bury her head in her mug for another sip of hot chocolate, which was no longer hot. Still, she sipped on her warm drink.

"What do you do, Ezra Buchanan?" she asked, changing the subject. She was finally getting a chance to hear what his actual job was, a mechanic, a doctor, or a detective.

"I am a firefighter at Fort Rock." He leaned his arms on the table.

He talked about his new promotion to lieutenant. Leila smiled as she watched his face light up when he spoke of work and spoke highly about his colleagues, whom he claimed were another family away from home.

"That explains your heroic actions. I think it's so brave and selfless to save people for a living," she said with a genuine smile.

Ezra blushed and tried hard to focus on his drink. "I wouldn't say I'm a hero."

They were both dancing around their attraction for each other, embarrassed and shy, each wearing a soft, genuine smile. Changing the subject, he asked, "Why are you so afraid of spiders?" A memory rushed in, and a feeling of nostalgia overcame him. He'd wanted to know all along; he remembered the piercing scream.

He had been on his way out to meet the cycling group when he'd heard a scream and saw his brother, among others, surrounding her. He hadn't been sure it was Leila, since he only had a view of her back, and had assumed his mind was playing tricks on him. He didn't want to go find out who the lady was when she already had all the help she needed. After his encounter with her earlier today on the trail, he had no doubt Leila was the spider girl.

His gaze was intent on hers. A silent language seemed locked in the sensational depth in her eyes.

"Did your siblings tell you about the scene I made this morning?" Her coy smile projected her natural shyness. She tucked a strand of hair behind her ear.

"They didn't need to—your scream was loud enough to bring the dead back to life," Ezra chuckled softly.

It was great that Leila could laugh about it now that it was history. He made it seem like spiders couldn't shut her out of life, getting restarted the moment they were gone out of her sight. She somehow didn't seem embarrassed that Ezra was aware of it. Though he teased her, he was careful not to make her feel bad for her phobia—and for that, she looked grateful.

"Why didn't you tell me at the trail that you saw me earlier?" she asked, continuing to smile shyly.

Ezra was glad for the double-booking mistake. It boggled his mind how quickly his plans had changed—and he was thankful. Spending time with Leila was like spending time outdoors—he felt at home and relaxed around her, yet he hardly knew her. The fact that he was enjoying a normal conversation with a beautiful woman, while he was supposed to be sleeping fascinated him.

"You were hurt, and that was not the best time for me to introduce myself as your neighbor at the campground. Besides, I wasn't sure it was you." He then added in a serious tone, "I still want to hear about your spider fears."

"It's hard to explain . . ." She sighed. "They just give me the heebie-jeebies." She scrunched her face and squirmed in her seat at the thought.

Leila was finding herself more and more comfortable with Ezra, and her filters and walls seemed to come down a little more with each question. She was enjoying the way Ezra got her to smile, and the way his smile tugged at the corner of his mouth—it did something to her heart, and she was not only beginning to love it, but she was also hunting for more of that feeling.

She told him about how Andrew had saved the day, which she quickly realized sounded more like something Ezra would have done. Perhaps heroic deeds ran in the family. "I don't like bugs, but spiders are in a different category of bugs for me. They are creepy. Ew!" She squeezed her face, grimacing and tweaking her eyebrows. "But on the bright side, I love the peace and quiet up here."

She thought of the view by the creek, the deer that came in the afternoon, and the generous amount of wildflower blossoms, mountain air, the feeling of inner serenity. Things that made her wish to stay for the rest of the week, or perhaps for a whole month, but she couldn't.

"I think you're very brave to be facing your fears," Ezra said.

"Well, I wasn't exactly facing my fear quite that eloquently."

He chuckled. "Well, you're doing well for someone who's camping for the first time."

"You think so?" she asked hesitantly. Why does it matter what he thinks of me? For some reason, she longed to hear of his approval.

"I know so." He wasn't smiling, but he was calm without looking stern. It was a reassuring expression that warmed her soul.

"I had a flat tire, an ankle injury, now the rain. Everything hasn't gone smoothly at all," she reminded him.

"Certain things are out of our control. God has a reason for everything. Just because you've had a few bumps in the road doesn't mean your whole camping experience will be as bad. You don't know what tomorrow will bring. Do you?"

That he was right, she needed to let God finish the job He'd started in her life.

She shook her head. "No, I don't." Her voice low "Thanks for reminding me."

"You could look on the bright side," he gently suggested. "For each obstacle, you've faced, God sent someone to your rescue."

"It's been you." She buried her face in her mug.

"Even so, I am glad to be that person." Then he realized what he'd just said; he thought it had turned out awkward and tried to rephrase it. "At times its one person God uses in your life for a season." Even as he said the words, he wondered why God had placed Leila in his path three times in the last seventy-two hours. And now they were at the same campground, site, and trailer, too. They seemed even closer than before.

Ezra glanced at the numbers on the microwave screen and realized it was already four a.m. He was surprised to see they had talked for over an hour, but that was the thing he was starting to learn about being with Leila. When he spoke to her, time didn't seem to exist. This was his third time talking to Leila, and as he realized it, an old phrase kept ringing through his mind. Third time's the charm. He nearly scoffed at the thought.

"I will let you get some rest," he said suddenly. He was afraid that he might embarrass himself or let another foolish phrase slip from his lips. What would she think of him? Or better yet—what did she already feel about him? He couldn't deny he wanted to know. He could see her thoughts, but that was something else—she either did not care or she was careful to keep any interest well hidden.

They bid each other good night, which was more of a good morning.

Back in his room, Ezra set the alarm on his phone, then finally drifted off to sleep. He dreamed— no surprise—of the girl in the trailer, with her infectious laugh. He knew he couldn't have her, but his mind blessed him with a dream of inhaling her scent as he kissed her lips.

CHAPTER 9

LEILA WOKE UP to the golden rays of sunlight streaming in through the thin openings of the window blinds. Covers to her chin, she found it hard to believe the sunshine still existed given the storm they had experienced last night.

Her mind replayed the previous events, from the warm shower, the hot chocolate, to the last seventy-two hours that Ezra had been involved. Before falling asleep last night, she'd prayed for a quick recovery for Bianca's daughter Daisy, and hoped to call first thing in the morning when she went into town. She'd finally drifted off to sleep as the rain slowly subsided and finally blew itself out.

Leila took a deep breath before pulling herself out of bed and heading into the hallway of the quiet trailer. The place seemed desolate, except for the smell of fresh coffee. She glanced at her watch and saw that it was 8:35 a.m. As she cracked the front door open, the sky cast sunbeams in every direction, illuminating the whole campground. She knew it was going to be a beautiful day.

Back in the kitchen, she noticed a blue handwritten note on the center of the table. Her lips creased into a smile at the sight of the scribbled handwriting, more like a doctor's handwritten notes than something she'd expect her fellow camper to leave. Still, she managed to understand the words, and it read,

I made you some coffee, help yourself.

Please don't leave just yet. I will be back by ten.

—Ezra

She then remembered Ezra's meeting with a friend this morning.

She put on her flip-flops and Ezra's sweatshirt that she'd borrowed last night. Taking a stroll outside, she began to assess the damage done to her friend's tent. The smell of rain hang smoothly in the air. Leila was thankful for the blanket of pine needles that kept the campground from being muddy. To her surprise, the rain fly of her tent was off and nicely spread out to dry on the logs. She knew there was only one person who must have done that. She returned to the trailer to make breakfast and shower.

With a Bible in her hands and a cup of coffee on the table, Leila read Psalms 19. She began meditating on it as her prayer for the day. It reminded her of how perfectly it suited the scenery: the heavens declaring the glory of God; the skies proclaiming the work of his hands. She especially loved verses one through six.

Being in nature was an ever-present reminder to think about the Creator. The breathtaking scenery, the cloister of lofty mountains towering up above them, the serene perfection of nature's beauty with the birds' twitters echoing across the mountains. She finished her Scripture study and prayer, thanking God for sending help in the midst of the storm. The song "Eye of the Storm" crossed her mind as she finished praying.

The jerking of the door announced Ezra's return. Leila lifted her head and noted that he was dressed in a white T-shirt with a plaid shirt hanging over his shoulder. The T-shirt was dampened, and his forehead wore a sheen of sweat.

Ezra's eyes went straight to the table where Leila's Bible sat. He smelled bacon, and his stomach lurched with an audible growl. Leila sent a cursory glance his way.

He cleared his voice, "I hope I'm not interrupting your devotional time." He smiled and tiptoed towards Leila.

"I'm done with my devotions." She raised her coffee mug.

He was impressed that her devotions were a priority. Whenever Ezra camped, he was terrible at keeping up with his devotional routine. He would draw up a schedule to fit it in, but then he would forget to keep it.

"I made some breakfast for us." She closed her
Bible. "Hope you're hungry."

His hands went to his toned stomach, and he
sent a soft smile her way. "I'm starving," he said, still
rubbing his belly.

Ezra stared at Leila while she cleared her bible
and papers from the table. With her dark hair hanging
over her shoulders, she looked prettier than ever. Her
brown eyes seemed deeper as if they held several layers
of undiscovered beauty within. She must have rested
enough— her eyes were bright and her face rejuvenated
from last night's events.

One of the papers landed on the floor, and Ezra
bent to pick it up about the same time as Leila reached
for it. Their hands brushed, and Ezra's heart lurched.

They stared at each other with simmering
tension for another second, before Leila yanked the
paper from his hand. "Thanks," she said, pulling herself
up.

Ezra rose and sniffed the air that clouded her, and it smelled of something fresh and aromatic. Then he became conscious of not having had a shower, although he hadn't planned to take one this morning since he was going to be outdoors throughout the day. Now he felt it necessary if he planned to talk Leila into staying so he could be her tour guide.

"I will join you shortly," he said, taking off for a quick shower.

He swiftly returned to the table in a blue plaid shirt and brown outdoor pants; he took a deep breath before taking a seat on the table across from Leila. He could make out the scent now, and it smelled like a cocktail of vanilla and mint.

Ezra prayed over their meal, and they started to eat.

He took a bite of his eggs. And let out a moan of pleasure which caught Leila's attention by the way she fidgeted in her seat. "You make such delicious eggs."

"Thank you," she said and took another sip of her coffee.

They both enjoyed their breakfast as they talked, sharing constant glances and occasional stares. Now and then Ezra's sweet jokes made Leila laugh. He silently observed her full lips when she wasn't looking at him, and quickly diverted his stares to his plate when she turned. Feeling the need to fill the silence, he asked.

"How is your ankle feeling?"

Leila nodded. "Almost as good as new."

They ate in silence, but it was as if a thousand silent words were being exchanged between the two. Words they couldn't yet say.

All of a sudden Ezra realized how small the kitchen table felt. He'd sat with Leila at the gas station just fine, but it was starting to feel crowded in the small trailer—though he didn't mind being near Leila. Even last night they had sat together drinking their hot chocolate just fine. What is wrong with me? He thought. He squirmed in his chair. He often sat in this same space with his siblings, which had seemed big enough until now. He needed to breathe. He needed to think. Too many thoughts kept swirling around in his head. The coffee now seemed too hot. Leila sat so comfortably like all this was normal for her. Now that he was acting awkward, he was afraid Leila would start to feel uncomfortable.

"What time will Andrew and Renee return?" Leila asked suddenly, nudging Ezra back to himself from his long brooding.

"That depends on how soon my parents will let them go," Ezra explained as he continued staring at his plate. It was safer to keep his eyes there than on Leila.

Ezra knew how much his mom got excited whenever she saw either one of them. His dad was excited as well, but his mom didn't work on a schedule. When you visited her, you had better not have any plans or experience an emergency. She always had reasons to keep you longer with either small chores or plenty of talking. "Given the fact that my mom is involved, they might end up spending the entire day there. I will find out when I call." He moved his eggs around with a fork and then asked, "What are your plans for today?" He asked, hoping to impose his own plans on her.

He stared at her elegant long neck while she took a bite of her last egg, then pushed the plate to the side with two pieces of bacon left.

"Looks like I need to do something with the tent, then find a Laundromat, and go home."

"I took your sleeping bag out of the tent. You need to let the tent air-dry. Otherwise, it will get moldy."

The weather looked promising and bright. The clouds were a bit scanty, but the sun had hidden behind some clouds just like yesterday's forecast before the night storm. It seemed to be in the mid-seventies, but you never knew what early summer in the mountains could bring. The mountain atmosphere was always different, more refreshing than that of the plains.

"You can't go home just yet." He scratched the growth of hair on his long jaw. "I want you to stay."

Did he just say "I"? He thought about his statement as he caught himself. He bit into his last piece of bacon as he thought of the best possible way to rephrase his words. He tried to string his mind together before he spoke again. "So," he continued, "we would love for you to stay with us for the rest of your trip." He reminded her about the extra space in their trailer. If the tent was her reason for leaving, her problem had been solved. "I know that both Andrew and Renee will agree with me on this."

He knew for a fact she and Renee had hit it off. Renee had talked about her like they'd known each other for a long time. He wanted her to stay so he could show her the different parts of the mountains that he had no doubt she would love. She'd seemed curious enough about the outdoors, and he'd hate to see her give up on her trip all over some pesky storm. Why he cared if she left—well, he wasn't quite sure yet.

He'd been attracted to women before, but he never seemed to care if they parted ways before he could talk to them. He always had more important things to focus on but with Leila—he couldn't even seem to think of the words for what he was starting to feel.

Leila wanted to turn him down. She had failed at this whole camping trip. Though she knew in her heart that Ezra was right about God having different plans for us and that things happen for a reason, she couldn't shake off this sense of failure engulfing her.

For a moment, an array of excuses filled her mind—all the things she could say to justify leaving. Megan's daughter is sick. I need to be there for her. My tent may dry, but what if it rains again? I don't feel comfortable imposing on you and your family. It's your trip—I shouldn't be here. Your eyes stir in me something that both terrifies me and calms me.

Leila gazed into his stormy gray eyes and lost track of her words. She had found just one substantial reason to stay: to see those eyes again. That's foolish, she told herself, you can't stay any longer.

"I will stay," she said confidently, although her brain and mouth were not in coordination. She'd been sure she was going to turn him down but had no idea what just happened.

"Are you sure I will not be in the way of your spending time with your siblings?" she asked, peering into his eyes. The atmosphere had become warmer.

"The more, the merrier!" he grinned. How long could he control himself when he felt so comfortable and at ease with Leila?

Ezra's instinct was to throw his arms around Leila because of her response, but then a red flag went off on his brain. She was still unfamiliar territory. He didn't want to ruin her impression of him by being too forward. He was excited, and his heart skipped a beat at her response. He could also feel a slight flush to his face.

"Also, I have another request." His hand went to the back of his neck. "I can take you to town to get your laundry done since I have to make a few calls anyway. I was wondering if you can come fishing with me, and maybe four-wheeling too . . . If you'd like that." He asked as if he were doing her a favor, but it was a form of bribery to keep her entertained and occupied so she wouldn't decide to leave.

He loved the outdoors and assumed Leila would, too, if she gave it another chance. If she had a good day, perhaps she would want to stay and finish the trip she started. As much as he wanted to spend time with her, he also wanted to see her accomplish what she came out here for and not leave early.

"What if I say no?" Leila asked with a teasing smile.

"Then I will just have to find another way to persuade you." He smiled as he buried his face in the mug to take a final sip of his coffee. He felt something was about to leap out of his heart, something he wasn't sure he'd felt before or was it something he didn't want to feel just yet? He was prepared to catch it whenever it leaped out.

Leila thought she saw a spark of excitement in Ezra's eyes . . . But perhaps it was only in her imagination. She had to push those thoughts away for now.

She didn't have anything planned. How could she say no to spending the day with a man who had been her knight in shining armor? She could see his soul through his smile, how he wanted her to join him. She did want to explore the mountains and what better guide than someone who knew it well?

She was working on her bucket list, and she might as well make it memorable. For that reason, she felt right about accepting the invitation. "You won't need to find more ways to persuade me," she said, tucking a strand of hair behind her ear.

"Given your tender ankle, fishing might be a less strenuous activity."

"I would love to go fishing. Just so you know, I am very terrible at it." She smiled. "My dad tried taking us once, but my patience level failed me. Once, I flicked the hook over and found it hooked to the back of my top." She laughed.

He chuckled. "We could all use patience." He rose from the table with the disposable plates. "And fishing is another way to exercise patience."

I'll make us some lunch then. Are you allergic to anything?" Leila rose to find the food items from her cooler in the car.

"I'm very sure I will like whatever you make unless you're packing eel."

"There's always a first time for everything," she said, lifting her brow.

"I can make it my first then."

"So you're not into seafood?" Leila asked as she leaned against the entrance door.

"I'm not fond of seafood, but I like fishing."

"I'll be sure to remember that." Not that she had any seafood in her lunch options, but it was fun teasing Ezra. She turned to head for her car before he could see her mischievous grin.

CHAPTER 10

EZRA OPENED THE passenger door of his Jeep for Leila to get in. Her eyes widened as she assessed her climb at the highly elevated tires that jerked up the Jeep. She gave Ezra a doubtful glance. Without a word, Ezra picked her up and placed her gently in the passenger seat.

She gave him a soft smile and shook her head in amusement as they drove off to Hidden Valley.

An hour later, laundry was done, and phone calls were made. Leila had changed into a pair of Capri leggings and a plaid hot-pink with a white shirt. She was almost sad to return Ezra's sweater to him—she loved how it smelled, reminding her of the outdoors scent. Wearing it made her feel secure as if she was wrapped in loving arms.

After a few twists and turns down the rocky dirt road, they were surrounded by a bracket of mountains where Hidden Lake stood still with its clear water. The lake was hidden as the name implied. A couple was leaving as Ezra and Leila pulled in. There was also an older gentleman still fishing. After Ezra had set the rods, he handed one to Leila.

"There's a chance we will walk away without any fish." He handed her the bait.

Ezra thought it would be more comfortable fishing with such a full lake after last night's rain, but he didn't want to give Leila false hope. Fishing was one of those things where you could never be 100 percent positive about the results.

"I'm okay." She managed a smile as she gracefully arranged the bait. "I don't have to be anywhere. We've got all day to try to catch us something."

Leila took a quick whiff of the lake before Ezra showed her how to attach the bait and the extra steps on when to place a cast. Within several minutes, they started fishing while they talked about life in general. Their favorite foods, and places they longed to travel to.

"Why did you become a firefighter?" Leila asked, peering at him.

Ezra's gaze went to the lake as if in deep thought, "I always admired my dad saving lives, then my brother and I . . ." He chuckled as he shared memories of them hosing the neighbor's house, pretending to play firefighter. Ezra was 10 and Andrew 12. They got in trouble for that, since they'd flooded her garden. "My mom made us replant the flower bed, and we mowed the neighbor's lawn for the rest of the summer." He shook his head with a smile plastered on his face. He couldn't forget the constant adrenaline rush that gushed through his being. He still felt it just by reminiscing about good old days. "I'm always drawn to the adrenaline."

"Adrenaline like parachuting or something?" She gestured vaguely.

He laughed. "Exactly!"

"Why did you become a teacher?"

She sighed, "Fair enough, I spent a lot of time taking care of my brother and helping him with homework, and I think that was the root cause of my passion to serving others especially kids."

Ezra was impressed by how she took care of her brother, where was her dad? He had so many questions he wanted to ask, but it was a day to relax. Choosing a safer question he asked.

"Why kids? "

I love not only teaching them but being their friend—someone they could trust. My brother has major trust issues especially when it comes to women. Her gaze was distant and then continued. "He was only ten when my mom left my dad and moved to Jamaica for five years. She's back now, but it still had some side effects on our family."

Ezra wanted to place his hand upon her back for comfort, perhaps, but he couldn't get himself to do it.

The two continued to talk with occasional silences hanging between them, mainly when Ezra was too close to Leila showing her how to cast. Those moments had seemed longer than usual.

"I think I got something," Leila squealed in excitement, and she beamed with delight when her cast felt heavier. She noticed a fish as she pulled her rod out of the water.

Ezra put his fishing pole down, displaying a wide grin to share Leila's excitement as he moved closer to her.

She exposed her white teeth. "I've never caught a fish before," she said, grinning, and then she moved closer and pulled him into a quick side hug. The fish escaped back to the water. They stood staring at each other for a while before bursting into laughter. Both incidents were unbelievable, the hug and the fish diving back to water.

"I hope to catch that fish again," Leila said, laughing, and Ezra joined in.

***

Two hours later, Leila had caught three trout, and Ezra two. Probably because he spent more time giving lessons and explaining things over and over again. Ezra had shown her how to take the fish off the rod.

"We have to get a picture for your students," Ezra said when Leila had her final catch.

He rushed to grab his iPhone and snapped a photo of Leila with one of the trout.

"I will take your photo now." Leila offered.

Ezra slid his phone back to his pocket. "I'm good thanks!"

After they'd released each fish back to the lake, they stood side by side, gazing at the fish diving back to freedom.

Leila turned to face Ezra. "Thank you for the lesson," she smiled. She thought he was a great teacher and excellent company at that. She did something that surprised her; She hugged him once more. She never hugged the opposite sex, except for her dad and brother.

Now why she was hugging a guy she'd just met four days ago, she had no explanation yet.

Ezra had been caught off guard by the hug, but he enjoyed her arms wrapped around him. He had a quick and deep sniff of her refreshing scent, and he wanted to hold her longer and feel the fresh energy that swirled around them for a moment more.

"You're welcome." He stared at her, "What are the other three things on your list?" he asked when she dropped her hands from him.

"I would love to hike a fourteener, swim in the lake. I already did horseback riding yesterday. She spoke with excitement. "In the future, I would like to do something outrageous like a parachute from a plane. Extreme sports, you know? Maybe when I've mustered enough bravery to do so." She chuckled. "Maybe surfing too!"

Ezra had never enjoyed fishing as he did just now. Watching Leila's excitement had sparked fishing into something exciting. But now he longed for more of the moment, with her of course. They both walked back to the car so Ezra could put the rods away. Leila browsed in their lunch box to grab a drink for herself and offered one to Ezra.

"Thanks," Ezra said as he joined her under one of the pine trees. They sipped their water in comfortable silence, watching the birds hover above the clear and still lake, then swoop low just above the water in calculated, aerial acrobatics.

"Where next?" Leila asked.

Ezra sent her a calculated look. "Do you get car sick?"

"I don't think so, why?"

"I'm going to take you four-wheeling."

Leila glanced at her watch. It was half past noon, "Are you hungry for lunch?"

Ezra nodded. "But I can wait until our next stop. Can you?" He winced, "We are going on some steep and winding roads."

"Maybe I better eat a snack first. I know one thing: being hungry could limit my enjoyment of the adventure."

He gave a gentle chuckle and patted her shoulder.

***

Leila's lips felt drier the farther they drove on the steep dirt road, so she pulled out her mint lip balm from her shoulder-strap bag and applied a layer to her lips while Ezra navigated through the narrow road.

At some point, the Jeep ascended a steep hill, which caused Leila to cover her face. She thought for a second; they were going to trip off the edge of the mountain. They ended up on a road that seemed seldom traveled except by serious jeepers. They had rolled the windows down to see the magnificent scenery.

They entered a forest, where the damp earth combined with old fallen leaves and rotten twigs created an aroma that wafted into their noses as they wheeled past. She inhaled the aroma, and she felt something close to the utmost ease with the trees shading their path as they drove by.

The forest had mostly pine trees with a few random aspens, and Ezra rode roughly through large pools of water. The damp smell that formed the great aura birthed an increased desire in them to drive longer. Although not the best, it wasn't too bad when combined with the other smells of the forest.

Mud splashed all over the car, and some of it landed on Leila's face and hair. Ezra's face was splashed as well. But neither of them seemed bothered, they just glanced at each other when it happened, and giggled.

"I think this is going to be one of the best days I've had," Leila said, with her eyes wide in awe of their surroundings.

Voice low, Ezra agreed. "Me, too."

He reached the summit and parked the car.

"Wow!" Leila was mesmerized by the overlook, regretting having left her camera behind. The landscape was full of sheer beauty with a deep tinge of serenity spreading across the overview.

She stepped on a rock, spreading out her hands as she took a deep breath of pine-scented air. Ezra moved to watch the view from a different rock not too far from Leila's. Before them was a green valley with towering mountains. Leila pulled a water bottle from her shoulder-strap bag and hydrated herself, then applied more lip balm.

"From here you can see Mount Evans and Mount Bierstadt." Ezra pointed toward the mountains.

Of course, the guy knew all the mountains in Colorado, and probably had hiked most of them.

"I would like to hike that sometime," Leila said.

"It's a fun hike. I know you'd like it."

Yep, he'd hiked all of them according to his response.

"I should have guessed that you've already hiked it," Leila said, wearing a knowing expression on her face.

"There are others I haven't hiked, believe it or not."

"Others like?" Leila queried.

"Pike's Peak."

"This is beautiful!" she said when Ezra stepped down from his rock.

"I know, isn't it?" He glanced at her mud-covered face.

Ezra wished to offer to join Leila whenever she decided to hike any mountain, but he didn't have it in him to say the words, and they became lodged in his throat. He could only agree with Leila at the beauty surrounding them, not to forget that seeing the scenery from her point of view was more enjoyable.

Ezra always felt refreshed and exhilarated each time he drove up here; Today Leila seemed to add more beauty to the scenery for him.

He led her to a grassy open space with multiple flat rocks where they sat to enjoy their lunch.

This side of the mountains was still a few degrees cooler than where they'd started. There were still traces of snow on some of the mountains, but the scenery was breathtakingly beautiful. Ezra wanted Leila to see and enjoy the mountains, to feel the air around them since he was aware that she hadn't grown up doing much outdoors. He wasn't so sure why it mattered to him that she have a great time, but somehow he wanted to be the one to introduce her to God's beauty through the Colorado scenery. And here they were.

After washing their hands, Ezra prayed over their meal. The place was quiet except for the occasional sounds of the birds chirping and a few rodents scurrying around waiting for food crumbs.

Ezra took a bite of his wrap, "hmmm." Leila squirmed uncomfortably and stared at him. "These are the best wraps I've ever tasted." He said.

Leila gave him a shy smile, "There's more lunch in the cooler." She handed him a napkin.

"Would you like some Coke?" Ezra offered since he remembered Leila drinking a Coke the first time he'd met her at the gas station. He figured she might want some.

She shook her head. "Unless you have a plastic cup and some ice."

"I'm funny that way," her nose crinkled. "I only drink soda from a plastic cup with ice in it; otherwise, I'll have to stick to water."

Ezra was up to surprise her and left for the car, returning with a cup of ice, two cans of chilled Coke, and a bag of spicy Cheetos.

Her mouth opened and amused at the same time. "What else do you have in that car of yours?"

Besides sports equipment, Ezra kept his car stocked up with all sorts of things in case of an emergency, especially when he came to the mountains. He carried his caffeinated drinks in his cooler all the time. The cooler kept the ice for up to seven days.

"Everything I need." He popped open his soda. "I have a tent, in case the car gets stuck while we're up here and no one can reach us. I have a walkie-talkie. As a matter of fact, I should remember to give you one, in case we get separated."

She frowned, a bit curious and a bit worried. "I hope you are not planning to leave me up here."

He shook his head and smiled. "Why would I want to do that?" The only thing he wished was to stay up here and talk with her until they ran out of things to talk about. And then . . . He brought himself back to the present.

Leila squinted at him instead. "That's some serious stuff. You must have been a Boy Scout."

"Eagle Scout."

"I feel safe already," she said with a half smile.

Realizing it was better to learn more about Leila than about himself, Ezra switched the conversation.

"Why do you have to drink soda in a plastic cup with ice?"

"It tastes much better that way," she answered, before sipping her soda. "It's hard to explain, but you should try it sometime."

"I just might have to." This lady was getting more interesting each passing moment. His eyes darted to Leila's bag of chips.

"What kind of chips are those?" he asked while he placed a few spicy Cheetos to his mouth.

"Plantains," Leila said and handed him the bag. "You should try some."

He wasn't the one to gobble strange foods, but he had a lady to please. Hesitant, he pulled out a piece of plantain and sniffed it before popping it in his mouth."They are a bit different." He didn't know what to make of the taste yet, but he ate a few more and squinted.

"They are not as good as potato chips." His brows drew together as he chewed. "Not as disgusting as they appeared though."

"At least you tried something new." She took another sip of her drink.

"Yeah, I will have to make a bucket list of my own."

She gave him a warm smile that did something to his heart. Without permission from the rest of his body, his eyes darted to her lips, to the delicate cleft that divided them, and he savored the sight as he quickly redirected them back to the bag of Cheetos in front of him.

After lunch, they got back in the Jeep, and Leila asked if they could take a selfie of them with the scenery. But as she pulled out her phone, it was blank, an indicator her battery was out.

"Let's use mine!" Ezra pulled out his iPhone from his pocket, snapping the shot since he had a height advantage over Leila; otherwise, he'd have to be cut off with probably just the side of his head visible in the picture, or only his shoulders.

CHAPTER 11

THEY DROVE OFF onto another dirt road at a lower elevation, where the forest was thick but not too cold. A few people were enjoying the scenery from their vehicles; some were resting by their Jeeps or cars, looking at the landscape, while others were posing with their backs to the view, taking pictures.

Ezra strolled toward the thick forest. Leila had refused to walk any further since she was only wearing flip-flops, her shoes still drying out from last night's storm. She stayed in the open area of the mountain to enjoy another picture-perfect view.

"Ouch." Ezra ran out from the thick forest of trees, his hands frantically slapping at his neck while he spun around.

Leila's face frowned, "Are you okay?"

"I think I got stung by something. Ouch!" He let out another disgusted grunt, his hands searching his neck.

Leila made a few steps to meet Ezra. "Let me check." She said, and Ezra sat on a rock so she could reach his neck. She knelt beside him and poked the red mark with her fingernail. Leila sighted a stinger on his neck. With a couple of scrapes of her fingernail, she managed to pull it out. Even as strong as Ezra was, the bee had sent him into an uproar.

"Hold on, hold on," Leila said before Ezra could move. She pulled a bottle of essential oil from her chest slider bag and massaged a couple of drops over the affected area.

She could feel Ezra's muscles relax while her hands gently kneaded and soothed his neck.

Leila paused when she noticed a big scar right next to the area where she was applying the oils. "This should help prevent infection and swelling," she said before continuing to massage an extra minute. For a while, she thought Ezra had drifted off to sleep until he spoke.

"Gosh, I can't believe the sharp pain is gone," Ezra said while Leila shoved her bottle back into the bag. She sensed his gaze on her and studied him through the corner of her eyes. Leila's heart was pounding as she busied herself with her bag and slowly rose to her feet.

"Thank you," Ezra said before he moved his hand to touch hers and gently squeezed it. Leila took that as a sign of his appreciation, and she squeezed his hand back before turning and smiling softly at him.

"You're welcome."

"That medicine." His mouth curved into a smile. "It smells good." He'd never experienced such soft fingers on his skin before.

"It's lavender essential oil. I use it, for multiple purposes." Her hand brushed a hair out of her face. "Bug bites, sleep aid, you name it."

Ezra could only wonder how a small drop of fragrance could have numbed the pain. He knew it was almost time for them to head back, but he couldn't move and didn't want to. He realized he could stay seated all night just looking at her.

"I think we've had enough excitement for today. Don't you think?" Leila asked, perhaps sensing Ezra's intent gaze and the thick air between them. She created a slight distance between them, leaving Ezra no option but to agree with her.

"Yes, it is...," he lied, but rose and took her hand as they walked back to Ezra's Jeep.

There was something about the mountain air swirling around them that brought a degree of fatigue and exhaustion. On the way back home, Leila drifted off to sleep. Her head was slumped against the shoulder of the seat. Ezra enjoyed the sight of her sleeping peacefully. He glanced at her from time to time. At least he could watch her without being sneaky about it. He admired her smooth dark skin and the crazy way her now muddy hair was tangled up. Her face shone as the evening beam of sunlight sent its rays through the window.

Ezra parked the jeep at the campground and killed the engine.

"Sorry I fell asleep," Leila said.

"I'm glad you did." His hand ruffled his hair. "If I weren't driving, I would have done the same."

Ezra unloaded the car, Leila offered to help him clean the fishing tools."No worries, I will get it, get some rest."

she rubbed a hand through her face. "Do I still look tired? "

Ezra smiled, you look beautiful, but he couldn't get the words out loud.

"You look fine," he said.

Leila pulled out her duffle bag with the clean laundry. "I could use a shower." She walked back to the trailer, while Ezra watched her until she disappeared.

***

Ezra had hesitated to shower since he didn't want to wear off the lavender that Leila had applied to his neck, but he jumped in the shower regardless. He knew the hot water might sting his wound, but he needed to freshen up after his day out.

An hour later, and his siblings still not in sight, Ezra's thoughts drifted to Leila, and their day together. He smiled thinking about her soft, warm hands, and all of a sudden wondered where she could be. He didn't get enough of her today, but he needed to tone it down a notch and give her space.

Pushing her out of his thoughts completely, he decided to distract his mind by taking a walk. He'd only walked for a short period when he sighted her on the wooden bench by the creek. His mind told him to move on, but his feet carried him until he was standing right over her shoulder. "Hey!"

She jumped from the rugged bench and turned. "Hi."

"Enjoying your solitude?" He scratched the back of his head. "I could let you be if you need a few moments to yourself." As he stood there silently, his gaze locked with hers. His feelings for her were getting harder and harder to ignore. The moment dragged on for an eternity.

Leila's teeth bit into her lips. "You're fine." She cleared her throat.

"I like to see the sunset; I've watched it every evening since I came."

She steered him to join her at the bench. He breathed the fresh scent of her conditioner.

"I've rarely taken the time to just sit and watch a sunset," Ezra said. "Come to think of it; I've never taken the time to just sit and watch a sunset."

All the times he came to the mountains, he was busy tiring himself with one activity after another. He never sat still for anything, but somehow he liked the idea of sitting down in silence and observing the scenery. The only time he sat down was when he had his quiet time praying. And now this moment, watching the sunset with Leila sitting close by, could go down in his memory as one of those times he did something unusual with someone sane.

He liked how he felt sitting beside her. An image of Leila being home when he returned from a busy day at work to sit beside him and lean on crossed his mind. No other woman had inspired such thoughts in him before.

"I don't do this often either; it's so hard to relax in the city. " She said.

Ezra scratched the stubble on his chin. "I would love to hear more about your family." He wanted to know more about her—did she have a boyfriend? Several questions had started to plague his mind. Ones that he couldn't voice, at least not yet. Good thing he didn't see a ring on her finger, or else any hopes he had of winning this beautiful woman over would dissipate in a second.

"It's just me and my brother, we're six years apart, but we are not too close." She told him since she'd mothered her brother Brian during his teenage years. "Brian somehow treated me like his mom and not his sister," Leila said. "At first I was mad at God for letting my parents split up, especially the times when I didn't feel like taking on mom responsibilities. I missed out on some parties and hanging out with friends because I had to drive my brother somewhere. "Perhaps it kept me out of trouble too."

Ezra wished he'd been there with her instead. "Where was your dad during this time? "

She sniffed. "He'd just started his business, and was very busy with clients."

Ezra could tell that her tears were threatening by the increased rate of her sniffles.

He found himself doing something unexpected—He slipped an arm around her shoulders and drew her in close. "I'm glad their marriage was restored."

"Yeah, me too. When they renewed their marriage vows, after the counseling sessions, they both gave their lives to Christ, which was an eye-opener for me as well. It helped me believe in a God of second chances." She cleared her throat then asked, "How long have your parents been married?"

Ezra wanted to hold Leila, to comfort her from her past pain. He swatted mosquitoes off his face. "Thirty-five years."

Ezra's parents had been together all his life. They were a team, but he couldn't imagine what it must have been like for Leila not to have that, not to mention the constant moving due to the nature of her dad's job. Deciding to lighten the mood, Ezra asked, "What did you think of four-wheeling?" He smiled as an image of Leila's muddy face came to mind. "I mean, besides the mud?"

She returned the smile. "The mud was one of the favorite parts of the drive." She gazed at the open meadow as if recalling a distant memory.

"It brought back some memories of my childhood, playing in the mud with my brother at the various military bases we lived on. My mom had not been too fond of the game because of the mess, but my dad had approved because he'd wanted us to be kids."

Ezra dropped his hand from Leila's shoulder. They talked about their high schools, and then silently watched the deer in the meadow, both stealing a few glances at each other. Ezra admired the way the fading rays of the setting sun dappled Leila's face with gold. He then glanced back at the field of purple and pink wildflowers.

They sat and watched as the sun lost its heat, listening to the stream of water below their seat and the sound of birds slowly fading as the night crept in. The sky had worn a bluish tinge of twilight with the sun already rolled out of sight.

"How did you get your love for the outdoors?" Leila asked as she brushed a strand of hair away from her face.

"Our parents have always loved the outdoors, but I tend to take it to the next level. I love nature; it's always a great way to remind me of God's handiwork." He inhaled the fresh mountain air. "You can sit all day in the clasp of this awesome beauty and meditate. It gives me peace."

Leila thought of Psalms 19. There was no better example of it than the magnificent view of the mountains.

"I wouldn't say that I know all about the outdoors. Like Surfing and scuba diving, I have no idea how they're done," Ezra continued.

"I could teach you scuba diving." She wasn't thinking; her words came out as if she were talking to her friend Bianca. Most summers they would go to Jamaica to visit her mom's aunt and cousins, and her uncle was a scuba diving instructor who'd given them lessons. That was the one thing she did well, and with such artistry.

"I would like that," Ezra said as he extended his fingers to squeeze hers. They watched the twinkling stars that had filled the sky above them.

"We probably better get back," Leila said as she felt the warmth of Ezra's grip.

***

The fire pit was lit at their site, an indication that Ezra's siblings had returned. They could see Renee leaning back in her camp chair.

"There you are!" she exclaimed with a smile plastered on her face, then rose to greet the happy couple standing in front of her.

"Hey!" Ezra greeted, embracing his sister in a hug, and stepped aside when Renee moved to wrap her arms around Leila.

"I have some meat pies left," Leila said, and turned to leave for her cooler to bring another homemade dinner. She was met with no objections.

"So, what did I miss, Ez?" Renee asked with a teasing tone to her voice as she sat back in her chair.

"What do you mean?" Ezra sat on a round log across from her.

"What do I mean?" She rolled her eyes and smirked. "You took Leila fishing, the extended walk, or should I say the heart-to-heart at the camp's most scenic location?"

When he had called them earlier, Ezra had mentioned to his siblings his plans for the day with Leila and explained what the storm had done to her tent. Now he wished he hadn't. Then Renee would have something else to talk about. He shook his head and chuckled.

"You are insane, and you know that." He ran a hand through his hair. "I just wanted her to have a good time. First time camping should be memorable. Her friend left, then her ankle, the storm — the least I could do was to remind her that the outdoors can still be fun."

"Even with a few forces of nature." Renee nodded, lifting her fingers in quotations "I hope you've noticed how beautiful she is." She put her hands closer to the fire. "And a nice Christian, too—"

"Let's not go there," he interrupted his expression stern. "You know how busy I am."

"So you've said." She sighed, "You know, love is not an activity you add to a schedule. It happens when it does, so don't miss what's right in front of you." She bent forward to whisper, "Keep your schedule open to some important things, Ez. You find time for rock climbing, your friends, and the outdoors." She lifted an eyebrow as if to say, why can't you find time for this?

Ezra knew that arguing with his sister never got him anywhere, so he bit his tongue. She was always the optimist, though she possessed a high temper. Andrew was always the practical one, and Ezra in the middle seemed like the skeptical one when it came to relationships. He got along with his workmates just fine and made friends easily, except for romantic ones. He hadn't figured them out yet. Besides, he often wondered if it'd even be fair to start a relationship with someone when most of his time was spent working.

Leila returned with a tray of individually wrapped meat pies in foil and Ezra rose to give her a hand, putting an end to the conversation. They heated their dinner on the hot coals.

"Ezra mentioned that you sprained your ankle." Renee's voice expressed concern. Leila could see her face through the dim light that came from the lantern and mosquito repellent candles around the fire ring.

"It's much better now, thanks," Leila responded. "Ezra has been good about reminding me to put ice on it. I can barely feel the pain."

"Leila!"

Another male voice interjected from behind. She spun around and saw the familiar face. Smiling, she said, "Hi, Andrew!"

"Heard about your ankle. You're okay?"

Leila was touched at how concerned all the siblings had been about such a slight injury.

She nodded. "Your brother," she said, glancing at Ezra, "and one of his biker friends were on the trail when it happened. He was my trail doctor." She laughed softly as a quick memory of how he'd carried her down the trail left her face flushed, even though she hoped it hadn't been evident.

Ezra felt like getting lost. If Leila knew his siblings, she wouldn't be having this conversation. They loved to tease each other, and he had no doubt this was going to be an exciting topic of discussion for the next few days. They could go on and on about it for weeks. He dreaded their banter and teasing.

"Did he?" Andrew said exchanging glances with Renee, then turned back to Ezra.

Ezra was now aware of their plan and tried to control a threatening grin. He figured it was safer to change the subject. "How did your concert go?"

"It went well, don't you think, Drew?" Renee said.

Andrew nodded. "Yeah," he responded dismissively. He was still obviously curious about Leila and Ezra's interactions from their time together. "Renee did a great job with the singing of course."

***

They all engaged in casual conversation with Leila as they enjoyed dinner. Leila was glad to have the diversion of the discussion, especially since her words just kept coming out wrong. Or maybe they were coming out right—she didn't know.

Ezra sipped his water to wash the food down. "These pies are so good, Leila," Ezra said.

"Thanks, Ezra," Leila responded.

Renee whispered into his ear. "And she's a good cook too."

Ezra ignored Renee, keeping an intent gaze on Leila. He hoped that Leila didn't get offended easily, with the whispering that his sister might be doing for the rest of the week. Renee was right about Leila being a great cook. Not that it was the primary reason he was being attracted to her, but it wouldn't hurt to add that quality among the others she held.

Ezra dreaded cooking. He could grill meat and microwave frozen meals. However, that was as far as he went. Whenever he took a turn to cook at work, they would have to eat frozen meals or pizza.

"You're a great cook, Leila." Renee said genuinely, "Ez hates it when I whisper, but I enjoy getting under his skin."

"Do what you need to do," Leila said.

"Seriously, Leila?" Ezra gave a soft chuckle "You do not want to give Renee permission to do whatever she wants, trust me."

Andrew was more interested in the food before him. "Did you make these?" he asked as he took another bite of his pie.

Leila nodded. "My mom helped." She didn't know what to do with all those compliments. Didn't any of the Buchanans cook? She felt odd like she possessed world-class culinary skills. They seemed to praise every meal she offered, but she figured that perhaps it was merely their way of saying thanks and being polite.

Now and then the siblings teased each other, but then Ezra, sitting across from Leila, stole glances and secret smiles just for her each time the fire sent crisp flames— Enough for Leila not to miss his intent gazes.

"Are we kayaking and canoeing tomorrow, then?" Renee asked before yawning. "I'm ready for a massage, and yet there are still seven more days to go,"

Renee said, more interested in beauty treatment than camping. "I hope the small town has a spa of some kind."

Ignoring Renee's spa statement, Andrew answered her question instead. "Yes, we are kayaking and canoeing!" he said. "Leila, since you're joining us for the rest of the week, I got to warn you. His face portrayed a mischievous smile as it illuminated through the fire.

"Warn me?" Her eyebrows arched in curiosity.

"Don't trust Ezra to take you fishing on a canoe,"

"Really?" Leila kept her eyes on her plate instead, avoiding Ezra's eyes, since she was well aware of his intent gaze on her.

"The last time we went fishing in a canoe, he tried to drown me. He rolled the canoe, getting both of us soaked. He didn't even care that I wasn't a good swimmer." Andrew found his joke to be rather hilarious, but a playful elbow punch greeted him to his chest. Ezra shook his head in amusement. "You're the big brother, remember?"

They went on to tease each other, recalling favorite camping memories.

Leila felt a strange stirring in her heart—was it jealousy? No, she thought. Something like jealousy, in any case, that much she knew. The siblings got buried in their laughter and talks. Leila could tell how much they liked and cared for each other, and how close they were to their parents as they spoke about them. She wished she had that kind of closeness to her brother. She had taken care of him for so much of her life, and it always amazed her that they hardly spoke now. She longed for a close relationship with him and wished she could go back and build a sibling closeness all over again. She'd had to knock some sense into him while he was a rebellious teenager. She wondered if she had acted as his sister rather than his mother, would they be closer now?

It hit her then—she was envious, and she felt guilty as she wondered what it'd be like to be part of this family. Blushing at the idea, she shook off the thoughts.

"You two!" Renee said. She shook her head, and Leila watched in amusement, taking in every bit of the moment. "I'm sorry you had quite a dilemma with your tent," Renee said turning her attention to Leila.

"I hope I'm not in the way of your family time by staying with you guys," Leila said, feeling a bit self-conscious and out of place. She felt comfortable with them, but this wasn't something she had experienced in her own life. She didn't want to ruin their bonding time.

"Are you kidding me?" Her eyes glanced back at her giddy brothers. "As you can see, your presence hasn't affected them in any way."

Leaning towards Ezra, she whispered, even though Leila could hear everything. "Actually, I lied. You're usually more talkative than either of us, but you've been pretty quiet with Leila around. Something's going on between you two, something that

God helped along by sending that storm while we were gone."

"I am glad you stayed." She turned back to Leila and patted her shoulder, showing that she meant it.

"I like having a girl to talk, too— not that I don't care for my brothers, but it would make for a long week when it came down to doing the physical activities they so much enjoy. Perhaps you and I can hike or swim when the boys do their hard-core activities."

Several campers had already gone inside their tents or trailers for the night. Renee and Leila headed to the trailer while the two brothers stayed to put out the fire.

Before sleep enveloped Leila, she replayed the events that had taken place earlier, and she found herself smiling and giggling to herself until she drifted off to sleep with the images flashing across her mind, and the one person behind the fun of it all. Ezra.

CHAPTER 12

THE TWO BROTHERS stayed another thirty minutes to catch up and put out the fire after the girls had left for the night. They talked about work, and Ezra asked about Andrew's girlfriend, Callie.

"We're doing well," Andrew said. "Speaking of girlfriends, you like Leila don't you?"

"Ezra shrugged. "I like lots of people. Plus, I just met Leila, what makes you think that I like her?"

They both stared at the hot coals in front of them. Andrew used a stick to move the coals around. "I saw how you were looking at her —"you're in trouble, little brother."

Ezra paused, his heart stopping as if he had been caught doing something wrong. Even though Ezra convinced his brother that nothing was going on, now he had to convince himself of that. The little battle that raged in his mind, the tug of war of lying to himself or convincing himself that he didn't feel something come loose in him just by looking at Leila. Her soft brown eyes that bore into him. They seemed like they would drown him in their depth each time he saw his reflection in them. Leila was beautiful, no doubt, but there was something more to her that kept drawing his heart toward her. Maybe it was the graceful way she scanned her words before she spoke or something else he intended to find out.

"What if she already has a boyfriend?" The words slipped out, contradicting his previous argument that nothing was going on. He clenched his jaw.

"Did you ask her? Perhaps you are the boy she's been waiting for." Andrew sighed. "I can sense that she feels the same way you do, which makes matters even more interesting for your perfectly single life. Besides, don't you think she would have mentioned a boyfriend by now?"

Like an expert, Andrew seemed to have it together. With his practical nature, he knew what to say to a woman and how to say it. He had given Ezra relationship advice now and then in the past. Ezra had been the teenager who'd given his parents trouble, and relationships weren't his strong point. It was no surprise that Andrew had a girlfriend. It still surprised Ezra that he wasn't married yet, but if anyone had it together, it was his brother.

Part of Ezra thought that he saw something in Leila's eyes too. It was something that looked like signs, signs that she might have mutual feelings for him. Signs that something also came loose in her whenever she heard his voice. Signs that she wanted more of him just like he wanted more of her. What if he had misread her? He needed to put all this behind. He needed to think straight, and maybe cooling off would help.

He was thankful that both his siblings would be with them for the rest of the week, so he didn't have to be left alone with Leila. All of a sudden she seemed more dangerous. The more he spent time with her, the more he got to know her better, and that only pushed his mind into more profound thoughts he wasn't ready to entertain.

"We better get to bed," Ezra said, and Andrew kept the rest of his words to himself; for another time perhaps.

***

Ezra lay on his bed, hands to his head as his mind wandered. It had been a beautiful day. Ezra always enjoyed his outdoor adventures with either the outdoor ministry, his brother at times or by himself, but he'd never thought it would be fun with someone else. He thought of the first day he met Leila at the gas station. Even in that brief moment of their meeting, he'd felt like a part of him had stayed behind when they'd parted, and he wasn't sure he'd ever see her again. And now she was right in front of him in their trailer. If this was not God initiating these encounters, he had no idea whom to give credit.

The last time he'd had a girlfriend, things had been different. She'd had so many expectations from him while doing whatever she'd wanted. He'd felt pressure to try to do something every time he had time off. Paige always loved talking about herself, so there were never flowing conversations with her. As for Leila, she seemed easy to talk to, flexible and curious. She wasn't afraid to try new adventures. She didn't seem to be the kind of person who would be demanding. He'd had a normal conversation with her than he'd had in a while. When Ezra closed his eyes, all he saw was Leila's curious eyes, and he could still smell the lavender scent on him way long after he'd showered. Maybe he was ready for new things, and that meant a relationship perhaps. However, then . . .

He contradicted himself with the thought of how happy he was with his single life. He already had a family at work, church, and his real family. He didn't need anyone else. He squirmed a bit and tried to arrange the bits and pieces of his thoughts.

Was he moving so fast in such a non-familiar territory? Perhaps he needed to tone it down a notch. Tomorrow, he was going to do his best to keep his distance from Leila as much as possible. He doubted he could nurture a relationship— Leila deserved someone who knew what they wanted. He, on the other hand, had no clue or experience whatsoever on what a healthy relationship looked like. He didn't want to end up in Jake's shoes. On that note, he drifted off to sleep.

***

Morning rays of sunlight shone brightly as Ezra made his way to the campfire. He'd tossed and turned last night with conflicting emotions, most of which involved Leila. He thought he had a mission today, but he needed some caffeine to give him a boost. He was relieved to see his brother by the fire with a kettle letting out steam over the hot coals.

"You look terrible," Andrew said as Ezra's hand moved to rub his heavy eyes.

"Good morning to you too, Drew."

Andrew lifted his mug in a toast to him."Coffee?"

Ezra let out another yawn and reached for the plastic tub with clean dishes to grab a cup for himself. "Yep."

"I'm here if you need to talk," Andrew said as Ezra silently filled his mug.

Ezra sipped his coffee in a brief silence. "You up for a run this morning?" He asked, needing to fill his head with something besides Leila Morgan.

"I'm always up for a run!"

***

It was eight o'clock when Leila and Renee finished their showers and began working together to prepare breakfast.

Renee went on a quest to search for her brothers, while Leila fixed lunches for them to eat later.

Leila was looking forward to another day of adventure. They were kayaking and then canoeing later. She'd kayaked before while visiting her great-grandparents in Jamaica, and she'd been canoeing too, but it had been a while.

Leila had made breakfast wraps.

"I'll make us some coffee," Renee offered. The guys probably already made their own on the fire earlier."

***

As Ezra stepped into the trailer, his T-shirt soaked, he breathed in the fragrance of Leila's essential oils that had dominated their trailer. She didn't have to be around for him to be affected, because she had that tiny thing she filled with oils at night that she claimed helped her sleep. If he was going to escape her, that scent had to go —it reminded him of her soft hands rubbing the lavender oil into his wound. Alternatively, he could avoid the trailer altogether, which seemed impossible because all he had to do was think of Leila for her to appear.

"Good morning, Ezra," she greeted cheerfully, standing at the entrance to one of the rooms. Ezra studied her in the morning light. She had her black hair in a ponytail, and she looked well rested with her bright eyes, while thoughts of her had kept him tossing and turning most of the night. She was wearing a colorful floral summer dress over her swimsuit, which complimented her dark skin.

Pretending like her presence wasn't affecting him at all, He dropped his eyes from her. "Hi, Leila!"

The action did not escape Leila's attention. She frowned, "There's breakfast on the table. Where's your brother?"

Without any word of explanation, he merely pointed toward the bathroom to imply his brother was taking a shower.

Why was he so quiet? Leila's heart dropped, and she started to wonder if he was okay.

"Renee and I already ate," she explained.

She realized Ezra seemed relieved that he would be eating breakfast alone, without her; she wasn't sure if he just wanted some alone time or if she had done something wrong. *That's ridiculous. What could I have done?* But the thought lingered in her mind long after he said thanks and Leila made her exit. She took a deep breath and decided to enjoy some alone time herself before she needed to get things ready for their little adventure.

Ezra tried to close the window shades but found himself staring at Leila. She was leaning against the tree while applying a coat of lip balm to her full lips. For a moment he wondered how her lips tasted.

"You got a good look?" A feminine voice from behind jolted him.

He gasped. "Good grief, Renee, are you stalking me?"

"We are in shared space, remember?" She raised a brow. "Leila could be asking the same question as far as you're concerned."

Ezra blushed and hoped his sister didn't notice. He pulled down the shades and then turned to pick up the medium-sized lunch bag from the table. "Let's get going."

***

The sky was bright blue, with temperatures promising midseventies when Ezra parked his Jeep in front of the rental place for their equipment.

Hours after their kayaking adventure, the foursome returned to Hidden Valley and shared lunch at the picnic table area by the rental store.

They finished their lunch and walked over to an ice cream shop for dessert.

"This is the best banana split I've ever had," Andrew said, as Renee reached with her spoon to scoop a bite. "Hey, this is mine." Andrew lifted his dessert and moved away from the table. Renee chased him so she could get a bite, leaving Ezra and Leila alone.

Ezra had managed to keep his distance from Leila throughout the day and almost made it, but now his sister had to play games. Leila's nearness stirred something in him. Realizing he'd created the awkwardness between them, he knew he needed to break the silence."

"How do you like your malt?" The way she was slowly savoring each scoop made it seem tastier than his ice cream.

"It's to die for," she moved the glass toward him, would you like to try some?"

Which meant he now had to taste it.

After taking his first scoop, he said, "This is the best chocolate malt I've ever tasted."

Leila couldn't agree more.

"I think I've had enough." She wiped her lips with a napkin. " Could you finish it for me? It's going to take several exercises for me to shed off the extra pounds I've gained from all the daily s'mores."

Ezra scooped another bite of the malt, accompanied by a moan of pleasure.

Leila's gaze was distant, which enabled Ezra to utter a comment."I wouldn't change anything about you. You're perfect." Before she steered to him, He returned his gaze to the malt and took another scoop as he was reminded of Leila's chocolate skin.

Ezra looked at Leila through the corners of his eyes, and he could tell she was uncomfortable with the compliment, by the way, she was biting her lips and shoving escaped strands of hair behind her ears.

He was scrambling for the next word to say when Andrew and Renee returned.

They planned to go canoeing to seal the day's fun.

CHAPTER 13

LEILA SAW LITTLE of Ezra over the next two and a half days. Except for brief moments at the campfire and over breakfast, he'd seemed busy with his brother doing intense activities. She sensed he might be avoiding her since he'd avoided making simple eye contact and gave precise responses whenever she'd asked him a question. The chatty guy she'd known over the last four days, had been replaced by a quiet guy. That was probably for the best, Leila told herself. Although she missed him, besides telling God about her feelings, she had to keep her concerns to herself.

It left her feeling uneasy as if she should break the ice wall Ezra had put in place. Even though it seemed God had put the two of them together, she couldn't be sure. She'd prayed over the last few days to be able to concentrate and not think about Ezra, and each time, she felt peace. Except for when she caught Ezra looking at her, her heart skipped a beat and jumbled up her emotions. It was hard to tell which feelings were from God and which were her own longings and desires.

Thankfully She'd enjoyed getting to know Ezra's sister, Renee since they'd done a few things together. They'd gone horseback riding, strolled along the small town, and taken a few mild hikes.

Leila stood shivering with a towel over her back after swimming in the cold lake, while Renee trotted out of the water to join her. Rocky Mountain pine trees surrounded the rocky sand lake. Leila sent a smile to Renee, who lay face down on her towel, stretching out her arms

"I'm dying for a massage," Renee said then told Leila that she was going to look for a spa and pedicure place in town. Unfortunately, Leila had plans of her own as well—to capture photos.

"Would you like to go four-wheeling?" Leila asked, spreading out her towel on the ground to face Renee.

"Four-wheeling?"

Leila nodded.

"That sounds more like what Ez would say." Giving Leila a speculative look, Renee added, "Speaking of which, you seem to have had an impact on his behavior this week." She shook her head. "I know it's not my place, but I can tell he likes you, as in likes a lot, but he doesn't know what to do with his feelings just yet." Her face dreamy, when she spoke, "I hope that someday I can find a guy who looks at me the way my brother looks at you."

Leila wasn't going to blurt out her feelings to Ezra's sister, but she didn't know how to respond either. She was thrilled to hear that he might like her, but what if his sister was wrong? He'd been ignoring her since his siblings came back.

Leila chuckled lightly. "Why do you say that?"

"Give me a break!" Renee rolled her eyes. "The way he looks at you when you're not looking, he looks like you're the only thing that matters. Also, I have seen how you look at him as well. You two have special gazes for each other." Renee confessed that she'd purposefully chased Andrew for his banana split at the ice cream shop so that Ezra and Leila could talk to each other.

"The only two people who don't know they are falling in love with each other are the two of you." She let out a sigh. "I got to tell you since you've now become my friend, he's not been in a relationship for quite some time."

Renee told Leila about the last relationship Ezra held. "It was such a disaster for him," she said. "He'd dated this awful girl for two years."

"If she was so awful, why didn't he break things off with her?" Leila asked.

"He was too much of a gentleman to dump her. He was hoping that if he didn't commit to her, she'd get the hint and break up with him, but it just dragged on and on with her using him. Ezra is like that, you know—he'd rather sacrifice his feelings than hurt someone else."

"So there's a slight chance he might still be traumatized from his last relationship, but I've never seen him look at anyone the way he's been staring at you. Not in my presence, anyway." Renee studied Leila, peering into her eyes.

"Why are you looking at me like that?" Leila asked.

"It's pretty obvious you feel the same way, from the spark in your eyes any time you talk about him. Anyway, don't hesitate to push him a little. He's fun and would make an excellent husband." She smiled. "Well, I suppose that was jumping the gun a bit. He'd make an excellent boyfriend too."

Leila did not doubt Ezra being fun since she'd been on the receiving end from him, but pushing him was not for her to do, especially if he'd been traumatized from a previous relationship. God would have to navigate the details if anything were to happen between them. The last thing she wanted to do was cause Ezra any more pain.

"Are you dating anyone?" Leila asked, changing the subject of dating to the beautiful girl before her. Perhaps she had a better love life to share than Leila's.

Renee gave a thoughtful frown and opened her mouth."Neither of my brothers thinks anyone is ever good enough for me." Renee explained, "The last time I introduced a date to them, the poor guy was so intimidated. He said my brothers were too overbearing. It was probably for the best if the guy couldn't stick to a relationship just because my brothers gave him the third degree." She sighed. "I don't blame them since I haven't found a decent guy. The ones I tend to be drawn to either have a shattered history of past relationships or are emotionally unavailable."

"Yeah, I can relate to that."

Two of Leila's relationships, she'd cut short— one, because the guy wasn't all in and depended on his family's financial stability; the other one seemed decent enough, but something was missing. She'd decided not to waste the time of either one since she didn't want to date a guy if there was no future to it.

"But you're still young," Leila reminded her.

"Twenty-three is not that young." She took a deep breath.

"Four-wheeling, are you in?" Leila asked, figuring that was the safest thing to say at the moment. Even though she knew what Renee's response would be, she asked anyway.

"We're taking the ATVs out tomorrow or Saturday. I would rather get a massage this afternoon to prepare me for that."

Renee told Leila how her brothers always made a whole day out of the ATV rides and how she didn't enjoy it nearly as much as they did, but she went nonetheless. "Crazy as it sounds, I'm getting a manicure too." She stared at her nicely painted fingers. "Just because I'm camping doesn't mean I have to lose myself."

Leila had no idea why she needed to re-paint her nails because the current nail polish looked just fine by her. What did she know about nail polish, when she rarely painted her nails? "I'll drive you back, then," Leila said as they both rose to get ready.

***

Ezra had worked hard to avoid Leila, hoping that distancing himself would keep his mind off her. As long as Leila was out of sight throughout the day, his mind would be free of her. He went with his brother on a hike in the high country for a whole day, and by the time they returned, both Leila and Renee were sleeping. They'd left very early the next morning for intense rock climbing, and they'd been joined by a couple of guys who were staying at the same campground.

They did more biking and rock climbing the next day. It would almost be three days today of him keeping Leila at bay, and he doubted he would make it through the week. He was getting the impression that Leila allowed herself to let him be. Unfortunately, there hadn't been a single hour when she hadn't been in his thoughts. Andrew had brought up Leila's name a few times, but Ezra kept telling him how he didn't want to talk about her. Like the good big brother he was,

Andrew had told Ezra he was there if he needed someone to discuss his love life with.

He'd only seen Leila briefly at dinner the day before and earlier that morning, but he'd avoided direct communication with her. Of course, he'd stolen a few glances at her when she wasn't looking.

"Ezra?"

Andrew's voice brought him back to reality.

"What?"

"I asked if you would like me to drive."

Ezra realized he'd been holding the steering wheel for quite some time without turning on the engine.

"Uh, yeah . . . I got it." He turned on the engine, and his brother buckled himself.

Andrew peered into his little brother's face. "As long as you don't drive us over a cliff. I sense your mind is not functioning to its full capacity."

"I can't stop thinking about her!" Ezra shrugged. "I mean . . ." His hands were tight to the steering wheel.

A brief silence followed before Andrew spoke.

"Finally, you get to use your words." He shook his head. "I was wondering if you would ever get there."

Ezra didn't want any sarcasm, but then again, he did the same to his brother all the time.

He ran a hand through his hair. "That's why I didn't want to talk about it." He started driving.

"Hmm, since when don't you want to talk about things?" Andrew asked.

Ezra and his brother usually spoke about everything. Even if they didn't see each other often, they talked on the phone and caught up whenever possible.

"Since Leila." When did Leila become the subject of discussion with his brother? That was alarming.

He was scared that his feelings for her were getting deeper than he wanted them to.

As if reading his mind, Andrew said, "Confessing your feelings is one step away from healing."

Ezra frowned, as he kept his eyes on the road since the path was narrow, with a cliff on one side and trees on the other. He had to maintain his focus.

"Now that you're aware of your feelings talking to her might be a great start. Get to know her and see where that leads. Keeping your distance is not going to get you anywhere." Andrew slapped Ezra on the shoulder. "The way you've been acting the last few days, she's probably scared of you."

If Andrew was right about Leila recognizing his strange behavior, then he needed to start over with her.

He felt relieved that he'd finally admitted his feelings to his brother.

Ezra nodded his understanding.

Realizing the distance he'd worked hard to keep had only robbed his time away from Leila, he felt the excitement as they pulled in to park at the campground. His heart leaped for joy at the thought of seeing Leila and perhaps talking to her. He was either insane or a mystery.

His T-shirt was still wet from the hard, refreshing climb when he entered the trailer in hopes to cool off in the shower.

"Hey," he greeted his sister, who was sitting on the couch with a Kindle on her lap, nails nicely painted in sea green.

Renee's eyes went to Ezra. "Hi."

"How was your time swimming?"

"It was fun, you?" Renee responded in a distracted tone, her eyes already glued to the screen again.

Trying hard not to make his interest too obvious by asking Leila's whereabouts, Ezra decided to take Andrew up on his offer of a water gun battle with the kids from the neighbor campers.

***

Two hours later, Ezra was fresh from his shower and returned to ask the question he'd been avoiding.

"Where's Leila?"

"She went four-wheeling," Renee responded nonchalantly.

Ezra's eyes widened at his sister's response.

"By herself?"

"Who do you think she was going with?" Renee said, "Apparently you have made an impact on her. She wanted to go four-wheeling and take pictures of where you took her last time." Renee's eyes returned to her tablet.

Ezra felt a knot in his stomach all of a sudden. He thought of the spare tire Leila had on her car and some of the tricky roads that required good tires for a steep climb. He hoped she didn't venture on the steep roads.

He understood her wanting to be adventurous, but spare tires were not designed for the backcountry roads. He exited the trailer without another word.

***

After dropping off Renee at camp, Leila had changed into her Capri jeans and grabbed her hot pink sweatshirt.

She could remember the route Ezra had taken her two days ago. She wasn't so bold as to drive herself on the steep road. Not only was she driving on a spare, but it would be nerve-wracking, so she'd opted to go to the lower-elevated scenery instead.

The higher mountains seemed a few degrees cooler, as she drove taking the backcountry road that she'd ridden with Ezra a few days ago. She remembered how to get to where Ezra got stung by a bee.

There had been two young adult girls and a guy with them at the time she'd arrived. They were fidgeting to get a selfie on their phone, and she'd volunteered to help them take their picture. She then walked to the thick forest which Ezra had mentioned led to the breathtaking scenery. Now that her ankle was better and she was wearing the right shoes, she was willing to check it out.

There were several trails, that Leila passed by, as she weaved through a meadow snapping pictures along the way— a confetti of blooms played peek-a-boo behind rock formations. She strolled in and out through the blossoms when until she ended up in a forested area below the top. Here she could see the panoramic view of the Front Range.

She was lost in the wonder of the Creator when she took another trail to venture. With her binoculars, she paused to watch a few birds. She cited a beautiful valley with an old tepee that captured her attention.

The tent was old. Leila neared to examine it. There was nothing inside, though it looked like an original tepee. After taking a few pictures of the tent and its surroundings, she realized she was the only person in view.

Panic rose when she found herself walking in circles, one trail after another. It seemed as if she was getting farther from her car and everyone.

She moved to sit on the higher rock and voiced a prayer of thanks to God for His handiwork, glorifying Him for his power and artistic creation. She also prayed to find her way back to her car. As much as she loved the scenery, she didn't plan on hanging out with the nightly creatures.

***

"Leila," Ezra called in a shaky voice. He called again, "Leila!" He'd started at the higher backcountry roads in his search, but then returned to the lower part. He'd seen her car, but thirty minutes later he hadn't traced her yet.

He remembered the walkie-talkie he'd left with her and hoped she'd carried it with her.

He pulled out his walkie- talkie and twisted the button. "Leila, do you copy?"

Leila rose from the rock when the radio made a static sound from her sling backpack.

Shortly after she'd prayed, she remembered she still had it in her bag and turned it on. She had tried calling out, but no one had been close enough to hear.

"Ezra," she said, her voice filled with relief.

Now she could hear his voice closer, and not through a radio wave. She spun around, and Ezra was making steps toward her. His grin was wider than ever before. Her knight in shining armor.

After the way he'd been ignoring her, she didn't think he'd be the one to come to her rescue once more. Her heart swelled.

"Oh, Ezra." She sighed with relief when he was within reach.

Ezra didn't remember ever being this panicked in his entire life as he did just now. Besides his job, which caused panic each time he and his friends entered a flaming building, he doubted he had ever been as worried as he had been today.

"You're okay?" He stretched out his arms, and Leila flew into them for an embrace. He held her closer, her head buried to his chest. Close enough to smell the faint scent of her shampoo.

"Now that you're here, yes." Her head lifted, and her eyes met his as she formed a soft smile.

235

"How did you find me?"

With his arms still wrapped around her, he responded. "Your bright-colored sweater." After connecting with her on the walkie-talkie, he couldn't sight her, and not until he used his binoculars and saw something colorful in the midst of the green pines on the rocks did he get a glimmer of hope.

She could have been attacked by a mountain lion or another wild animal. Even as he reminded himself that God was still in control, it was hard to put that faith into practice.

He softly brushed her cheek with his fingers as her hands dropped from their embrace.

He wanted to scold her like a child, for driving off on a spare tire and for coming here alone where she'd never been before. With his gaze intent on hers, instead, he said, in a low voice, "I will be happy to come with you anytime you want to come."

"That would work for me." She murmured.

"It's always safer to have a partner when coming this far in the mountains." He came up by himself most of the time, but somehow with Leila, he felt the urge to protect her from any danger.

As they walked together, Ezra put his hand at the small of Leila's back.

"I don't want to meet your family—" he shrugged—" and boyfriend for the first time bringing them bad news." It was his way of finding out if she had a boyfriend.

"I don't have a boyfriend." She twisted a lock of her hair with her other hand.

Ezra was relieved to know she was single, and he knew he was falling for her, but he still had no idea on how to go about that.

"Why don't you have a boyfriend?" He couldn't believe he just asked why, even though he was curious why a beautiful girl like her was still single. They came across a rock in the middle of their path, Ezra climbed and held out his hand for Leila, and then helped her down. There was no designated trail since they couldn't find it. They had to jump over a few rocks and logs as they walked.

"Remember how I told you when my mom left?" Leila said. "I had to fill her role of driving my brother all over? I was always the one to babysit him so he wouldn't make bad decisions when left at home alone. That left me no time to date. until the past couple of years." She brushed off a bug buzzing in her face. "When one of the guys asked me out, we had two dates both at a movie theatre. He wasn't too sure if he was ready for a commitment since he had his dad's business to run. So I opted out since I didn't want to be dragged along that route. Then my last relationship a year ago lasted for one month."

She seemed ready to be done with this subject, but Ezra wanted to know everything or at least listening to her talk.

"What happened? "

She shrugged. "Well, he was a nice guy, and I didn't want to waste his time since I knew something was missing in that relationship."

His brow arched, "Like a spark?"

Leila nodded. "I told him we should each move on. I'm either too particular or not as exciting."

He admired her courage to tell a guy that they were not suited for each other. Ezra thought of his own life, his previous relationship that he'd wanted to end but didn't because he was afraid to hurt the girl's feelings. He was still not bold enough to tell some of the girls who flirted with him that he wasn't interested. He felt like a coward at heart, despite the tough-guy image his job gave him. How was he ever going to commit to anyone if he was a coward?

"I find you exciting," Ezra blurted out.

"Do you have a girlfriend?" Leila asked, peering into his eyes before they strolled.

This girl was as bold as they came. He did ask her, and it was noble of her to ask back.

"No." He hoped she would fill that gap, but he was not sure of himself either. She had just mentioned she had no time for people like him—the type of people who are not sure they want to be in a relationship.

"You want to know why I'm still single at twenty-seven?" It wasn't that he lacked suitors, he just hadn't felt drawn to anyone as he did to her. She was very different from the kind of women he'd thought he was drawn to; she seemed to settle his mind. She was not too talkative, yet talkative enough to hold a steady conversation.

"You don't have to tell me," she said.

"I know." She didn't seem to be the pushy type either. He felt compelled to tell her anyway.

He told her about Paige, his ex. "I was once caught up in a relationship, and I thought I wanted to be in at first. It had started as a joke when Paige asked me out."

He sighed. "I'd been requested to play the guitar at Church for two weeks until the guitarist returned. Anyway, Paige sang on the worship team, and that's how we met. One date led to many forceful dates afterward."

Leila's gaze seemed distant until she asked. "Why were the dates forceful?"

"They were not necessarily forceful, but I didn't want to go on another date with her. She was very pushy if you know what I mean." Ezra thought of how he'd gone on the second date, Paige had ambushed him at work, then she'd found out where he lived. "She would come and wait for me at work, or just showed up at my house without notice, and she would assume, I would have to drop any plans I had including rest so that we could go do something together. By the time we had been on five dates, I felt it was too late to back out." Two years later, Paige had gotten tired of the nonprogressive relationship and decided to call it off. Ezra had felt like a heavy burden had been taken off him.

"Wow," Leila said, still listening.

"Let's say; I'm not as strong as I appear to be." He clenched his jaw. "I wasted her time and my time, by not telling her that I wanted out. We didn't have any chemistry at all." She loved the outdoors among the so many other things she'd dragged him to. But then it always had to be about her. "Two years of my life wasted. Since then, I'm afraid of getting involved in relationships." Realizing that Leila was the first person besides his brother he'd confessed his weakness too, he somehow felt he could talk to her about anything.

He thought about Jake's marriage falling apart, then another one of his friends from the opposite shift who'd just experienced a bitter divorce. Some of the people he knew were in their second marriages. "I'm more like that guy who isn't sure whether he wants in or out of a relationship." He nodded. "Plus the nature of my work makes it hard to find a spouse who's patient enough with my schedule" not that he'd bothered with finding someone since, but he knew that some of his colleague's marriages had been affected by their work schedule.

"I think the easiest way to learn anything, is by using experiences of others—taking the good and making it your own while leaving their mistakes behind." she cleared her throat. "It could be a great combination taking the bad and good, and transforming it into something wonderful, you know?" Leila arched a brow. "You don't have to define your future based on the ones that failed. Look at your parents; I'm sure there are also other people in your life who have had successful marriages. I know that I could learn from my own parents' relationship as well—even when my mom tends to forget that she and her husband have two different personalities. I hope to try and not make the same mistakes they made."

Ezra knew Leila was right. He hadn't thought of things that way at all. For example, his Captain had

been married for almost twenty years and had a
beautiful family.

"You're right." However, he still didn't want to
be that guy to mess with her and not see things through.

They arrived at a meadow sprouting with
blossoms and sat on the grassy area in the center. Leila
asked about the tepee, and Ezra said it was an original
Native American home.

They talked and laughed.

"What's the most memorable thing about your
job?" Leila asked.

Ezra smiled, his shoulders relaxed. "Do you
know that of all the times I've done dangerous climbs,
biking, and leaps, I've never been hurt before?" He
chuckled. "This one time, we get a call—just like a 911.
We get to this house for a false alarm, and the lady says
her cat was stuck in the tree. We don't respond to such
calls, but again, it was a false alarm, and the lady was

disabled. I easily climb the tree, I get the cat, then a tree branch comes down on my neck, and I end up needing stitches."

His laughter roared, echoing in their surroundings. Leila felt something ignite within her, as she watched Ezra laugh. She remembered the scar she'd seen on his neck when he got a bee sting. She smiled and found herself joining in the laughter.

They talked until they were bathed in the evening sun and surrounded by the scent of grass and pine.

They looked at several birds through their binoculars. They saw the mountain bluebirds, western tanagers, hummingbirds, and a bald eagle. Leila was excited to see some of the birds she'd read about.

"How do you know so much about birds?" Ezra asked.

"I just love to read books about nature in general. When I found out where we were camping, I read about the animals that I might see in the area, the type of birds and plants that grow around here."

Perhaps they had more in common than he thought. They silently watched the beauty around them, as the sky above them shifted to bright clouds of pink, purple, and orange.

"This is breathtaking," Leila said

"Yes . . ." Ezra cleared his throat. "You are breathtaking," he said, his voice husky. Even with a small gap between them, she was close enough that he could have turned and bent his head slightly to plant a kiss on her full lips. His eyes lingered on her lips for a while. He sensed she was aware of him looking at her, by the way, she was biting her lips. Her gaze, however, was intent on the scenic view.

Instead of a kiss, he settled for grabbing her hand and gave it a soft squeeze.

Ezra's pulse raced as he felt shock waves, the same waves he'd felt when Leila's hands went to his neck the day he'd been stung by a bee. Not to mention his heart racing whenever their eyes met. Now he was wondering why he blurted out everything that came to his mind. At least that was one character trait he and his siblings possessed from their dad—speaking their minds. He wasn't sure if it was a good trait or not. Even if Leila was breathtaking, he didn't feel bold enough to make his thoughts or actions known at the moment. Not that there was anything he was going to do about her beauty when he had a busy life. If Ezra were wise enough, the sooner he blocked his feelings for her, the better things would be for everybody. He had no desire to start something he couldn't finish; he reminded himself.

"We better get going," he said as he rose up and held out his hand for her.

"Ezra," Leila called in a whisper as they started walking.

"Hm?"

"Thank you for coming after me."

They walked back, hands linked together.

"It's my job," he said as if he were on duty.

"I feel like . . ." Leila paused to catch her breath.

"I've known you forever," Ezra interjected.

She smiled. "Yes, that's what I was going to say. I feel like I've known you forever, too."

As they both got into their cars, Ezra realized, he wasn't wise enough and was determined not to worry about what he couldn't control anymore since God was in charge. With two more days of camping left, he was going to focus on having fun and hoped to let God direct his steps as far as Leila was concerned. Less smooth had been his efforts to distance himself from Leila. Who was he kidding!

CHAPTER 14

LEILA WOKE UP Friday morning to a beautiful bouquet of pink wildflowers by the door of her room. A smile creased her face as she took a whiff. She didn't have to ask to know who put the flowers there. Her mind went back to yesterday's afternoon rescue and her time with Ezra. He was quite the guy—a knight in shining armor. When he'd come after her, she'd noticed something else besides concern lingering in his eyes, something profound that she couldn't explain. Regardless of his non-committal blurb, he'd shared, Leila sensed he felt something for her.

She moved her bouquet to the kitchen and put her flowers in a cup that she filled with water, placing the arrangement in the center of the dining table.

After she'd showered, she and Renee got breakfast ready. The guys hadn't returned from their morning run.

"I would enjoy camping if I received the kind of treatment you're getting," Renee teased as she placed the bowl of fruit on the table. "Glad to see that my brother can be romantic." Her eyes dreamy, she took a whiff of the flowers.

"Why wouldn't Ezra be romantic?"

Renee lifted her hands in mock surrender. "My mistake, he's romantic."

Leila smiled. "No doubt."

***

After breakfast, everyone pitched in with packing lunches. Renee stocked up drinks in the cooler, while Leila fixed sandwiches.

Someone was standing over her shoulder. She could feel the rise in her body temperature. Ezra

"Something smells good." He spoke.

In an effort to breathe normally, Leila dropped the butter knife to the ground.

Ezra picked it up, and dropped it to the sink, handing her a clean one. He stepped beside her, trailing a warm finger over the back of her neck causing her insides to melt, as the air around her thickened.

"I can't focus when you're right next to me." She whispered.

"Is that so?" He whispered in response, invading her personal space. All she knew was that her feet were wobbly. Thankfully, Ezra made himself useful, by placing the sandwiches in the cooler. Otherwise, she was about to topple over.

The guys helped clean their breakfast dishes, and they all worked together to get ready so that they could get good use of their second-to-last day. After everything had been loaded into the Jeep, the four of them rode off to Hidden Valley to rent the ATVs.

Even though Renee knew how to drive an ATV, she'd opted to ride with Andrew. Leila, this being her first time, didn't want to take a chance driving, so she decided to ride with Ezra instead.

Ezra leaned forward so Leila could climb onto the seat behind him, then waited until she'd fastened her helmet to turn the machine on.

"Thanks for the flowers," Leila said. She'd wanted to thank him in the morning, but he'd been standing too close for her brain to remember anything.

"I hope you liked them," he said.

"I loved them."

"You need to hold on to me tight if you don't want to fall off," Ezra said.

With her arms wrapped around his waist, he headed to the trail. He could sense Leila's slight tension and nervousness and tried to go a bit slow until she was comfortable. He rode farther, following his siblings as he climbed up the steep dirt road.

Ezra felt Leila's body relax as her hand rested comfortably on his waist. Clouds of dust flew up as they rode, soon replaced by splashes of mud, which wasn't a problem, since they were all dressed appropriately for the occasion. Now that Leila was having fun, Ezra wondered if her proximity and scent would be too much of a distraction. Of course, she only held on tight for fear of falling off. They arrived at the very top where there was another opening with a few shade trees where they could enjoy their lunch. They visited over their lunch break, and the siblings teased each other whenever possible.

***

After three hours, they drove back down the hill, and halfway to the rental, Ezra pulled to the side.

"Do you want to try to drive?"

Leila 's eyes widened in doubt. "No way I'm I going to be in charge of driving an ATV, what if I—"

"We will be fine," Ezra interjected, cutting off any further protests.

"Are you guys okay?" Renee, who was now driving Andrew, asked as they passed.

Ezra nodded. "We'll be right behind you. Leila is going to drive us back."

One more glance into Ezra's stormy eyes was all the assurance Leila needed to calm her doubts, and she took over.

As nerve-wracking as it'd been for Leila driving, she considered this the best adventure ever. Not only did she ride on an ATV, but she also drove one. It helped to have Ezra right beside her to navigate in case she messed up.

After returning the ATVs to the rental store, they all took showers at the bathhouse by the rental facility since they'd packed extra clothing to change into. Before they left town, they stopped at the ice cream shop to top off the afternoon.

***

The rest of the afternoon back at the campground was relaxing. Ezra skipped a rock that bounced through the stream, while Leila relaxed at his closeness with both their shoes off seating on a log that Ezra had hauled over the creek.

He stretched his arm and reached for another smooth rock, handing it to her. "It's your turn."

She'd watched him throw about six rocks, but Leila had never skipped stones in water before. She sighed before accepting the rock. "Well, I doubt it will be as good as yours, but—"

"It will be perfect." He said, his gaze intent on her. "Because you are perfect."

With her insides melting, she confidently threw the rock in the water and before long, she'd lost count on how many stones she'd thrown. They took turns throwing until Renee called out.

"Ez"

Both Leila and Ezra turned to Renee as she walked toward them. "I could use some of your epic fire starting skills. Andrew is helping some guy set up his tent."

"Why don't you start it yourself?" Ezra teased.

"You're the eagle scout," Renee crossed her hands over her chest. "Since you ate all my girl scout cookies that summer, I missed out on girl scout camp, and you know very well that I never went back to scouting."

Ezra winced and returned his gaze at Leila. "Hope you don't believe every bad thing she says about me."

Leila chuckled as Ezra rose and reached for her hand, pulling her next to him.

While the flames flickered, the foursome played a game of Truth or Dare. Renee said Truth, so Ezra asked her if she had a crush on anyone. Ezra said truth also, so his question was whether he talked in his sleep. Which he admitted to often doing.

Leila could imagine, how easy it would be for Ezra to have nightmares due to the nature of his work. Andrew's question was whether he'd ever told a lie to get his way.

Then Andrew dared Leila and Ezra to a staring contest to see who could hold out the longest without smiling, which turned out hard for both of them since they both smiled the moment their gazes met.

Leila was now comfortable with the three siblings. She felt embraced by their love and presence. They all teased each other, including Leila, but instead of feeling embarrassed, she threw a few teases back at them. Andrew talked about his girlfriend, Callie, "I hope to propose next spring."

It was nice taking part in the witty banter that Ezra enjoyed with his siblings—still Leila felt a sense of nostalgia, thinking back on her relationship with her brother. She wondered if they'd ever been like this. At the moment, it still felt like a mother-son relationship. Maybe one-day things would change.

A few bugs buzzed in front of Leila and she excused herself to get her mosquito repellant. Renee followed her.

When they returned, Ezra motioned for Leila to seat on the long log beside him, and Renee took a seat beside Andrew.

Ezra inhaled Leila's sweet fragrance of essential oils that he had become accustomed to over the last seven days. "Hmm, you smell good," he murmured. The words popped out of his mouth instead of staying in his thoughts where they belonged. He felt a blush and hoped nobody noticed the color transformation to his face.

"Doesn't she?" Renee said, with a wide grin as she looked at Andrew.

Andrew decided to remain silent, determined not to ruin the moment for his brother who was falling in love. Ezra may have been unaware of the situation, but no one else was. Ezra was always busy working or taking an adventure of some sort in his free time. Andrew knew just how hard it could be finding love when putting in extra hours at work and hobbies which his brother enjoyed a lot. Mountain climbing and biking at some point were going to land him a permanently single life. It would be okay, but after this week, seeing him with Leila, he saw something in Ezra that he hadn't seen before. He had no doubt his brother's priorities would change after this trip.

Leila noticed the stares Renee and Andrew exchanged. "It's just the bug spray, that's all!" she slid her hands into the pockets of her sweatshirt.

The colorful sunset swept through the pine trees, making a lovely backdrop for the campfire smell and the faint buzzing of insects and a few mosquitoes. It was a perfect summer evening.

They put hot dogs on roasting sticks and roasted them on the open fire.

They shared recaps of their week and the day as they roasted their marshmallows. Ezra offered to roast Leila's as he showed off his marshmallow roasting skills— taking all his time turning the stick with a marshmallow on it "Now this is how to roast a marshmallow." He pulled the perfectly toasted marshmallow from the fire and fit it between his two waiting graham crackers, then handed it to Leila.

"Thanks!" Leila said.

"That takes way more time," Andrew said and showed off his burnt marshmallow.

"That explains why you didn't stick to scouting," Ezra spoke to Andrew.

"Hey, at least I have some cooking skills to show for it, unlike the eagle scout in question," Andrew said leaning back in his camp chair.

"I'm not taking sides since I can't roast a marshmallow." Renee chimed in, telling her story behind not roasting marshmallows since she'd done as a teenager. "It stuck in my hair, and It was such a hassle to wash out," she added.

"You've got a little something…" Ezra pointed to Leila's mouth. And while Leila moved her fingers to locate whatever mess Ezra had pointed out, he brought his fingers, to the corner of her mouth, turning away with melted chocolate.

Leila swallowed, at the feel of his fingers on her mouth.

Their exchange didn't go unnoticed by Andrew and Renee, although they seemed to dismiss any comments they might have thrown at them. The conversation flowed, as they laughed with each other.

Two hours later, they were under a blanket of stars above them. Leila enjoyed this new group of people she'd just met just over a week ago. Especially the guy on her right, who ignited sparks within her each time he spoke or dipped his head close when she spoke like whatever she might say was the most important thing to him at that moment.

"Ezra, you should play the guitar for us," Andrew voiced. " I think Leila would love to hear you play."

It had been a tradition in the past whenever they camped, Ezra played songs on his guitar. He didn't feel like playing the guitar, not tonight. He started to object, but his brother sent him a determined gaze—one Ezra had often seen which meant Andrew wouldn't give up.

"Yes, come on!" Renee interjected, her chin leaning against her arm, she lifted a brow toward Leila, a gesture which only Ezra saw.

"I would like to hear you play," Leila chimed in with a brimming smile.

Ezra realized he'd already been outnumbered and couldn't protest any further. He was doing it; then he would have to deal with his brother later.

"Okay," he said reluctantly as he brushed a mosquito off his chin.

Andrew brought Ezra's guitar to him, and Ezra played "Stars" by Skillet and "This Is Your Life" by Switchfoot.

The words from the song 'This Is Your Life' especially pierced him like a sword.

What did he want to be? He'd asked himself the same question as a teenager, but now that he was an adult, what did he want to be when he was older than twenty-seven? Something he had to ponder.

Leila soaked in every word Ezra sang from 'Stars.' It was perfect for the occasion since they were blanketed by them as they worshiped the Maker. Ezra had such a deep, rich voice.

"That was amazing," Leila said as they all clapped for him when he finished singing.

Leila wondered what Ezra wasn't good at. If there was anything, she hadn't found it in just seven days.

The group prayed together before they called it a night.

Leila offered to put out the fire; excusing everyone for the night, and everyone did as told, except for Ezra, who stayed and helped her put out the fire.

They walked back to the trailer holding hands. Ezra let go of Leila's hand as they approached the door, and turned to face her as if to hug her, but instead bent and brushed his lips against her cheek.

"See you in the morning," Ezra whispered.

Leila's body shivered, trying to form her words. "Okay," she croaked.

After the tiring activities they'd done today, the whole trailer was silent within a few minutes, except for

Leila and Ezra, who were pondering a galaxy of thoughts.

CHAPTER 15

AFTER A WHOLE week and a half of being in the woods, it was easy to tell who was cut out for the outdoors. Ezra and Andrew were not affected by the absence of their beds. They were still as energetic as ever.

Today was the day before their last day at the campground. Earlier they had done archery and returned to the campsite at three. The three siblings decided to go for a run. Even though Leila was invited, she'd opted to stay and ponder instead. She'd joined them on a couple of afternoon hikes over the week, but this afternoon she just wanted to savor her favorite spot and watch the sunset one more time. She'd done so almost every evening; one time Renee had joined her. Ezra hadn't joined her since the last time they'd sat here together.

What started as a mutual friendship between Leila and Ezra now seemed to be filled with simmering tension. Leila was still affected by last night's gentle brush of Ezra's lips to her cheek. She could have sworn they left a permanent, glowing mark.

After her shower she'd strolled over, now sitting on the bench, She thanked God for the week's events. And for the Buchanans who'd become her new friends, including Ezra with whom she enjoyed an even deeper level of friendship. Although she was unsure where that friendship stood. *God, please give me patience with all this.*

Ezra was a godly man, handsome, with all the qualities Leila would want in the man of her dreams. She revisited all the encounters she'd had with him. At the gas station when he'd paid for her lunch and changed her tire, on the trail when he'd carried her so she could be safe, during the midnight storm, and then him coming after her when she'd been lost in the mountains.

He had taught her fishing, four-wheeling, and all the adventures this week that Leila had never expected to do.

Lately, she hadn't thought much about being in a relationship, until now. Ezra was quite adventurous. Outgoing, funny, confident, and kind. Now that she'd figured out all these things about him, she needed to know what he thought about her, but how was she going to do that?

As the afternoon sun lost its heat, she silently watched the deer in the open meadow, and it's young in the field ahead. Her shirt had been perfect in keeping her warm earlier, but she doubted she would last long since the temperature started dropping. Her eyes went to the pink-orange sky.

"What did I miss?"

She jumped and turned towards the familiar voice that had interrupted her thoughts from behind her.She'd enjoyed the silence, but she didn't ever remember being so happy to see someone during her time of solitude, another explanation for her butterfly-filled stomach.

"Hi," she said with a soft smile.

"Hey," he responded with his hands in his jean pockets and a plaid shirt hanging over his shoulder.

Leila's gaze turned back to the scenery since she didn't trust herself in making eye contact with Ezra. "How was your run or walk—whatever you guys did?"

Ezra slid next to her on the bench. "A run, it was good."

He breathed in her mint mixed with all the luscious oils of her bug spray. That was the one thing he was afraid would remain in his nostrils way after this week was over. Even though he kept telling himself that he had no intentions of thinking about her when she was out of sight, that didn't stop him from wanting to be around her.

"I let Andrew and Renee finish off. I felt distracted."

Ezra recalled the run with his siblings; he'd not been attentive in his responses. It was bad enough that he had tripped a couple of times and Andrew had given him a hard time about it, thus forcing him to leave. "If you need to be somewhere, why don't you just leave before you break your back on the trail?" he'd said. It came out a bit harsh, but Ezra knew his brother meant well. He'd almost fallen flat on a rock one of the times, and it was a good thing he'd missed it when he carefully landed.

Renee had asked him why he was with them when he could be hanging out with Leila on their final day together. She'd told Ezra that he didn't have to prove his loyalty by running with them. He'd argued with his siblings until Renee rolled her eyes. "So you think because I'm your little sister, I know nothing about the two people who have chemistry with each other?" Shaking her head, she'd said, "I've seen your eyes follow her every move, and I know she feels the same about you, too."

Between Renee and Andrew, they'd convinced him to leave them to find Leila, which hadn't been too difficult, since that's exactly where his heart wanted to be. After a fast shower, he knew exactly where to find Leila.

The thought of knowing it was the last day with her bothered and terrified him at the same time. However, it didn't have to be the last time, came the small voice within.

"My body was running, but my mind was here." He scratched his ten-day scruff of a beard on his jaw. "With you, I mean."

"Thank you for all the fun adventures this week," Leila said. "This has been the best experience I've ever heard."

This has been my favorite time in the mountains too." He was glad she'd come camping, and they'd ended up at the same site. He would have to thank the camp host someday for messing up the reservations, but right now God would get the glory.

He raked his hands through his hair. "I enjoyed watching you the most, the ease with which you jumped into new situations without the slightest hesitation." His voice now low and husky, "Seeing the outdoors through your eyes helped me appreciate it more." Another reason he was falling for her.

Leila remained silent as if thinking of what to say. Instead, they both watched the now dark sky serenaded by only the sound of water flowing peacefully as it trailed off the rocks. With no one keeping track of time, Ezra's phone battery had died. Leila didn't have a watch on her wrist, which surprised Ezra since she'd worn it every single time he'd seen her. They both enjoyed the comfortable silence.

Ezra liked how he was feeling right now. He wanted this feeling to last. Was he halfway to falling in love with her? It probably was more than halfway, even though he tried to ignore the feeling altogether.

Leila moved her head and found Ezra's gaze intent on her; the illuminating moon shone on his face. Leila was now shivering and blinking at the same time.

"You're cold," Ezra said as he took his flannel shirt within a matter of seconds, blocking the gap between them and gently placing it over her shoulders.

She dropped her gaze, feeling goose bumps and her pulse rise at the slight brush of Ezra's hands over her shoulders. Her head lifted and met Ezra's gaze again. He cupped her chin and bent slightly, his hands moved toward her face and pressed his lips to hers.

Leila felt the bristles of his stubble but didn't care. Her arms went around his neck as she wondered if this was a good idea, but she was far gone to differentiate a bad idea from a good one.

She hoped Ezra would be stronger than her, and perhaps stop the kiss, but he seemed to have lost himself just as much. Neither had the strength to stop and then, just for a moment, they both forgot everything around them.

The kiss lasted about two seconds, but it was the kind that took Leila's breath away and left her giddy with possibilities.

Thankfully Ezra regained some of his senses and broke the kiss.

"Leila," he called, his lips still resting against hers.

"Hmm?" She responded, her eyes still closed.

"We better get going," Ezra said, but made no attempt to make any movement, which was fine by Leila. He kissed her again, softly, and gently before pulling himself up. He then put out his hand to help Leila up, and they walked back with his arm wrapped around her waist.

Andrew and Renee sat by the sizzling flames and silently watched Ezra and Leila join them. This time, neither of them dared to make any teasing comments. Now that Ezra had opened up to them about his feelings for Leila, he was grateful for his siblings' silence.

They sat around the campfire, Leila by his side as they all gave recaps of their favorite things at camp this week. Leila mentioned four-wheeling, which surprisingly had been Ezra's favorite since Leila had been a part of it.

Ezra felt like he'd accomplished something even more significant this week, something he'd promised himself six years ago to do with a girl he thought he would marry. Leila seemed to have all the things he wanted in a wife, but was he ready to take that leap? He'd kissed her because she had such a reaction toward him.

Besides the light pecks on the cheek he'd shared with Paige, he'd never been drawn to kiss her as much as he'd been attracted to Leila. Even though he enjoyed kissing Leila, somehow his emotions were jumbled up.

He could have kissed her all night long if he had the choice to do so. He could still smell her mint scented lips on his.

They polished off all the leftover food and enjoyed their last round of s'mores as they talked and laughed easily. Except, Ezra didn't laugh easily, because he had Leila next to him, crowding his mind and yet somehow unsure of where to start with her. Was he really going to date her? Did he have the ability to nurture a relationship? All these questions needed time to process. Perhaps he could find some answers within the next thirteen hours left before Leila departed from him.

***

Ezra kept running on the mountain trail without a destination in mind. He had no idea how long he'd been running, but he was panting and gasping for air. He'd left before Leila and Renee woke up, and told Andrew he needed to clear his mind. Andrew had offered to go with him, but Ezra had told him he needed to do it alone. Although Andrew had respected his request, he'd insisted Ezra give him the location he was going so he could come looking for him if he didn't return within three hours.

He needed to process his newfound feelings, and that required more than thirteen hours. He hoped by the time he returned to camp, Leila would be gone. He didn't want to think with her in sight. Last night's kiss was still fresh in his mind. Although he reminded himself it'd been a mistake to kiss her, he still felt the urge to kiss her again. He shook his head as he slowed down to a steady pace.

Leila had told him she needed to be back home by eleven o'clock so she could catch the twelve o'clock service. At least he'd managed to get her number, which she'd written on a napkin. He would call her if he felt the need to pursue her further.

As much as he wanted his relationship with her to go deeper, he was afraid of taking that next step. What if he took the next level and things didn't work out? He didn't want to let Leila down by misleading her until he was sure about this relationship.

Deciding not to worry his brother by his delay on the trail, Ezra returned to the campground.

As soon as he stepped out of his car, Leila was the first person his eyes landed on. His heart skipped at the sight of her closing the car trunk. She looked cute in the grey leggings and a hot pink tank top.

Her eyes met his when he was a few yards away. She sent a soft smile his way, which brought excitement and fear all at the same time. Ezra managed a fake smile back, though he sensed Leila could tell it wasn't his real smile by the way her genuine smile faded.

Even with his damp shirt, he sensed a rapid rise in body heat, which he assumed to be related to Leila's proximity. He moved one hand to the back of his neck, his eyes focusing on Leila's car instead of her eyes. "You're already leaving?" he said as if he were clueless to her time of departure. He'd hoped to avoid this encounter altogether.

"Yeah." She fidgeted with her hair, which was all tucked into a ponytail.

Ezra ran a hand through his damp hair. There was so much he wanted to say, but he had no idea where to start. He wanted to tell her last night was a mistake, without permission, his eyes went to her moist lips, and memories of last night's kiss flooded him, he wanted to wrap his hands around her and give her a much better kiss than the previous night.

Leila bit her lips and Ezra stared into her dazzling brown eyes, "Umm . . . I will call you?" The words didn't feel sincere the way they came out, especially coupled with the fact that he'd added a question mark to it.

"If you get time," she said.

Leila swung the door open. "Thanks again for everything." Perhaps she sensed Ezra's hesitation and doubts. She entered her car.

Leila put her car in reverse, and Ezra placed his hand behind his neck as he wondered how his feelings for her had gone astray in just ten days. Putting his thoughts aside, he waved to Leila as she exited the campground premises.

Ezra watched her drive off, regretting his reaction; it was as if she was driving off to a distant land he may not visit for a long time. He needed to help his siblings pack; perhaps he could use his energy toward something constructive rather than ponder uselessly.

***

"What were you thinking?" Renee shot at Ezra, giving him a hard punch to his shoulder as soon as he approached her in front of their fifth wheel.

"Ouch, I'm already sore from my run." He massaged the shoulder his sister had punched.

"Seriously, is that your best defense?" Renee rolled her eyes. "Don't worry, since she believes in giving you space as if you need it, which I'm sure you don't need." Renee shook her head in annoyance. "You're second-guessing yourself, Ez, and I think you need some serious dating sessions."

"And you're the dating expert?" Ezra smirked shooting a sharp gaze at his sister.

Both hands to her waist, Renee lashed out. "At least you could have stayed and given her a proper farewell and not run off like a coward."

Ezra knew his sister was right, but still, she had no right interfering with his love life. The fact that Renee mentioned Leila giving him space, what did the two talk about?

Annoyed, Ezra asked, "What exactly did you tell her?"

Renee sighed. "That you are too stubborn to know when the right woman came along, and that you are still traumatized by your previous relationship."

His sister got carried away at times, and whenever she had her temper rise up, it was no use arguing with her.

"Stay out of this. Leila and I —It's my business," he said sternly.

Andrew emerged from the trailer and just stared at them. Whenever Ezra and Renee had their conflicts, Andrew never broke their arguments. He would let them resolve them on their own. If Renee knew that Ezra's emotions were jumbled up, she would drop the issue and move on because at the moment; he had no patience left in him.

"There might not be a Leila and you if you keep up with this . . . ," she said while moving her hands in the air as if to say "this whole thing."

Ezra's jaw clenched, and he went around Andrew to enter the camper. He needed a shower anyway. He could still hear Renee and Andrew talking.

"Just give him a break, he's had so many changes so fast." Andrew said."He'll come around."

"It's his loss if he doesn't," Renee said. "We better get going. I have a spa appointment this afternoon."

***

Surrounded by mountains, Ezra sat silently on the rock. The silence was only interrupted by a few woodland creatures moving around. His thoughts were mixed with emotions of fear, doubt, and something else. He was too distracted to voice a prayer. After he'd apologized to his sister and said goodbye to her and Andrew, he'd had every intention of returning home, but that was not the right place to think. He needed to process his thoughts before he reported back to work. Being in the mountains helped him think— the city was too loud to process things. Focusing, he tried to clear his mind, but even as he did so, Leila Morgan occupied his thoughts. He'd come back to the same place he'd taken her four-wheeling.

He found himself smiling as he thought of her smile, the way she lit up when he made her laugh, and the genuine spark her eyes portrayed when she saw him. She had a calm demeanor and transparency; she was confident and knew what she wanted. She would be good for him. His thoughts traveled to the future; if he married her and they had kids, would they have her hair that he loved?

"I bet they would be so adorable," he whispered aloud. He smiled, but his face tightened when he felt a knot in his stomach and decided to pray for wisdom, to keep his mind from wandering in the wrong direction. He had a perfect life as it was, and relationships took a lot of work and time. The thought of living and being with Leila both terrified and excited him at the same time.

"Lord, I'm not good at relationships." He silently prayed.

He left in a different mood than he'd come. Not exactly how he'd expected to leave the mountains. He'd intended to ask Leila for lunch before they left the campground, but with doubt hovering over his thoughts through the night, a lunch date would have only complicated things further. He didn't need to give her false promises. He wasn't ready to date or start something he couldn't finish— he was the new lieutenant— and he wasn't going to let one kiss ruin things for him.

With one more breath of the fresh mountain air, Ezra was off to the rocky dirt road only divided by aspens and pines. He drove home wondering what Leila was thinking of him and why he'd left things vague between them.

He felt like running to work off some steam. At least work would keep him too busy to focus on the girl invading his thoughts.

***

Two weeks had gone by since Leila had returned from her camping trip. Although things hadn't ended the way she'd hoped with the handsome man she'd met on her trip, she'd still enjoyed the outdoor experience more than she'd expected.

When she had departed from camp, she'd sensed regret in Ezra's gaze, regret that he'd done the wrong thing by kissing her. She had to leave it up to God, and perhaps Ezra needed time. At least he'd been honest confessing to her his fear of commitment. This was probably for the best.

Leila hadn't been into the outdoors until two weeks ago. Most of the things she did every summer took place indoors. She volunteered at the recreation center, tutoring students, and she went to the gym by her apartment. Only once every three years when she visited her relatives in Jamaica did she take a vacation and manage to enjoy the ocean. Now that her mom had returned to remarry her dad, it would be a long time before she went to Jamaica again.

Over the last two weeks, Leila had immersed herself in volunteer work; aside from tutoring, she'd signed up last minute to help at her church with the one-week Bible camp. After encouragement from Ezra to connect with her church, she was jumping at every opportunity to serve when possible. She was thankful to have something to do besides checking her phone for any missed calls or messages from Ezra Buchanan.

Leila had also spent the whole week taking care of her god-daughter Daisy; something she did every summer to give Bianca a break.

Bianca joined them today for the July Fourth weekend, They'd been to the parade and watched the fireworks show yesterday, and then went to the Colorado Springs Zoo today.

Now that Daisy was already asleep, Leila sank to the sofa and took a deep breath.

"I don't know how you do it, working and taking care of a four-year-old," Leila spoke to Bianca who sat in the armchair across from her with a small coffee table in the center.

"I don't do it alone, Bianca said. "Between you and my family, I think I'm in good hands."

This was the first time they'd be catching up since the camping trip.

"So, tell me more about your trip?" Bianca asked with her hands stretched out on the chair.

Leila's mind wandered off, wishing she had exciting news to share with her friend.

She sighed, "It was fun."

"Did you get any more spider visits?"

"No, I moved to the trailer." Even though staying in the trailer had simplified things, she doubted she would have stayed for the rest of the week if she'd been in her tent, regularly taking trips into town to take showers.

When she was finished telling her everything, except for her departure, Bianca's eyes were dreamy.

"If he's as handsome as his brother, then I'm so happy for you."

Renee had mentioned Ezra to both Leila and Bianca when she referred to the brother who was bicycling, but Bianca hadn't met him before she left.

"I still can't believe, he's the same guy who changed your tire at the gas station."

Bianca put her hand to her mouth. "You two belong together."

Leila needed to put an end to her friends' excitement. She inhaled and exhaled deeply, "Before you get all excited, " Leila filled her in on the details of their last day together and the departure, she crossed her legs. "I guess it was fun while it lasted."

There was silence for a moment before Bianca spoke. "My advice is to be patient. If he spent almost two weeks with you in the outdoors and failed to see the real you, then it's his loss." "You're so transparent, " Bianca added, "anybody who hangs out with you more than three hours already knows ninety percent of who you are!" Leila appreciated her friends' confidence in her.

"And if it came to shared space with you, he had to have gotten the whole package of your personality. He kissed you because he found you irresistible." Bianca grinned as she relaxed back in her chair. "I bet he liked you a lot and he's still trying to figure out how to take your relationship to the next level."

Leila's silent musings drifted back to Ezra's embrace the last night of camping, and how the departure made her wonder if he had regretted the kiss. She knew it was pointless to stir up yearnings that could never be fulfilled. But then why couldn't she get that kiss out of her mind? Also, why did she get butterflies in her stomach every time she'd looked at him?

"Well," Leila said as she redirected the conversation toward her friend. "What's new in your life?"

"We got another groomer," Bianca told Leila about the ups and downs of her job at the vet clinic, and they visited a while longer.

After praying together, Bianca went to join her daughter on Leila's bed she'd given up for the night.

Settling on the couch, Leila decided to put the camping trip behind her. She thanked God for making her path cross with Ezra's even for the shortest time. He would always be in her heart. She trusted that there was a reason for every single person God brought into her life.

God had used Ezra as Leila's guide through her camping adventure. And if something beyond camping was meant to be, God would have to intervene. With matters placed in God's hands, she felt a sense of peace that she was getting back on track.

CHAPTER 16

EVEN THOUGH HE'D buried himself in work, Ezra
was ready for another break. It had been four weeks
since his camping trip. Between doing paperwork, fire
safety training sessions, on top of regular fire duty calls
and filling in for others, he should have been busy
enough to put Leila out of his mind, but that hadn't
done it. The guys at work kept giving him a hard time,
saying he'd changed ever since he returned from his
break. He'd told them it was jet lag from such a long
break. Because of dealing with his conflicting
emotions, he'd even developed migraines from time to
time.

Having Leila's photos on his phone didn't seem
to help. Especially the one from when they went
fishing, and their selfie at the overlook when they went
four-wheeling. He missed her scent so much that he had
gone shopping and ended up with a mint conditioner for
himself and a bottle of lavender oil to sniff and bring
back some memories. It was quite unusual for a guy
who wanted to keep his distance.

The one thing he'd found time to do outside work was his workouts with Jake. He'd worked two twelve-hour shift for the last two days; he and a couple of guys from Shift C were filling in for others from the opposite shift.

Thirty minutes prior, they'd just returned from rescuing a woman who'd been swept away by a raging wave during a tubing adventure. After washing up, Ezra closed his eyes while sitting on the couch. He took a moment to pray for the woman since she'd been in terrible shape when they found her. He wouldn't know what happened to the woman unless it showed up on the news.

"Some of the guys are going to grab a burger at The Side Rock Cafe, are you in?" Miguel asked when he joined him.

Usually, that would sound better to Ezra than going back to his house for a quiet microwave meal alone, but tonight he just wanted to go home and think. Leila had been weighing on his mind, and he needed to figure out a way to contact her. He'd washed the napkin with her phone number in his pants, and all he had was her pictures on his phone to look at. He had tomorrow and Friday off. Perhaps by then, he would have a better plan.

"Maybe not tonight." Ezra's hands went to his face as he straightened on the couch."If you can do me a favor, though, hand this folder to Curie on your way out," he said, handing Miguel the folder with full reports from the emergencies they'd responded to during their shift.

Miguel shrugged, his shoulders stooped and his eyes heavy with hidden emotions.

"Everything okay with you? " Ezra asked.

The short and stocky guy sighed and sank into the chair across from Ezra."Well, my grandma is having hip surgery."

As far as Ezra knew, Miguel's grandma lived in Mexico.

"Unfortunately, they can't do the surgery until we make a partial payment of $500. Anyway, I could borrow —"

"I will give you $1000." Ezra offered. "And you don't have to pay me back."

Ezra always had an emergency fund set aside. And as far as Miguel's grandma was concerned, this was an emergency. The guy had a family to take care of, the last thing he needed was to worry about his grandma.

Miguel sighed with relief, and his voice choked when he spoke. "Thank you, but that's a lot of money."

"You're family." Ezra nodded.

Miguel rose and patted Ezra on the shoulder, then took a couple of steps to make his exit. He turned and narrowed his gaze towards Ezra, "You're not quitting are you?"

Ezra frowned. "Why would I quit? "

Miguel studied him, "I'm not ready for a new Lieutenant. Personality clashes are not in my cards yet." He stared at Ezra for another long moment before he spoke. "Ever since your vacation, you've been more distant and less talkative. You're always the happiest person around."

That was not good that his colleagues noticed his change in personality. "Yeah, it's jetlag from my camping trip." He could keep telling himself that, but deep down, he knew it had everything to do with the beautiful woman he'd met during his trip.

***

Since Ezra's friend Jake Larson had given his life to Christ two weeks ago, Jake had been so excited about his newfound faith and had so many spiritual questions after his new believer's class, and Ezra had been his go-to person. Jake had also moved out of Ezra's place. One of the firefighters from Shift B got married and was moving into his wife's house. Since he still had another six months on his lease, Jake had paid him a minimal rate and moved into his duplex a few blocks away from Ezra.

Ezra had kept his schedule open this weekend so that he could meet with Jake and answer some of the questions he had. Not that Ezra had all the answers, but this was an opportunity for him to learn more as they researched for answers together.

Earlier in the day, Ezra had managed to take a drive to the mountains and had found himself back at

Site One at Hidden Valley campground. He sat on the wooden bench where he'd shared a kiss with Leila. When he left the campground, he was sure of one thing: the outdoors were never going to be the same without Leila. If he wanted to forget her, he knew he might as well find a new way to enjoy the outdoors. A different approach that didn't include him going to the mountains. This seemed impossible, given the fact that the mountains were his stress-free zone.

As he lay down on the carpeted floor of his living room, he was grateful for his late great-grandma, who'd left him and his siblings some money in her will. Ezra had used his money to buy a townhome. He doubted he could have managed to afford the mortgage without her help, at the rate the housing market was skyrocketing.

"The sound of the door opening reminded Ezra of his meeting with Jake at three.

"Hey, Jake," Ezra called out as Jake hung his keys by the hook at the entrance. "Aren't we supposed to meet at three?"

"Yeah, I keep time, man." Jake looked at the clock on the wall. "It's quarter to three. "Did I catch you at a bad time?" He gave Ezra a once over. He was probably wondering why Ezra, who was always ready for engagements, seemed so distracted.

"I can come back later."

Ezra shook his head and motioned for Jake to take a seat on the leather chair in the living room, where he'd put the snacks on the coffee table.

On his way back home, Ezra had stopped to pick up a few snacks for their meeting.

He moved toward the fridge and swung the door open, looking at the only two options of drinks it held.

"Coke or water?" he asked.

"I'll take water," Jake made his way to the refrigerator to help himself.

Ezra took a Coke and reached for a plastic cup from the cupboard, since he'd bought a few of them, in case he thought of Leila and needed to have an iced Coke.

Jake eased into the chair, and Ezra followed him back to the living room shortly.

As Ezra poured his Coke into an ice-filled disposable cup, Jake narrowed his gaze. "Man, I notice you've changed ever since you returned from that camping trip, I know you've told everybody about your jet lag story, so I didn't want to say anything in front of all the other guys, but hey, it's just the two of us. Tell me, what happened to you?"

"How? What do you mean?" Ezra said defensively.

"Looks like we're getting somewhere, my man," Jake said with a wide grin exposing his white teeth. "Since when do you drink soda in a disposable cup with ice? The Ezra Buchanan I know drinks soda straight from the can."

Jake's eyes moved to the bag of plantains, and he picked up the bag to read.

"Then with the plan—"

"Plantain chips," Ezra said, finishing the word for him. He'd found himself adding plantains in his shopping cart in Leila's honor since he'd acquired their odd taste after all. "Why are you asking so many questions? Do you want to try some or not?"

"No, sir." Intrigued, he said, "It's strange, that's all."

"I met a girl. Let's say that."

"Whoa! Not too fast," Jake said, lifting his hands in the air. "Give me the whole scoop." He placed his water on the coffee table and settled back in the chair.

"While camping." Ezra sipped his soda and then told Jake about Leila and their encounters from the gas station, then the trail, for which Jake happened to be present. He also included the story of the rain, plus the fun they'd had together the rest of the trip.

"Oh," Jake said, his eyes wide.

Ezra had been too busy to talk about his personal love life to anybody. He'd brushed off his brother when he'd called and asked how things had gone with Leila. Andrew had teased Ezra, saying he doubted Ezra would make it through the week after the way he'd left the campground.

"Yep." He nodded.

"Is that a good thing?" Jake asked.

"I don't know." He shook his head. He didn't remember ever feeling this way before. He'd had a high school crush, but he'd never had the chance to do anything about it. Then with Paige, he'd just blindly moved into that relationship because he thought he needed to be in a relationship.

The feeling with Leila was just too hard to explain. He thought four weeks away from her would be all it took to erase her from his mind. Unfortunately, each passing day without seeing her left him terrified that he might never see her again. At times he'd hoped she would somehow show up at his workplace since hc'd told her where he worked. But then, why would she after he'd left her the impression that he needed space?

"I'm scared that I might be falling in love with her." He ran a hand through his face. "The kind of love where I see a future together . . . Marriage and kids. I know I sound crazy."

"No, you don't sound crazy," Jake nodded. "I've just never seen you worked over a woman before. Way to go, bro!" He slapped him on the shoulder.

"Finally. It's about time you got a life outside of work for a change."

"But it's complicated." Ezra scratched his chin as memories of his farewell at camp washed over him. "I don't think she will like me after what I did."

"It can't be that bad if you told her how you feel."

Jake continued, "I know I'm not the best person to offer relationship advice, I mean, Aniya claims she left me because she hated the way I cut my avocado. You know I would've given up avocados altogether to save the marriage, but she insisted I sign the divorce papers since she'd already moved on with somebody else. But I can try."

Ezra's gaze moved to the window, "We had a great day together; then I avoided her for a couple of days. I kissed her and avoided her the next morning, at the brief encounter I had with her before she left, I gave her a fake smile, which no doubt she noticed. I told her I would call, but then I haven't." He ran a hand through his hair. "I could tell she didn't believe me when I said that I would call her, I didn't sound convincing." Not that he could blame her, after his shaky behavior toward her throughout the week. He remembered Leila telling him how she didn't have time to date someone who wasn't sure whether they wanted in or out of a relationship. Yet it seemed he'd been that kind of guy before, but for the wrong girl.

"Who kisses a girl and then plays cold shoulder?" Jake said. "I knew you were terrible at relationships, but I didn't know you were this bad."

"Yeah! I told you it was bad!" Ezra massaged his temples, sensing a tension headache coming on.

Jake gave a comforting grin. "It doesn't sound that bad. I'm just giving you a hard time." "You have been single for a long time, and you got caught up in the wrong relationship last time, so of course it's scary when you finally fall in love." He scratched the back of his ear. "I would have done the same thing. Just give her a call, I know it will be fine. You will have regrets if you do nothing, and she will never know how you feel about her." Clearing his throat, Jake added, plus, I'm ready to have the old Ezra back."

Ezra patted Jake's shoulder and nodded his thanks.

Feeling hopeful, Ezra led them in a prayer before they started their discussion. Perhaps Jake's spark of excitement for Christ would ignite Ezra's as well. Why a loving God allows evil and suffering was their topic of discussion.

"The Scriptures make it plain that God did not create the world in the state in which it is now, but evil came as a result of the selfishness of man. God is love," Ezra said, as he referenced the scriptures about God's love for His people. They read Romans 5:8, Psalm 36:7 and a few others that went along with their lesson.

Jake interjected, "Which makes sense since the verse implies that genuine love can't exist unless freely given through free choice and will."

"That's right! Man was given a choice to accept God's love or reject it." They continued discussing and reading Scripture.

After their discussion, they started planning another workout before Ezra's brother's visit. Andrew Buchanan was coming to visit Ezra for the weekend.

Living forty miles away from each other, the brothers still managed to get together now and then for a bike ride or a run if they were not having a get-together at their parents.

"What time do we need to be at the pancake breakfast?" Jake asked as he flipped the remote in search of any sports on TV.

Ezra frowned, "What breakfast?"

Jake shook his head, even though his eyes were still glued to the TV.

"Oh, yes," Ezra said, snapping out of it.

Ezra had to take one day at a time, and he had entirely forgotten about the annual pancake breakfast put on by the firefighters for the community in mid-July. "I had spaced that. Thanks for the reminder." He had Leila to blame for that.

"Whatever man, just be there tomorrow." Jake settled into his chair for a baseball game, though it wasn't the Rockies who were playing.

***

In the golden rays of the new morning sun, the pancake breakfast put on by the Fort Rock firefighters had been in effect an hour. The park had covered shelters, which would help when the temperatures rose. The newly planted trees didn't provide much shade for the crowd of people in attendance, but the breakfast had been projected to end by noon, and the temperatures would still be minimal at the time.

Several families had blankets spread out, while others sat at the folding tables. The park picnic tables were also occupied, and there were still other people standing as they ate. The kids were running back and forth at the playground, letting out screams and giggles, depending on what moods they were in.

The firefighters were all dressed in their Fort Rock Fire Department navy-blue T-shirts. Some firefighters mingled in with the volunteers to pass pancakes to those who were unable to walk to the line or to help the little ones carry their plates to their designated seats.

Leila had signed up to volunteer for a service project organized by her small group from church.

Thanks to Ezra, she was now a part of a small group. Upon realizing the service project took place in Fort Rock, Leila had invited Bianca to join her since this was Bianca's community.

Leila spotted Bianca walking towards her, Daisy by her side.

When Leila and Daisy's eyes, met, she tore her hand away from her mom and ran to Leila.

"Aunt Leila!" she called with arms wide open for a warm embrace, which always melted Leila's heart.

"Hey, sweetie!" Leila said as she lifted Daisy to kiss her cheek. "What have you been up to since I saw you last?" Leila said tickling her and was rewarded by the sweetest giggles.

After leaving Daisy, at the playground in the care of Bianca's neighbor, Leila and Bianca joined others who were serving pancakes to the people in attendance.

"So tell me —" Leila stopped short when she recognized a familiar face in the crowd, not too far from where they were. "Bianca, don't move," she whispered, ducking behind her friend's back.

Bianca, who seemed confused, turned around in a circle. "Only one thing could make you freeze like that. Where's the spider?"

"Don't move." Leila ducked even lower.

"Why are we playing hide-and-seek all of a sudden?" Bianca furrowed her brows.

Leila had spotted Ezra handing out food by the picnic table. She'd thought for a moment her eyes had met his, but whew, was she relieved she'd sighted him first and not the other way around. Her hand moved to her racing heart, and she sighed.

"It's Ezra," she said when they'd arrived on the opposite side from him.

"Okay, start talking." Bianca put one of her hands on her hip.

"It's Ezra Buchanan, remember?"

"The camping Ezra? "Bianca said,

 Leila nodded.

Bianca moved her hand to her mouth. "I see that spark in your eyes. "You're always talking about a spark before you can fall for someone. Why are you hiding from him?"

As much as Leila wanted to see him, she had no idea if he would feel the same, and what would she say to him? If she didn't leave soon, they were bound to run into each other again. For now, she hoped the crowd would mask her presence as long as possible. The fact that he had her phone number and hadn't called her was proof he didn't want to see her as much as she wanted to see him. And that hurt whenever she thought about it.

"I'm not facing him yet." She started to walk forward, and Bianca followed.

"I know your reason is that he hasn't called you yet, but it's a good sign. It means he's still thinking. It's only been like a month, right?"

"Yep."

"I did the same thing when John and I shared our first kiss." Bianca smiled and rubbed the back of her ear, reminiscing. "I knew I liked him a lot, but it scared me when we kissed. I had some doubts and was afraid to mess things up. It drove him crazy when I went all silent on him for a month. I was playing hard to get, but deep down I knew he was the one. He kept coming to the house and said he would keep doing so every evening until I spoke to him."

Leila listened to her friend, but her situation was different. A guy like Ezra was too handsome for her to put herself at risk. He was confident, adventurous, and funny—why would he want someone as dull as she was? She was the total opposite of him and was not in his league. That's why he hadn't called, she thought.

"That means I better wait for him to make up his mind. He has my number, and I don't have his."

"Just be patient," Bianca said. "I think I should go check on Daisy at the playground."

Now that Ezra was out of sight, Leila decided to inch her way to where another group of firefighters stood flipping pancakes on griddles. Cords were stretched out from where the electricity was plugged into the walls underneath one of the big shelters. The air smelled of syrup and sausage, igniting Leila's hunger all of a sudden.

***

Ezra tossed a piece of trash as he made his way through the crowd. The pancake breakfast was well attended, and Ezra was grateful for the great weather and the extra volunteers who'd stepped up to help. All the three shifts from Station #15 were busy working at the breakfast, but they were also prepared should they be called in case of an emergency.

His mind had probably been playing tricks on him, the fact he thought he'd just seen Leila. Mind games, he thought. He didn't trust his vision lately as far as Leila was concerned. Two weeks ago, he'd mistaken an African American girl to be Leila. She'd had the same body frame and hairstyle, but as he'd walked closer, he'd realized it wasn't her.

Setting that thought aside, he washed his hands and moved on to check and see if any of the guys flipping pancakes needed a break.

"I'm here to give you a break, Larson," Ezra spoke as he slid an apron over his head.

Jake flipped the pancakes on the griddle."Let me finish this batch."

The sight of a little boy in a superhero costume with a toy hammer in his hand caught Ezra's attention. Smiling, he bent to greet him. "Hey, Thor." He guessed him to be five years old. "How many pancakes can you eat?"

"Six!"

Ezra chuckled. "I understand Thor needs his . . ."

His words died in his mouth when his eyes landed on Leila standing in front of Jake, who was putting pancakes on her plate. Her eyes locked with Ezra's for a second, then she turned to walk away.

"I could use a breakfast break." Jake Larson stepped aside to trade spots with Ezra but then realized Ezra's eyes had strayed far from the service table.

"Leila," Ezra called as his gaze stayed intent on Leila's back.

"Dude, you know that chick?" Jake asked.

Jake pulled his apron off. Ezra slid off his apron too.

"Yeah." Ezra handed his apron to Jake, then walked in Leila's direction with eyes focused on her so as not to lose sight of her in the dispersed crowd. He wanted to see her, to explain why he didn't call. At first, he hadn't known he wanted to see her, but after two weeks had gone by, he'd decided he wanted to call and tried to find her phone number. But then he remembered he'd never retrieved it from his pants. By the time he checked the pockets, the piece of tissue had turned to shreds since he'd washed his pants. Now was not the time or place, while he was working, to talk to Leila, but he didn't have a choice.

Jake tried to keep up with Ezra's pace. "Now I get it," Jake said, "That's the same beautiful woman you rescued on the trail when we went cycling."

Ezra ignored him as he navigated his way further through the crowd. "Leila, wait! Please!"

Something in Ezra's voice broke through Leila's determination to ignore him, and she turned to face him. Ezra sighed in relief.

"Thank you." He noticed her face soften when she looked into his eyes. It was nice to see her in a different setting other than the mountains. She was wearing a hot pink tank top that hugged her chest and a knee length black skirt. She looked more beautiful than the last time he'd seen her. Ezra wanted this moment to last; he'd been thinking of her. Looking at her lips brought back memories of his time at camp. He could smell her mint-flavored, moist lips in his vision of memories.

"I' m sorry—"

Before he could finish the sentence, another voice forced its way in from behind him.

"Wow," the high-pitched voice squawked "It was so hard to catch up with you."

Leila noticed a tough-looking, beautiful blond woman appear beside Ezra. She was wearing the same dark blue T-shirt as all the other firefighters. She gave Leila a quick, assessing glance. "I'm Angie," she introduced herself with a sharp gaze and then slid her hand around Ezra's waist, leaning into him. They belonged together, which made Leila wonder why Ezra was chasing after her. Did he want to introduce his girlfriend?

Angie was part of the paramedic team, and Ezra considered her as a friend, just like all the other firefighters in his tour. However, Angie had made it clear with her flirtations that she wanted more than friendship with him, given her way of flirting with him and constant requests they have dinner together. Ezra had turned her down, using his busy schedule as an excuse instead of being straightforward. He figured he saw her only once in a while, whenever she filled in for the paramedics. He'd been afraid of hurting her feelings and assumed she would back off on her own since he never responded to any of her flirtations. Now he knew he'd been wrong.

She was back to haunt him at the worst possible moment. Was she becoming his escort? Ezra was very uncomfortable with the way she had her hand around him, something she'd never done before. This would be a reason for Leila to think they were a couple. And that was the last thing Ezra needed.

He sent a stern gaze to Angie but then turned back to Leila, hoping to keep her from walking away.

"I'm Leila." She moved her eyes from Angie to Ezra, as her posture maintained her balance. She put a hand to her forehead and sighed heavily.

"It was nice to meet you, Angie." With a quick glance to Ezra, she said, "Nice to see you again."

"Angie." Ezra tried to move out of Angie's hold tactfully, but she held on tight. When he opened his mouth to say something to Leila, his words stayed in his mouth, since Leila had already turned her back and mingled with the crowd. He didn't need an audience since he was terrible at drama and his colleagues would have a feast of him if he tried to chase after Leila when he didn't know how he could explain Angie to her in such a short amount of time.

Once he had himself free of Angie's hold, he threw his hands up in frustration, now more mad at himself than Angie. Jake had warned him of Angie's flirtations, but he was too much of a coward to say something. What could he have said? Avoiding her had always seemed like the only option. Why didn't she take a hint?

Angie was pretty, but she was the very opposite of Leila. Angie was loud and pushy. Leila affected him very differently than anyone else ever had: she was calm, and her excitement about God was a significant factor to entice Ezra to pursue her. She was everything Angie wasn't. Why did he have to be such a coward? What was Leila supposed to think with where their relationship already stood?

"Now about that dinner," Angie said as Ezra created a distance between them.

Ezra figured by the end of the day someone would be hurt, and it was the one person he didn't want to be hurt at all. He knew that the best way is always the truth, a hard lesson to learn for him at the expense of losing the one woman he felt connected to. He moved his gaze to Angie who was waiting in anticipation.

"I'm sorry, I can't go out to dinner with you." He clenched his jaw. "I mean it. You can join the rest of the crew and me the next time we go out, but not the two of us."

Angie had joined everybody from Shift C before when they went out to eat on their days off, but all of a sudden she was zeroing in on Ezra.

"Why can't you go out with me?" She seemed surprised.

"I'm off the market." He only had a professional relationship with Angie, and he hoped she understood and left things at that. "You're like my sister."

"Sister?" She shook her head. "Since when have you been off the market?" She folded her arms angrily across her chest.

"One month."

"I saw how you looked at that girl. What does she have that I don't?

She has everything you don't. The calm demeanor for one, Christ of all things. He felt like saying all that out loud, but he chose a noble response instead.

"I like her, a lot." He scratched his ear. "She's the type of girl I didn't think was my kind, but yet she seems to have everything I want in a woman. I would appreciate it if you don't interfere the next time I'm talking to her." His final words held an edge even though he hadn't planned to sound sharp at all.

His mind was back to how Leila had invaded his thoughts lately. At the end of each heavy day, he'd kept wishing he could talk and share with her the hardest challenges he'd faced. His mother did that job well, but he was starting to think how nice it would be if it were Leila. "I doubt there will be a next time, especially after this whole thing." He sounded defeated as he put his hands up in mock surrender.

Angie rolled her eyes. "I just hope she's worth it." She turned her back to walk away, then swiftly turned around for a second. "Hey, thanks for telling me. I know that probably wasn't easy." Her eyes were sad, but she gave a gentle smile of understanding.

He gave her an apologetic shrug and lifted his hand to wave as they both parted ways.

Even though Ezra had no idea where his future stood with Leila, the one thing he was aware of was that the thought of not having her in his life created all sorts of emotions he couldn't contend with, especially the fear that some other guy would come along in her life before he did. He could either let Leila be or figure out a way to reconnect with her. Letting her be was not even an option, so he focused on the latter instead.

***

After they were done cleaning up the mess from the pancake breakfast, Ezra had gone looking around the park in search of Leila, hoping she missed him as much as he missed her. He gave up on the hunt after what seemed like an hour of picking up all the candy wrappers around the park. They returned to the station, and his colleagues cleaned the equipment while he recorded the proceeds from the breakfast. He still needed to type up Thank you cards to their biggest donors, who'd made the breakfast possible. Most of the donors were the local businesses in Fort Rock.

Later that day, he and Jake had their Bible discussion. They'd been going through the Bible one chapter at a time. Though they were still in Genesis, they'd had great discussions, and the last thing he needed was to let his issues interrupt a spiritual meeting. After their study, Ezra needed to burn off some steam at the gym.

"If you keep up at that rate," Jake told Ezra between breaths during his weightlifting, "you're going to hurt your back, bro."

Jake gently set his weights on the floor to watch Ezra, who just kept bumping up his treadmill.

Ezra finally cut the speed and walked another half mile before shutting off the machine. He grabbed the towel he'd draped over the treadmill and wiped sweat from his face before stepping down.

Jake stood leaning against the wall, sipping his water. There were rarely people working out in the property gym. Whenever Ezra and Jake worked out during their time off, they mostly had the place to themselves.

Ezra twisted the cap off from a water bottle that Jake handed to him.

As the silence lengthened, Jake managed to ask, "How did it go with that chick I saw you chasing after?"

"Why do you call her chick?" he grumbled.

"What else can I call her?" Jake asked as he moved to open the door.

Ezra wiped his chest with a towel before putting on a shirt and followed Jake.

"Her name is Leila."

They sat on the couches in the lounge to cool off.

"She's beautiful, by the way." Jake sipped a drink of his water. "I remember her from the trail," he added as he settled into the tan couch. "Are you going to tell me the whole story or are we going to play the guessing game?" Jake prodded, and Ezra felt encouraged to share what was bothering him.

"How do you think it would have gone?" He stretched out his hands on the couch, trying to release the tension. "Angie showed up and made it look like we belonged together. The last time Leila saw me at the campground, I barely managed to voice a farewell to her and then I don't call her . . ." His jaw tightened. "When she runs into me a month later, I have a girl attached to my hip, who sends her a mean glare."

Jake wiped his short hair with a towel."At least you don't have Angie over your shoulders anymore. When you get another chance to see Leila," he said, "at this point, I'm starting to believe you will...I mean, it's unusual enough to run into the same person more than twice in different places, but you've run into Leila three times in the mountains, and then here at the pancake breakfast." He sighed. "I'm still new to this God thing, but maybe God is telling you something." There was a fixated gaze on the water bottles followed by a brief silence. "Be sure not to stammer, and tell her how you feel. Tell her everything, including Angie."

Ezra managed a smile. "You're good at this, Larson."

"Hmm." Jake shook his head, his eyes distant, then said in a low tone, "It didn't work out for me, but I know it will work for you. Hearing how you feel and what you've told me, there's a big shot for you, man."

Setting thoughts of Leila aside, Ezra asked, "Any news from Aniya?"

A heavy silence followed. "I think we're over." He went on to tell Ezra how he'd called to see if they could talk and start over. However, his idea had been shoved back into his heart where it belonged when a guy answered Aniya's cell phone at ten p.m. "He sounded more at home than I ever had and he just hung up."

"That's awful," Ezra responded with concern. He'd always made himself available for Jake, no matter how busy his own life got. He'd taken Jake along to their family gatherings and had also helped him connect at church, where everyone had been warm toward him. He hoped it made Jake feel a part of the family there.

"I'm thankful for you and the guys at work," Jake said, confirming Ezra's thoughts. "Even though you're terrible with your own love life, you're very good with the right words whenever I or any of the guys need to hear them. Apply that with Leila, bro."

Jake slapped Ezra on the back.

"Don't let that girl go; you may live to regret it."

Ezra hated how he had left things off with Leila. It was a whole mess. And he had to fix it. He was terrible at fixing messes, but for his own sanity, he just had to because he needed to have her in his life, and that was worth trying to fix things if he wasn't too late.

"We better get going." Ezra rose and grabbed his duffle bag, and Jake did the same as they both realized they had lingering thoughts. But they were confident of Who was in charge as they walked out of the gym.

CHAPTER 17

LEILA MANEUVERED FROM one obstacle to another at the Inflatable 5K Run with a bit of clumsiness.

Her mind was not sufficiently attentive as memories of last Saturday's pancake breakfast ran through her mind. Since she had no idea how to process Ezra and Angie, she'd left shortly after her encounter with Ezra. Why did he kiss her at the campground if he had a girlfriend? She had no answers to her questions despite her active mind. She'd thought of Ezra all week, and wondered why her heart was aching all over again.

July brought an additional heat, and running unfocused wasn't helping Leila's progress at all. She'd been a part of the Inflatable 5K Run for the last three years since a few teachers from the school participated in the race, and they'd promoted the event through the school. Leila dragged her friend Bianca to join her each year.

Rope climbing was Leila's final obstacle before making her way to the finish line. The event had taken place at a spacious park, which was over ten acres wide. There was a grassy area with shade trees. The obstacles were set on the wild, slightly rocky grass. Several people were on the sidelines cheering on participants.

Leila was panting, and she could feel herself running out of breath. Bianca caught up with her and noticed her rundown pace.

"We're almost to the finish line," Bianca said.

Yes, she could see the finish line, where fans stood with grins for their friends and family. Before she could respond to Bianca, she felt something smack her foot, and she went down.

"Are you okay?"

Several voices echoed, but there was only one voice that brought her back to her senses. Her vision brought the last person she'd expected to see.

"Ezra?" She squinted, ensuring her line of vision wasn't a dream. Ezra's warm hands held her moist ones. Her eyes turned to Bianca who was watching the exchange with far too much interest.

"Are you hurt?" Ezra said with a worry-filled expression.

"I . . ." She gave a nervous laugh. "I think I tripped, but I'm okay."

His furrowed face turned into a smile, the kind of smile that melts any heart and stays in your mind for quite some time, a smile you still want to see whenever you wake up. Just the smile she needed at that moment.

Ezra held his hand out for her. "Let's see if you can walk, I'll get you something to drink," he said after stabilizing her and slid his hand to the small of her back as he guided her. She'd never experienced this kind of attention from any guy before. Besides her dad of course. She was always giving attention to her brother, but right now, she really liked to be on the receiving end. Ezra knew exactly how to give her the attention she needed. She turned in search for Bianca, who was nowhere in sight.

"What are you doing here?" She asked curiously, trying not to show her excitement. She'd already forgotten that she was supposed to be mad at him for not calling her, and for not telling her, that he had a girlfriend all along.

"I know you're mad at me, but I'm here to see you." He squeezed her hand. His gaze turned to hers, seeking approval and Leila felt her whole self soften, her eyes melting into acceptance and understanding. Whatever Ezra made her feel, it was hard to explain to anybody.

"I have a lot to tell you," he motioned her to a blanket under one of the shade trees.

She gave him a questioning look, he didn't appear like the picnic kind of guy, but Leila did as told and sat on the blanket.

Ezra had contemplated finding Leila's home address so he could show up at her doorstep but then remembered the Inflatable 5K Run that she'd mentioned she participated in each summer. He'd looked up the time and place, hence the surprise visit.

"This is my blanket," he told her. It was Jake's suggestion to do something thoughtful for Leila, and Ezra couldn't think of anything but a picnic. He'd gone out and purchased a picnic blanket, not that picnics were something he did often, but with Leila, he was ready to try anything new.

"I brought you lunch," he said as he pulled out packaged take-out meals, a bag of plantains, and a six-pack of Coke; then he lifted the cooler and said, "Ice and some plastic cups."

He finally got a smile out of her.

"But . . . Bianca . . . ," she started.

"Yes, I bought four lunches since you mentioned you ran with your friend. I threw in an extra lunch for her daughter in case she's here too."

Leila shook her head in amusement. "You're something else, Ezra Buchanan."

He smiled, noticing the effect his smile brought to Leila when she rewarded him with a vibrant smile that held a spark in her soft brown eyes, sending him to a halt;—the spark Ezra longed to see, which he knew existed because of him. His eyes lingered to her lips, and then quickly moved his gaze back to the bag of plantains in front of him.

"I am now in the plantain chips club," He ripped open the bag. "I figured if I am going to pursue you"— he flashed a smile—"I'd better join that club."He said placing the bag in front of her.

"Welcome to the club." She shook his hand, laughing, and he returned a firm handshake, smiling.

They washed their hands and prayed for their lunch before they started to eat.

"I am sorry I didn't call you," Ezra said sincerely.

He told her how he'd washed the napkin with her phone number in his pants. Ezra also explained his relationship to Angie, "She's like a sister to me, just like all my colleagues. We are like family, you know?" He was not about to tell her that Angie had a crush on him. She seemed content enough with the simple explanation, and Ezra didn't see any reason to get into unnecessary details. "I'm sorry, for how I left things off at the campground." He'd wanted to give her a warm farewell kiss, and perhaps take her to an early breakfast before she'd left, but he'd done much thinking, and his emotions had turned doubtful.

"So, you're still single?" she asked

"I am as single as the numbers one to nine," he said, smiling.

She giggled, and Ezra's heart contracted. He knew then; there's no other girl he would rather pursue than Leila Morgan. He wanted to hear that laugh every day for the rest of his life.

After more catching up, they had no more cloud over them.

"There you are!" Leila said as Bianca approached. Her face beamed at both of them.

"Bianca, this is Ezra."

"I know." She gave Leila a knowing look. "I heard you call out his name when you fell." She extended a hand to Ezra, who eagerly shook her hand.

"I've heard so much about you," Ezra said.

" Same here," Bianca responded.

The three continued with their lunch having small talk. Ezra asked Bianca about Daisy, and work. Bianca looked impressed by the way Ezra knew a little bit about her. Leila did not doubt Ezra being a good listener.

"Glad you finally showed up," Bianca said. I was about to find you myself, since Leila—"

Leila put her hand on Ezra's shoulder. "Don't believe all the wrong things she's going to say about me," Leila said as if using Ezra's own words when he'd told her not to listen to whatever his siblings had to say about him.

"Please, I know who needs to hear about you." Bianca swung her hand in the air.

Ezra smiled and enjoyed the exchange between the two ladies who seemed comfortable with each other, and he was glad to know that Leila had a good friend since she didn't have a close relationship with her brother.

***

After their picnic lunch, Bianca bid farewell to get back to her daughter.

"So, I'm off this week," Ezra said. "I would love to spend some time doing things together, as normal couples would." He paused, unsure of Leila's response. "I want to take you on a real date. That is if you don't have plans this week."

He sure hoped she didn't have plans. He'd decided to take the week off so he could get to spend it with a girl he had no right to claim. He wanted to take her out, to go to a movie, to walk with her on the streets of downtown while holding hands and getting to know her more.

With a spark in her eyes, Leila gave him a broad smile. "I would love to spend a week with you, and I don't have plans, I'm a teacher remember?"

"I remember everything about you, Leila." He assured her because she was the first girl to capture his full attention. He still had no idea why, but he assumed that was what it meant when you fall in love with someone.

Taking a whole week off had been a leap of faith for Ezra. When he'd talked to his captain about the reason for his time off, Curie had said if it meant he'd get his mind straight, he could have a break. He would have to fill in next week for the guys who covered his shifts this week.

He'd booked a room at a hotel, which turned out to be within two miles of Leila's apartment. He hadn't been too sure if Leila would take him up on spending time together, with everything that had happened, but seeing a spark of thrill in her eyes made him wonder why he'd been so worried in the first place.

They left the park—Ezra heading for the hotel as Leila headed home to get a shower—with plans to hang out that evening.

***

Later that night, stretching out on the queen bed in his hotel room, Ezra put his hands behind his head and stared at the off-white ceiling for quite some time. He doubted he would get a decent sleep tonight since he kept thinking of Leila and daydreaming of a future together. He was getting too ahead of himself for a guy with a history of shaky commitment patterns. His thoughts went back to how cute she'd looked when he'd taken her to the arcade that afternoon since it had been her first time there. Afterward, they'd eaten hot wings and pizza at a mom-and-pop restaurant that Leila had suggested.

She'd said they made the best pizza and wings, and she wasn't kidding. Those were the best wings Ezra had ever had.

Tomorrow Ezra would meet Leila's parents after Church services at Leila's Church, and he was excited that maybe Leila thought of him in the same way he thought of her —with a future together. It was a casual invitation, but there was nothing casual about meeting your girlfriend's parents for the first time. At least he considered Leila, his girlfriend. He assumed Leila considered him as a boyfriend.

What if they didn't want their daughter to marry outside her race? With so many unanswered questions, Ezra decided to focus on Leila's eyes as he closed his own, only to be interrupted by his phone ringing.

He stared at the screen, and it was his mom. He pressed the button and before he could say hello, his mom spoke. "Honey, how did everything go with Leila today?"

His mom always wanted to know every single detail of her kid's lives. Ezra had told her about his visit to Leila. Crystal had offered to pray that everything would work out fine. Given the circumstances, before he showed up, Ezra would say, that God answered that prayer.

Ezra squeezed the back of his neck, "Actually, it went very well, thanks for praying."

"I knew it would go well."

Ezra told her what they did today and their plans for the rest of the week. "I'm meeting her family tomorrow."

"That's great news honey," Crystal said. "Bob, he's meeting the parents tomorrow."

Ezra could hear her relaying the message to his dad.

" Ez, you're still there?" Crystal asked.

"Uh-uh"

"Listen, I want you to bring her over next Saturday since you have off then, we'll have a BBQ."

"Mom, I don't want to scare her or anything like that."

"We will invite some of your friends from the fire station then. Then she will assume it's another casual get together."

Come to think of it, Ezra wanted nothing more than for Leila to meet his family and friends. If he made it a casual invitation, there would be no reason she wouldn't agree.

"I will let you know if she says yes."

"Love you, sweetie, see you next weekend, with Leila hopefully."

"Love you too mom."

***

As Leila and Ezra walked into the ranch style home, a dark brown woman, embraced Leila in a hug. "Leilani!" her smile soft.

"Mamma, this is Ezra," Leila said after the embrace.

Ezra had a bouquet of yellow roses in one hand, and he extended his other hand to the woman, who smiled at him and shook his hand. "I'm Amelia," she said. "It's nice to meet you, Ezra." Ezra handed the bouquet of yellow roses to her.

Amelia took a whiff of the flowers. "Aren't you so thoughtful? Also, my favorite flowers, too."

Ezra sent Leila an amused smile since he'd asked her what her mom's favorite flowers were. "Come on inside; Amelia gestured them in the house. "There's lemonade and sodas outside. Your father is out there too." She said.

The doorbell rang, and Amelia sent Leila to attend to the door as she led Ezra to the patio for their gathering.

As more people arrived for their brunch, introductions were made. Ezra got to meet a few of the guests who'd attended the church that morning.

He'd already met Leila's dad, Chris Morgan, and was currently sharing a table with him. The Morgans' backyard reminded Ezra of an enclosed cottage. Their brick house was small with a decent-size backyard. Enough for Chris Morgan's furniture workshop, that he'd told Ezra about. There were flowering bushes, not as much as his mom's garden, but vibrant enough to attract the bees.

Twenty-some people were in attendance for their Sunday brunch. The mature trees gave enough shade to accommodate the guests who were seated on the extra card tables they'd set up. The smell of BBQ filled Ezra's nostrils and many other fried foods.

After the guests ate all the barbecue they could manage, Leila moved to help her mom. Ezra and Chris were left alone for the moment.

"Ezra, how long have you been a firefighter?" Chris Morgan asked as he leaned back slightly into his chair.

Ezra cleared his throat. "Seven years." He took a sip of his water.

Ezra told him about his family and how he became a firefighter. Both he and his brother had followed in their dad's footsteps. Chris talked about his time of service in the army and his current carpentry work and offered to show Ezra his current projects before he left.

Between catching up on spiritual conversations, Ezra's intentions with dating Leila, and sports, Ezra didn't seem to lack anything to talk about with Chris. Leila came around with two plates of chocolate mousse. After helping her mom serve everyone, she handed one to her dad and the other to Ezra. Then she whispered in Ezra's ear, "I'll be back shortly."

Ezra smiled at her, looking at her dreamily, while Chris shook his head in amusement.

"Leila has never brought home a guy before. I couldn't wait when she called us last night and told us she was bringing someone. You must be very special to her," Chris said.

Ezra felt his heart lift upon hearing he was the first guy Leila had introduced to her parents.

"It's the other way around. She's very special to me." His voice filled with emotion.

"You know she's a gem, right?" Chris asked his face serious. "I am not just saying that because she's my daughter."

Ezra took a bite of his last piece of chocolate, as he thought of how to explain to Chris what Leila meant to him. "She's more than a gem."

His eyes darted to watch Leila as she was interacting with one of the guests. He flashed a smile at her when their eyes met, then looked back to Chris. "I want to know Leila more, to spend more time with her.

She makes me excited about the dreams I thought had failed." Dreams like marriage when he thought a single life was perfect for him, and all the things Leila made him feel.

Even though Chris should have been panicking after what he and his wife went through, his faith in God was a significant factor for his peace, after his conversation with Ezra, in having Leila date him. He couldn't help but notice the way Ezra's face lit up each time Leila was in sight, so he had no doubt the man in front of him loved his daughter. Besides, he found it wrong trying to compare his and his wife's relationship with that of his daughter and Ezra. Every relationship is different in its way. After all, Leila was mature, and she and Ezra were different from him and his wife. Chris returned his gaze to Ezra, who had his eyes intent on Leila's every move.

"Leila has good judgment. I have no doubt you're the man she needs." Chris said as Ezra turned his gaze to him.

"If she loves you, I love you already." Chris leaned back and finally took the first bite of his dessert.

Seeing Chris relax, and his comment, Ezra took that as a granted blessing from Chris to court his daughter.

"Thank you," Ezra said just as Leila returned with her mom at her side.

"I see where Leila gets her cooking skills," Ezra spoke to Amelia.

"She does very fine without me." Amelia swung her hand in the air and smiled.

Ezra could see the resemblance between Leila and Amelia, especially when they smiled.

"Amelia is the trainer, but her student has surpassed her in skill," Chris chimed in. "She cooked us several meals over the years—"

Ezra noticed Chris' smile replaced by sadness, perhaps not wanting to go in detail about his separation with his wife to a stranger, but then Amelia moved towards her husband, and placed a hand on her shoulder.

"Chris is right," Amelia commented before she excused herself when one of the guests motioned for her. Chris joined his wife to tend to their guests while Leila talked to Ezra.

After everybody had left, Chris gave Ezra a tour of his workshop and current projects. They enjoyed a relaxing afternoon. Amelia had an opportunity to visit with Ezra even though she had been busy after engaging with the guests. Ezra and Leila stayed until dinner. They played cards and talked about Leila's brother, Brian.

"So where's Brian?" Ezra asked, wanting to know all the people in Leila's life.

"He's on a group tour with his school friends to California," Amelia responded.

"Yeah, he gets whatever he wants," Leila said, and Ezra noticed the way both her parents sent her a glare. He figured there could be more family dilemmas than he cared to involve himself at the moment.

"After their farewells, Ezra had forgotten why he'd been anxious about meeting Leila's family. He liked Chris and Amelia. They were both easy to talk to. He couldn't understand how a couple who got along as they did could have almost lost their marriage.

Ezra dropped off Leila at her apartment, with plans to enjoy the rest of the week together.

***

The week spent with Ezra had been more fun than Leila had experienced with anyone before. It was going too fast; it was already Thursday. Leila knelt to thank God for the fun week she'd had so far. Ezra had left most of the planning to her since he said it was her week and he didn't care whatever they did as long as they were together. On Monday, they'd hiked at Garden of the Gods, visited Cave of the Winds, and gone shopping.

They went to Seven Falls and did a zip line on Tuesday, a first for Leila. It had left her a bit dizzy, but she could care less; she'd insisted on the zip line activity as her way of trying something outrageous.

They'd hiked a fourteener and eaten dinner at a new ethnic cuisine the following day. This had been the week to venture out with different cuisines since it was something Leila liked to do. Ezra had been flexible about anything, especially when it came to trying new food.

Earlier today, Ezra had joined Leila at the recreation center and helped tutor kids. He was good with numbers since he'd majored in accounting before he joined the fire academy. His math skills had come in handy with the teenagers who'd showed up for the tutoring sessions.

As Leila looked in the mirror one more time to make sure everything was perfect, she smiled at her reflection while thinking about her day with Ezra at the recreation center.

It had been fun working together with the kids, and he was good with them. Leila could not think of anything she did with the firefighter she didn't enjoy. Tonight was their first formal date, as Ezra had called it. He'd made reservations at a Brazilian steakhouse. He said it was a business casual dress-up place, but Leila wanted to dress up for the occasion. It had been a long time since she'd gone on a first date. This date with Ezra was different because her feelings for him went deeper than she'd ever felt before.

After trying on various outfits, Leila had texted Bianca, since she knew Leila's wardrobe well. At Bianca's recommendation, she ended up wearing her silk black-and-white print dress with a hot pink belt. She added her pink hoop earrings and dabbed mint lip balm on her lips. Content with her attire, her heart leaped for joy. She felt like she was going to the prom, only this felt much better, since her prom date had been her friend's brother and they'd gone as friends.

Even though relationships were bound for ups and downs along the way, Leila felt confident for the first time. Being in a relationship with Ezra was already enjoyable, and she was ready to overcome the obstacles, with God's help of course. Making God the center of their relationship would be the best decision they could both make. She slid into her hot pink strappy sandals when the doorbell rang. She gave a glance at her watch—it was already five thirty p.m, her date was here.

With her pink purse over her shoulder, Leila swung the door open. Her eyes sparkled at the sight of Ezra, handsomely dressed in a blue button-up shirt with a sports coat and dark blue jeans. The blue shirt brought out the light blue spark in his gray eyes. He was more dressed up than she'd seen him before. How quickly her life had changed, she thought. What had started as a summer for bucket lists had landed her a guy she was falling in love with. All thanks to God.

"Hey!" Leila greeted.

Ezra studied Leila from head to toe, and he was left breathless. Leila couldn't look more beautiful in her black & white dress with the hot pink belt, showcasing her slim waist and curves. She looked beautiful in her casual clothes, but she was striking in her formal dress tonight.

Ezra couldn't take his eyes off her. The woman was everything he had ever wanted and more.

"Hey, yourself!" he leaned in to give her a soft kiss on her cheek, inhaling the scent of the oils she smelled of, which he'd so come to love. "You look stunningly beautiful!" he whispered in her ear, then stepped aside so Leila could shut the door.

"You don't look bad yourself," she said, linking her fingers through his as they started descending the stairs.

Before they got in the car, Ezra remembered something he'd brought her. He pulled out a small pouch from his blazer and yanked a bracelet out. He'd noticed how much she loved hot pink, and had found the time to venture to the mall today before picking her up.

"I brought you something." He said handing the bracelet to her.

Her hand went to her mouth, and her eyes widened. Ezra reached for her hand to help her put it on her wrist.

"I love it!" she said and rewarded him with a fierce embrace.

She studied the diamond chain with two pink birds and a heart "It reminds me of the day, we watched all those birds when I got lost, and you came after me." Her gaze turned to him, she opened her mouth to speak, but then held back.

Ezra smiled, at her reason, given the fact that he'd picked out the bracelet with the same idea in mind. To remind her of their time together while camping.

"Blue is my favorite color on you," she whispered to him as he held the car door open for her."It brings out a unique color to your eyes."

"Thanks!"

***

The restaurant had dim lights and played soft ethnic music. The interior was fancy with white tablecloths and unique decor. The place looked busy enough with a steady crowd.

Ezra and Leila feasted on a gourmet salad, while they shared small talk until their waitress returned to explain how the main course worked.

As soon as they turned the flag on their table to green, a flood of servers with long skewers of meat appeared at their table. From flavored steaks, filet mignon, and chicken to sausage, pork, ribs, and more beef, it was a never-ending supply of meat. Not until they turned their flag to red did the chefs stop bringing meat to their table.

By the time the waitress offered them a dessert menu, they were too full to eat any more.

"I've never eaten so much meat in my entire life," Ezra said, and Leila agreed it was the most meat she'd ever eaten as well.

"What are these?" Ezra asked when the waitress placed another plate of exotic mushy brown food in front of him. At this point, he wouldn't eat anything without getting sick.

Dinner had surprisingly been so good that Ezra couldn't tell the difference between Brazilian food and American food. He wasn't adventurous as far as food was concerned, but he was going to try to be open to some changes if he was dating Leila.

Ezra had wanted tonight to be special. He'd done some research in the area to find an ethnic gourmet cuisine since he knew Leila enjoyed trying exotic foods.

"Those are plantains," Leila said.

" They sure look more different than your chips.

"They have different ways to prepare them," Leila explained. "I prefer the chips though."

Ezra figured, whatever Leila preferred, would be his preference as well.

***

They decided to take a stroll in downtown Colorado Springs. The warm August air turned into a soft breeze to cool the heat, convenient for their eight o'clock walk.

Ezra slipped an arm around Leila's waist and pulled her gently against his side, and Leila was more than willing to lean into him as they strolled down the streets. She tilted her head to his arm.

The walk was much needed. They'd parked the car a few blocks away, but they'd both agreed to walk off some of the meat.

"That was such a great dinner!" Leila said.

"It's surprising how much I liked it too."

Leila was impressed that Ezra had found an ethnic cuisine for their date night. He liked Ezra a lot, and she hoped he wanted her just as much because she could see him in her future. But right now, she was not going to worry about the future and what would happen to their relationship. All that mattered was that Ezra was here with her.

"What's going on in your busy mind," Ezra asked.

He was always good at reading her mind. She sighed."I'm thinking of how much I like walking with you and holding you." she said. Although she was usually not one to speak much of how she felt towards him, it seemed Ezra was helping her get better in that department. He was transparent for the most part, the least she could do was try to be open with him.

Ezra tightened his hold on her, "I love holding you a lot, his voice low when he bent and inhaled her hair. "And I love how you smell."

Leila could feel a blush inform of body heat, and was thankful; only she could tell that she was blushing.

"So, of all places your dad had been stationed, Colorado Springs had been your favorite then?" Ezra asked.

Leila had been in several places, and loved most of them, depending on the seasons of weather. By the time they'd settled in the springs, not only was she exhausted of constantly making new friends, but she was also tired of being on the move.

"Yes, for more reasons than just enjoying the sixty-degree weather in the winter time."

She loved the fact that she could see the mountains at every angle she stood. She was open to moving, but that would have to be when she got married someday. For the time being, she needed to settle down in one place, and Colorado Springs was home for her.

Ezra loved this feeling. Leila was like a magnet. He'd thought he loved the single life until Leila happened. The fact that he was drawn to her in a way he had never been attracted to anyone before surpassed his understanding.

Leila looked happy, and that warmed his heart. She was becoming a part of him now. Anything that made her happy made him happy, too. She was becoming a part of his dreams. He wouldn't mind spending every second of his life with her. That's how important she was becoming to him.

They spent another two hours strolling, but they were content whenever silence rose between them. They wandered in and out of the shops that interested them. Hand in hand, they embraced and relaxed like they didn't have anywhere else to be. Downtown traffic was slowing down. By the time Leila looked at her watch, it was almost ten thirty.

Ezra drove her back to her apartment as they made plans for tomorrow since it would be Ezra's last day before he returned to work. They planned to go back to the recreation center to tutor kids and then watch a movie.

"I'll pick you up tomorrow at ten am?" Ezra said, standing two stairs away from Leila's door as she dug into her purse for keys.

"Ten o'clock it is," she said as she opened the door, but she didn't go in.

He'd offered to walk her to her doorstep since it was late. His protective nature wanted to make sure she was safely inside, or maybe it was the fact that he didn't want to leave just yet. He would go with both. He doubted he would ever get tired of seeing Leila. Maybe because she had him wrapped around her fingers, and he hoped she knew that.

His mind busy, he said, "Good night, Leila." The words came out in a whisper as he contemplated giving her a good-night kiss.

"Good night, Ezra. I had a good time tonight." She hesitated before she turned, to enter and shut the door.

Ezra stood there for a minute with an inner battle: he didn't want to push her away by making a mistake he would regret, but he couldn't leave.

Breathing deep, he knocked on the door.

It swung open so fast that if he were leaning against it, he would have fallen inside.

"Did you forget something?" she asked, with biting her lips. She stood in the middle of the doorway, her voice breathy as if she was having the same internal battle as he did.

"Yes," Ezra said huskily. "This." His hand shot out and captured her wrist bringing her away from the door and into his arms, planting a soft, dragging kiss.

When he stopped, Leila still had her eyes closed, and he smiled. "I've wanted to do that ever since we parted from the campground." His voice was low. "Mint is my new favorite flavor," he added, referring to her mint-scented lips.

Catching her breath, she whispered in a dreamy voice, "You are trouble." She offered him a soft smile.

"I am afraid to say that you're the root of that trouble." He took a deep sigh, "I've fallen in love with you, Leila. It's not something I expected to happen, and not something I saw coming." He shook his head. "I honestly thought I enjoyed my single life until I met you," he said, gently stroking her lower lip.

Leila's hands to her chest, she took in a shaky breath, "I am in love with you too." She paused. "I liked you from the first day I laid eyes on you at the gas station."

After another gentle brush of her lips, he said, "I want to spend more time with you. I will try to come down to the Springs on my days off, or if you wish, you can come to Fort Rock on your days off." He figured it was only a forty-five-minute drive for both of them.

"I would love that very much," she said.

"Also, my parents are having a barbecue at their house next Saturday, and I would like for you to come and meet them." His hands held hers. "My mom has been dying to meet you ever since I told her about you." He paused for a moment, then said, "You've already met my siblings, so you know what to expect."

Ezra had shown Leila's picture to his mom, the selfie he'd taken with her during four-wheeling.

Leila seemed excited about meeting his parents, given the tight embrace and random kisses, he was rewarded from her.

Ezra guessed his mom was glad her son was finally excited about someone. To Ezra, Leila was not just anyone, but the girl he pictured himself with in the future. She was willing to share his world, and he was willing to share hers. It was a relationship. He wondered how it was possible to love someone that much within just a few months. All he knew was, he'd never felt like this before and wanted to hold onto this feeling forever.

Leila gave him a doubtful gaze as if wondering whether his parents would like her? Ezra could read her thoughts since he'd felt the same way before he'd met her family.

"My mom already likes you. She has seen your picture, and Renee has told her all about you too."He assured her. He didn't tell her that his mom had decided to have this barbecue specifically to meet Leila.

His dad's emotions had been unreadable when he'd seen Leila's picture, but Ezra had no doubt both parents would love her.

"I will come," she said, shining her beautiful smile that always warmed his heart.

"Thank you." He smiled in response.

She play punched him on the chest. "I want to go and see if you're momma's boy." She chuckled softly

He loved seeing her laugh, so he ran his fingers in her neck, to tickle her; sending her into a fit of giggles.

She jerked. "Hey, stop it!" Realizing people might be watching, since her door was still open, she lifted her neck to pop her head, as she tried to slap his hands off playfully.

His hands moved under her armpits, tickling her again and again, grinning at her inability to stop laughing.

"Ezra! Stop!"

She was laughing uncontrollably now. With one more tickle, he stopped and watched her calm down.

"That wasn't fair of you," she said, smiling.

"Wasn't fair, you mean I shouldn't have stopped?" He moved to tickle her once more.

"No, no!" She held his hands.

Ezra couldn't help but chuckle in response to Leila's laughter. "I love seeing you laugh," he said, as memories of their first encounter at the gas station rolled through his mind. "Remember the first day we met at that gas station?"

"How can I forget when you gave me such a captivating smile that stayed with me?"

"Turns out your laugh stayed with me, too." His gaze intent on hers, "And after I left that gas station, that night when I closed my eyes, I could hear the echo of your laugh, and I hoped I'd hear it again."

"And here we are," she said, her hands going around his neck. "Now I need to let you go; it's already late."

With a groan, he said, "Do you always have to keep track of time?" He wished to stay longer, but he knew Leila was right. It was getting late, and it would be best to call it a night.

With a searing hot kiss, a warm hug, and a final good night, Ezra made his exit, and Leila closed the door, behind her, taking a few seconds to capture his breath, Ezra descended the stairs with a wide grin on his face.

CHAPTER 18

AS IF TODAY was the most significant turning point in Ezra's life, he was dressed in his blue jeans and a light blue t-shirt, which he chose since Leila had mentioned it was her favorite color on him and brought out the blue in his gray eyes.

He paced, his heart pounding as he made his way through the kitchen to the sliding doors, that opened to the back patio. He straightened the cushions on the patio furniture.

"Dalton," he called over his shoulder for one of his colleagues, the youngest firefighter at the station who was in swim trunks. "Keep the kids entertained in the pool as long as possible."

With a mock salute, Dalton responded, "You got it Lt," He seemed thrilled to take over that role since it was hot enough that Ezra felt the need to swim, but he had things to set in order before Leila showed up.

He'd invited several of the guys from work and a couple from his church small group. His work and church friends were a part of his family, and he wanted Leila to get to meet them. Because she was becoming a part of his life, he wanted her to know everything about him, and that included the people in his life.

Ezra's parents did a great job maintaining their four-acre lot. They'd lived there since the seventies. Thankfully their community was still reserved from the new developments. Some of their neighbors still had horses, and it felt like a different part of the city whenever Ezra came to his childhood home.

Leila was the first girl he had wanted to introduce to his parents. He hadn't had much of an option with his ex-girlfriend since she had nagged him continuously about introducing her to his family. He'd eventually given in and brought her to one of their family get-togethers.

Most of the firefighters who could make it had already arrived. His captain and the chief came with their families and were already seated by the pergola and were visiting with some of his friends from church. His mom was chatting with a couple of Ezra's friends' wives.

Jake arrived holding a watermelon, and Ezra greeted him, taking the watermelon from him.

Renee came from behind. "Jakey!" she swung her arms around Jake. "Did you bring any guacamole?" Renee asked Jake.

Renee got along with all Ezra's friends, but she'd taken a shine to Jake the most. The fact that Jake spent more time with the Buchanans, he treated Ezra's family like his own.

Jake shook his head. "I'm sorry little Buchanan. I know how much you like my guacamole, but I came straight from work, and I didn't get time to make it."

"Your training job you mean?" Renee asked.

Jake nodded his response.

She tilted her chin down and frowned. "I was ignoring all the snacks while saving my appetite for your guacamole." She said.

"I can assure you; I will bring it next time," Jake said.

Miguel arrived shortly with his wife and their kids. The captains' kids raced around with water guns, squirting anybody who came within their proximity.

Two preteen boys were swimming in the pool with Dalton.

Ezra received a text from Leila when she was five minutes away. He decided to wait for her on the front porch. He waved at their neighbor next door from a distance as he remembered the times he and Andrew had poured food coloring in her pool because her son told them he had a crush on Renee. And another time when they'd hosed down her garden playing firefighter. Both Incidents, they'd had to face some consequences on top of paying to get her pool cleaned out and having to re-plant the garden. Thankfully, they still maintained a good relationship with her, since she still came to some of their family BBQs.

Leila's car pulled in shortly, and he went to meet her. "Hey gorgeous!" he said, planting a soft kiss on her forehead and another on her lips. She looked lovely in her floral summer dress, with her hot pink earrings and the bracelet he'd given her. She was dressed simply but looked beautiful. Ezra doubted there was anything about Leila he didn't like.

"Hi," she responded with a soft smile and then opened the back door and pulled out a clear container with homemade mint brownies and a big bowl of homemade chicken Caprese salad, Ezra knew that because she'd told him what she was bringing. Ezra took them from her.

As they'd walked halfway down the stone-paved driveway, a middle-aged woman with a vibrant face approached them.

"My, oh, my," she said, assessing Leila. Her gray eyes sparkled with delight. "I finally get to meet you, Leila Morgan."

Leila gave a warm smile to the woman, who mirrored Renee in looks. She had Ezra's gray eyes. Her hair, dark brown, with a few strands of gray, draped over her shoulder. She was dressed in a silk summer top and jean capris.

The woman glanced at Ezra, before turning to Leila, wrapping her arms around her in a tight warm embrace, leaving Leila no choice but to return the hug in kind. "I'm Ezra's mother, Crystal."

All Leila's doubts about how her visit was going to be faded after the embrace.

"Mrs. Buchanan—"

"Call me Crystal," she said, as she smoothed Leila's cheek. "Ez forgot to mention that you're more beautiful than the pictures he took on his phone."

Ezra flashed his mom a shy smile.

Leila could tell the two of them were close, and how much Ezra would need his mom's approval to marry any girl. If Crystal was as warm as she'd just reacted, then Leila had nothing to worry about.

Unlike Leila's parents' house, Ezra's parents' front yard had a spacious garden, with flower beds that sat in full-blooming glory, wafting a scent into the warm afternoon air.

"You have a beautiful home, Crystal." Leila commented as they walked through the tall doors into an impressive room with a vaulted ceiling." The house was immaculate in the interior, with glass windows streaming natural light.

"Well, thank you, it was all Renee's ideas. She had the walls taken down to give the house an open feel. Make yourself comfortable."

There were several family pictures hang up on the wall, but Leila's eye caught the three pictures by the kitchen wall. There were two cute boys in their baseball uniforms, about ten to twelve years old and a girl in a gymnastic outfit. "Oh! these are so adorable." Leila said.

Ezra was still standing beside her.

" Don't let the uniforms fool you," Ezra whispered in her ear.

Crystal pointed out which kid was Ezra, although Leila could already tell.

"You guys lost the game that day." Crystal said to Ezra.

I was terrible at baseball. Ezra said with a smile. "That's why I never pursued it." Leila knew that Ezra was capable of several sports if he chose to pursue any of them.

"I'm sure you were good at so many other things."

"He made it to state level in track and field though."

Ezra lifted his hand."Mom!"

"What?" His mom swung her hands in the air. "Leila wanted to know." Crystal took the food from Ezra's hands. "Ez, show Leila around." She excused herself for the kitchen.

Ezra led Leila through the sliding glass door that led to the back patio, putting his hand at the small of Leila's back, and guided her to the pergola where several people sat lost in laughter and casual conversation. "Let me introduce you to everybody."

"Hey, guys," he said as the loud group quieted and gave him their attention. "Meet Leila."

"I've met Leila." This came from the tall, dark gentleman Leila remembered to be Jake. Leila nodded, and the dark brown man shook her hand.

"Jake," he said with a grin.

Ezra introduced her to the rest of the group.

"Good to see you again, Leila." Ezra's brother Andrew greeted her with a hug.

"Good to see you too, Andrew." The introductions continued as some of the guys made silly remarks, while others tried to make small talk with Leila.

"Tell us how Ezra swept you off your feet at the trail!" the man Ezra had introduced as his captain said, with a teasing grin plastered on his face.

Andrew Buchanan watched in amusement.

Leila chuckled nervously, but before she could respond, another young man cut in.

I'm Dalton," he said as he joined the group in his dripping swim trunks.

With introductions made, there were eight new names that Leila would have to remember, which wasn't a challenge since she had to learn the new names of her students each year. The men spoke to Leila and each other freely.

Jake clapped his hands. "Let's start the grillin' guys," everyone followed him except for Dalton.

"I promised the kids I'd play Marco Polo," Dalton said as he made his way back to the pool.

"Dad, this is Leila," Ezra said the minute a tall and handsome middle-aged man joined them by the pergola. The man's face went pale, and his hand went to his forehead.

"Are you okay, Dad?" Ezra led him to one of the chairs.

Leila pulled a water bottle from the cooler, twisted off the cap, and handed it to Ezra's dad.

"I think I have a slight headache," Ezra's dad said and dismissed both Leila and Ezra, saying he needed to cool down.

Given the eighty-degree weather, perhaps he'd had a heat flash. Not the best way Leila had expected to meet her possible future father-in-law.

Ezra ignored his dad's discomfort and continued with the introductions."Leila, this is my dad, Robert." The man waved at Leila as he leaned into his chair to catch a breath.

Crystal joined them shortly and checked on her husband. After assuring Leila and Ezra that he was okay, Crystal linked her arm through Leila's. "I am snatching Leila away from you for a few minutes; I have a few questions about Essential oils," Crystal told Ezra and then led Leila towards the house.

"I've been experiencing some pain in my hip, do you know what oil I could use?" Crystal asked as they stepped from the deck through the back sliding doors to the house. "I'm still new to this whole essential oils world."

Leila was glad that Ezra had told his mom a lot about her, which helped to give them something to talk about.

"I usually make some for my dad," Leila said. "I mix Valor, Peppermint,Panaway, and frankincense, with a carrier oil—"

Leila stopped talking when she realized Crystal 's blank expression as if clueless to what she was talking about.

"I'm sorry, I will just come by sometime, so we can make the mix since I have all those oils," Leila said

Crystal sighed. "I will be happy to pay for any of them, but I'm still a newbie to oils like—"

"Leila!" Renee stormed from the kitchen where she'd been with two other ladies and threw her arms around Leila. "Hi, girlfriend!"

At least, Leila was comfortable enough with Renee, since they'd spent over a week together during the camping trip.

Leila hugged her back. "Hey," she greeted, and Renee led her to the kitchen.

"This is Andrew's girlfriend, Callie."

Leila acknowledged the red-haired woman with a nod, and Renee continued with the rest of the introductions. Renee apologized for having been absent at the time of Leila's arrival. "I had taken the other ladies on a walk in the neighborhood."

The ladies spoke freely as they got the plates and salads ready.

***

The afternoon was filled with stories and laughter. The air smelled of propane and grilled meat. The firefighters shared some of their most exciting life stories, pranks, and mistakes they'd made as rookies. The captain shared about Ezra's first month as a rookie and how he was subject to bullying. Each time they would tell him he needed to do a chore that hadn't been assigned to him or added to the chart, he would ask why and told them he would only do tasks listed on the schedule. They eventually gave up trying to manipulate him.

"Except for when I opened my locker and was greeted by a flying chicken," Ezra said, chuckling, and everyone, including Leila, joined in on the laughter.

"Did you ever find out who put the chicken in your locker?" Leila asked choking on her iced coke.

"Yeah, it was Miguel." Ezra's eyes moved to the guy in question, who lifted his hands in mock innocence.

"He does it to every probie," Jake said. Then he shared the goose incident in his locker.

Miguel had been with Fort Rock Fire Department longer than most of the guys on Shift C.

Dalton nodded in agreement as he told his chicken incident that Miguel had placed in his locker, during his first week at work. He also shared his ongoing probie struggles, "I can't wait to be done mopping the floors." Dalton lifted his brows. "Hey, I can't complain much, these guys are my family now."

Since Ezra was seating between Dalton and Leila, he slapped Dalton on the shoulder. "Glad to have you at shift C," Ezra said.

Every now and then, Robert spoke, and the guys clung to every word that came out of his mouth.

Everyone pitched in at cleaning and clearing. They rolled the grill back to its original place and covered it. Marvin Speers was the first one to leave with his tweens, then the captain followed. The rest of the guys said their good-byes, thanking Mr. and Mrs. Buchanan for their hospitality. They told Leila they hoped to see her at their local arcade hangout for a game of bowling. Later Andrew announced his departure. He said he needed to drop off his girlfriend to get her car from the parking lot where she'd left it.

Leila had enjoyed spending time with Ezra's friends and family. Crystal Buchanan was just as easy going as her three kids. Leila had felt an instant connection as they talked about their spiritual journeys and their fear of spiders. They spoke about essential oils since Crystal was starting to use them, a field Leila was knowledgeable to talk about. Jake and Renee had gone to the neighbor's to look at the horses. Now it was just Ezra, his parents, and Leila left on the porch.

Except for the few stern glares Robert had sent Leila's way, she wasn't sure what to think of him yet. He'd recovered from his heat flush, or whatever it was, and he'd enjoyed chatting with the firefighters and even shared a few of his own stories. He'd been quiet around Leila, and she had a feeling he wasn't fond of her being with his son as much as his wife was. When Robert finally managed to speak, he asked out of the blue, "So, Leila, why Ezra?" He cleared his throat. "Of all the guys you could date, why him?"

Ezra's brows furrowed, tightening his grip in Leila's hand.

Crystal's jaw dropped.

"Bob?" Crystal called in shock and then turned her eyes toward Leila. "You don't have to answer that, dear."

Leila pulled her shoulders to settle in the chair. She assumed she was the reason for the man's pale face earlier. Yes, she didn't have to answer to the man since she wasn't at a job interview, but she figured it would only be polite, regardless of whether the guy just wanted to intimidate her or not. She felt a slight rise in temperature due to the abrupt moisture on her hot summer dress. Feeling Ezra's assuring grip and nearness, Leila felt the courage to speak. "I love him, more importantly, we both have a common ground in our faith. Why him above anyone else?" Her dreamy eyes moved to Ezra. "There's only one Ezra in the whole world. I don't want to date just any guy."

Ezra gave her an assuring smile and a gentle squeeze. Leila could feel his muscles relax, probably from the tension he'd acquired at his dad's question.

Crystal gave her husband a stern gaze, and Leila suspected she and Robert would be having a conversation later.

Robert forced a chuckle. "Well, I just had to ask, that's all." His tone was curt.

"Now, Bob, why don't you come help me in the kitchen while Ezra and Leila catch up?" Crystal said, taking his arm.

Robert raked his fingers through his hair and followed his wife.

Meanwhile, Ezra hoped his mom would help smooth out the awkwardness his dad had created. He moved closed the small distance between them and placed a gentle kiss on her ear, another on her forehead, before placing one on her lips. Leila squirmed. With their foreheads touching, Ezra opened his mouth, wanting to kiss away any doubts his dad had created. "I'm sorry about my dad," he whispered against her lips.

"It's okay, it shows that he cares about you," she said, eyes filled with understanding.

***

While inside the house, Crystal asked her husband why he was acting odd.

"Well, I'm more concerned about our son's happiness!"

Crystal's eyes darted through the sliding glass doors, and she saw Ezra laughing, Leila's head resting against his arm and Ezra's hand over her shoulder. Crystal returned her gaze to Robert.

"Ezra might not be a lot of things," she arched an eyebrow in Ezra's direction, "but he looks very happy to me right now."

Robert's eyes gazed through the glass doors, and then back to his wife. He clamped his mouth shut as if to bite back a comment he might regret.

"Maybe you can work on your attitude when you get back out there." Crystal cast a worried glance his way.

"Mom, is Dad upset about something?" Ezra asked when he met his mom in the kitchen upon returning some utensils.

"I know he might be dealing with some issues," she assured him with a warm hug, "but trust me, it has nothing to do with Leila."

Ezra could only hope so. Not that it would change the way he felt about Leila, but he wanted her to feel welcome in his parents' home. A place he called home, which he hoped to become Leila's home too.

Leila announced her departure.

"Now you don't need to be a stranger, Crystal Embraced Leila."You are welcome here anytime," Crystal said and kissed Leila on the cheek.

"Thank you, Crystal," she said and turned to Robert.

"It was very nice to meet you, Mr. Buchanan," Leila said, but Robert barely responded. Not until his wife sent another stern gaze his way did he manage a grumble.

"Yeah, me too."

Ezra walked Leila to her car.

He embraced her and planted another soft kiss on her lips, making her feet wobbly. "I 'm so sorry about my dad's rudeness. Honestly, it took me by surprise. He's usually not like that."

Leila swung her hand as if to brush it off. "I'm not bothered, as long as you love me, that's all that matters."

Ezra's spirit was lifted at the warm welcome his mom had given Leila. He knew his mom already liked her before they'd even met, but seeing her genuine love toward her did something to his heart. He could tell Leila was touched by his mom's attentiveness. Ezra was more relieved that Leila handled his dad's rude behavior more lightly than he'd expected.

***

"What was that all about, Dad?" Ezra asked his dad as they stood in the driveway. He needed some answers about his dad's rude behavior toward his guest. His dad was always a great host to all his colleagues and friends, and now the most important person in his life comes along, and he puts on an act.

Robert sighed in angry frustration. "Have you met her parents?"

"Yes, I have."

Robert closed his eyes with a brief silence."What do they think of you two together?"

"We're adults." Ezra's mind reflected on his dad's stern farewell to Leila. "I had a good visit with them actually, warmer and more inviting than the daggers you threw at her." He shook his head. "But really, what's up?"

Robert tightened his jaw. "I dated a girl before your mother. Her name was Nelly." He let out a heavy sigh. "She was beautiful, and we were in love, with plans to get married. But her parents, especially her dad, were determined to keep us apart." He told Ezra how Nelly didn't care what her parents thought. But Robert didn't want to keep being harassed and gave up on her. "I didn't fight for her, and I should've. Don't get me wrong, I'm so blessed to have met your mom, but I felt terrible for breaking Nelly's heart. Instead of staying and fighting through it, I didn't." Another heavy silence followed. "That's why I came off strong on Leila. I don't want you to go through the same thing I did. I am sorry, son."

Ezra hugged his dad, then folded his arms to his chest.

"I like Leila, and I appreciate you trying to protect me, but I think you raised me well enough to handle the fight for myself," Ezra said, smiling softly. "If it comes down to having to fight for her, I will be ready." He hoped there wouldn't be a battle to fight.

"That's if my attitude didn't send her flying for the hills." Robert managed a forced chuckle.

Ezra doubted Leila would run off because of his dad's attitude. She'd defended Robert by saying he was protective.

"I don't think so, Dad." Ezra patted his old man on the shoulder as they both made their way inside the house.

***

It had been almost two weeks since Leila had visited Ezra's parents. She'd heard from Ezra daily, either through texts, phone calls, or in person. Four days after her visit to his parents' house, she'd received a call from Robert Buchanan, apologizing. His exact words were, "Sorry for misjudging you based on my personal experience." He'd told her about Nelly as well, and Leila told him she understood that being a good dad meant protecting his children at all costs.

They'd ended the call on a good note when Robert invited Leila to join him and Ezra for golfing. Not that Leila knew anything about the sport, but he'd insisted he wanted to prove to her that he could do better than the last time she'd seen him.

Summer was going too fast since Leila was having so much fun. Despite the August heat, Leila hoped the days could slow down a little, especially now that she was spending most of her free time with Ezra. Usually, she would be prepared for work by now, but this summer had been the most enjoyable by far and the first that Leila did not want to come to an end.

She'd picked up Ezra from work three times in the last three weeks and gotten to meet a few guys from the opposite shift on one of the days when he was the substitute.

Leila had also joined Ezra's colleagues at their hangout arcade on one of their days off. They bowled and played table hockey and pool. On one of the afternoons they'd bowled competitively, but for fun, Leila and Ezra's team lost and had to buy dinner for the winning team. It had still been a great experience altogether. Ezra's colleagues were loud, but a fun group of guys, who seemed to care for and love each other genuinely. No wonder Ezra considered them to be his family.

Today, Leila had her end-of-summer party with her former students and their families at the park. Ezra had switched his schedule with someone else, so he could come and meet Leila's students.

The food had been potluck style. While the parents visited with each other in small groups, some of the students shared photos from their summer bucket lists. One of the students who'd been afraid of flying shared the pictures she took from the airport, and some on the airplane when she and her family flew to New England to see her grandparents. "I'm so glad we did that challenge Miss Morgan" the little girl's eyes sparkled.

Leila shared a photo album of her camping photos, including one of the pictures that Ezra had taken of her with a trout in her hands.

The kids took turns surrounding her as she explained the story behind each photo. " Were there any spiders?" one of the kids asked.

"Now about that," Leila smiled and shared her spider incident with them.

There were giggles, from some of the students. "I wish your friend took a video." said another student.

"I'm so glad you guys challenged me to go camping because that's how it landed me Ezra," Leila said, her eyes darted to Ezra who was busy entertaining another group of kids at the playground. Some were role-playing how to put out a fire, and others rolled on the ground with him.

By the end of the day, most kids wanted to be firefighters when they grew up.

After the students had left, Leila an Ezra sat on the grass to watch the sunset. She leaned her head on his shoulder, as she experienced a wave of contentment, unlike anything she'd ever known. She wished they could stay seated all night long, but Ezra had to drive back to Fort Rock for work tomorrow.

With summer tutoring sessions at the recreation center being over, Leila still had one more week of summer left. She was looking forward to spending all available time with Ezra. Since he'd been off yesterday and today, they'd done paintball yesterday, but Ezra and his colleagues had gone to help a family rebuild their home from fire damage. Ezra had texted Leila earlier with an update —they were finalizing the deck, but the project was taking longer than they'd planned. Leila wouldn't be seeing Ezra until Monday at the end of his twenty-four-hour shift. It would be almost three days before they could see each other again.

Leila couldn't wrap her mind around not seeing Ezra for three days; that's why she was making peppermint brownies to surprise him at the fire station tomorrow. Sunday afternoons were less busy according to what Ezra had told her when he'd asked her to stop by anytime she was able to.

Leila's phone chimed as she placed a lid on the brownies in the airtight container. She reached for it from the counter and saw that it was a group text from Renee to both Leila and Bianca reminding them of their dinner engagement at Renee's place.

Before Leila could type her response, another text came from Bianca: "What can I bring?"

"Just yourself, I'm ordering takeout," Renee responded.

"I will be making a quick stop at the fire station to see Ezra. I will bring brownies," Leila added.

"Yum, looking forward to our reunion."

"See you tomorrow."

After Leila's visit with Ezra's family, Renee had asked her to connect with Bianca so that the three of them could schedule a girls get together to catch up on their camping trip. Renee hadn't seen Bianca since then.

After they'd all agreed on the date, Renee had suggested they meet at her place so they could chat and perhaps play a board game in case they got tired of talking, which seemed impossible when three girls with different personalities got together. Leila planned to meet her friends after Church service and the Fort Rock Fire Station. She wanted to surprise Ezra and his colleagues with some of the homemade brownies.

***

Ezra sat on the couch by the kitchen at the fire station with his eyes glued to his phone, scrolling down to reread Leila's previous texts. His grin wide, he thought of sending her a text, but it was only eleven a.m., and she was probably still at church. At that thought, he decided to focus on reading all her old texts instead.

He'd been busy at work over the last three weeks, but he'd managed to update Leila about his day-to-day emergencies. She'd sent him texts of encouragement or prayed with him when he was having a hard day at work, depending on the nature of their call.

They shared and encouraged each other, both spiritually and emotionally, by exchanging scriptures in texts and praying together both on the phone and in person. They both felt their spiritual lives being strengthened as a couple and as individuals.

Ezra had been so discouraged when they'd tried to answer the emergence of a man who'd had a heart attack but didn't make it. The paramedics had transported a dead body to the hospital instead. When he'd called Leila to talk about it, she'd prayed with him, and that had pushed him through the rest of his shift.

Despite Ezra's tight schedule, he'd managed to spend most of his days off with Leila. She'd joined him at his monthly outdoors small group, joined him with the guys when they went to the arcade and had also come to watch him as he taught indoor rock climbing. He'd enjoyed having her watch him as he led the group. He loved spending each passing day with her. He knew he would sit in the most boring place and not complain as long as Leila was there with him.

He chuckled as he read another one of her texts.

"Why are you smiling so much lately?" Curie teased with a grin as he made his way to the refrigerator.

They all knew about Leila, and Ezra didn't have to answer that question. He wasn't the type of guy who sent text messages at work that often, but somehow he'd picked up the habit ever since Leila happened. He was feeling like a schoolboy, and time spent with Leila moved so fast. Lately, he looked forward to his days off. He didn't remember ever feeling this happy with anyone as much as he did with Leila. He'd had to sacrifice some of his sleep to see her on his days off, even though Leila insisted he stay home to rest, but she'd lost each time. The more he spent time with her, the harder it got for him to be apart from her. She had become a part of him."

"I smile often." His face lit up and, like a kid caught in a cookie jar, he just shook his head in amusement.

"Leila is the reason, right?" Angie chimed in from the dining table where she sat pretending to read yet silently watching Ezra.

Both guys on the paramedics' team were giving a CPR class at the Recreation Center. Angie was taking over for the guy on the night shift, but she'd showed up early.

Ezra ignored Angie's comment and continued scrolling through his texts.

"Glad to see the original Buchanan," Curie said, then poured orange juice in a cup.

"Hey, that's my cereal!" Dalton came chasing Miguel who had a cereal box in his hands.

"LT, can you tell Miguel to stop eating my fruit loops?" Dalton spoke to Ezra, while Miguel yanked open the box.

"We're a family here; we get to share," Miguel said.

Ezra turned his gaze to the two guys in a cereal battle. "The kid is right, give him his cereal." His tone distracted, and his gaze back to the phone again. "Don't you two need to watch a training video, anyway?" Still unable to keep the smile off his face, he said.

"I better join Larson in the gym." Ezra rose just in time for the Buzzing alarm.

Dispatch announced the nature of the call.

"Accident on Fort Rd and I-25"

Miguel groaned and tossed the cereal bowl back to the sink. Curie quickly rinsed his cup. "Meet you guys out there."

Ezra climbed into the shotgun seat of the Engine truck since the ladder truck hadn't been requested.

Jake slid into the driver's seat as the rest of the crew took their places. Pulling out of the bay, Ezra hit the lights, and the siren blared.

Station 15 was the first to arrive on the scene. Not only because they were the closest, but they were also the only ones available at the moment.

CHAPTER 19

LEILA WALKED TO the two-story brick building with the white trim and a sign that read Fort Rock Fire Rescue Station 15.

The doors to the bay were closed, so she used the entrance on the west side of the building. Her heart raced, the same way it always did when she was within reach of Ezra's surroundings. She hesitated for a few seconds before she knocked on the heavy metal door and waited.

Her stomach dropped into knots the moment Angie opened the door. She remembered her from the pancake breakfast, and judging from the cold gaze from Angie's blue eyes, Leila knew that she recognized her, too. Not knowing what to say or do with the cold invitation, Leila kept a steady gaze. She was not going to bc intimidated when she hadn't done anything wrong.

"Hi," she greeted, but Angie didn't respond. She looked at her critically up and down before she stepped aside to let her in.

The place was quieter than the last couple of times Leila had visited, an indication that the shift might be out on a call. As Leila scanned for any other person in the room but Angie, her eyes darted to the open living area. There were two large leather couches and two lounge chairs, and above the wall was a TV mounted to it, but it was turned off. Her eyes moved to the kitchen, and beside it was the rectangular dining table and almost a dozen chairs, but there was still no sign of life. Her gaze returned to the only occupant in the room.

"Is Ezra around?"

"You know he's on duty, right?"Angie asked with a frown.

Leila was doing her best to stay calm by ignoring the sharp tone of the blonde woman. She felt like making a remark about her rudeness but then realized it wasn't her place to do so. She was going to need to exercise self-control by keeping her tongue intact, which was going to be a bigger challenge since self-control wasn't one of her strongest virtues. Thankfully, today's message at church had been about controlling the tongue and how words could be used to bless or curse someone. God knew Leila would need that message today. She was going to need all the help from God to apply the pastor's sermon.

She closed her eyes, then opened them and responded, "Yes, that's why I came here instead of his place. I made some brownies for you guys." She gracefully walked to the kitchen and placed the container on the counter. When she turned, Angie was right behind her, with her hands on her waist as if ready to take her down in a fight if it came down to it.

Angie had a strong body form, and she could take Leila down if she wanted to, but Leila had no intention of fighting. Creating the needed space between them, Leila said, "Tell Ezra I stopped by." She doubted Angie would relay any such message, but she only said it to fill in the tension-filled silence.

"Just so you know," Angie sneered, her muscles tight, "Ezra is handsome, but what girl wouldn't think so? Have you wondered why he's still single?"

Determined to ignore her tormentor, Leila made her exit before she could say anything she would regret.

The firehouse was Ezra's home away from home, and the last thing she needed was to get into an argument with one of the people he considered family. Without a word, Leila made her exit, but Angie followed her out of the door.

"He's dated other women like you, but things didn't work out, because he's not the commitment kind of guy." She sent an edgy chuckle. "Six months into your relationship, you will be history, just like me. Our relationship was going very well before he took that stupid camping trip. We were the power couple at the firehouse, but thanks to you, I will have to work hard to get him back."

Leila kept walking toward her car, racing through the parking lot. She was tempted to turn around and yell or say something back to Angie, but she knew where that would lead. Another fire lash.

"I hope he comes to his senses soon." Angie's words were coming too fast without a breath in between. She trailed off with more insults until Leila entered her car and turned on the engine.

Finally, in her car, Leila felt the temperature rise another twenty degrees. She cranked her air conditioning and pulled out peppermint essential oil to massage her temples. She could feel a slight tension headache coming on. Angie's words were like a sharp sword through her heart, yet they held partial truth to them. Leila had been looking forward to seeing Ezra, but right now she doubted there would be an Ezra for her.

Ezra was afraid of commitment, at least he'd been honest about it, but Leila had assumed he could change. Did he ever date Angie? Why would she have said they had a good thing going until Ezra's camping trip? Ezra had seemed truthful from the start, but he'd told Leila that his relationship with Angie was work-related. With so many questions stirring in her mind, she needed to be alone, and the last place she needed to be was with Renee Buchanan or anyone related to Ezra, for that matter. Before driving off, she pulled her phone out of her purse and dialed Bianca so that she could relay her regrets to Renee.

***

Jake held the hydraulic claws while Ezra manned the cutters through the door. Curie, Miguel, and Dalton joined the police in assessing the young guy who'd been thrown from the motorcycle during the accident.

It took ten minutes for Ezra to get to the middle-aged man in the passenger seat. Untangling the man from the seat belt, Ezra checked for a pulse but found none. Panicking, he pulled the man from the car and laid him on the pavement.

He yanked open the man's shirt and began CPR compressions. "Where are the paramedics anyway?" Ezra asked Jake whose concentration remained where it should be, on the other victim in the car. Her arm was covered in blood, but the fact that she was crying was a good sign —it meant that she could still feel her body functioning. Curie continued barking out updates on the radio, about the paramedics' whereabouts.

Ezra's sweat was almost turning to blood, and his arms were on fire as he kept pumping the man's chest, all along praying to God that this man's pulse would return. The paramedics arrived and stood by Ezra's side. He looked up, expecting them to take over, but the resigned look in their eyes told him they believed the man was beyond help.

Miguel tapped Ezra's shoulder. "Hey, the captain says we should call it."

"I'm not giving up, not yet," Ezra said, his face dripping with sweat as he continued to perform compressions on the man in front of him. As Ezra's arms were about to give out, he felt a pulse.

"Found the pulse," he announced with a wide grin on his face. The paramedics loaded the man onto a stretcher and rushed him to a waiting ambulance.

As more paramedics showed up, they tended to those with mild injuries while the police collected information. The road was blocked off. Fire trucks and emergency vehicles were angled between police cars, while blue and red lights flashed.

Between the semi truck that had bumped into a Hyundai and the suburban, altogether three vehicles and the motorcycle had been involved in the accident.

Ezra's eyes landed on the guy who'd been riding the motorcycle; he imagined him to be in his early twenties. One of the guys from EMS shook his head, a familiar signal to Ezra that he was already dead. The images were too raw to take in.

With the victims all rushed to the hospital, the fire crew stayed for hours to help clean up the scene before returning to the firehouse. All Ezra could think of was Leila. Life was too short, those images fresh in his mind of people who were on their way to somewhere but somehow didn't make it back home. His job was the kind where he didn't know what to expect when he went to answer the call. And today was one of those days that had taken him by surprise.

An hour later, Ezra sat at his desk, staring at his computer screen. He had to make updates for the recent emergencies they'd had, and was also checking to make sure all his crew was up to date on their training. The rest of Sunday night's shift had been slow—except for a call they'd received from a seventeen-year-old girl whose eighty-three-year-old grandmother had fallen and was too heavy for the girl to help up. His colleagues had managed to get some sleep, unlike Ezra.

Leila had been on his mind most of the night since she didn't answer or return any of his texts. They had talked or texted each other daily, especially before Leila went to bed. Even this morning he'd checked his phone twice, hoping to have received a text from her. Besides his mom's text messages, which he'd completely ignored, there was nothing from Leila.

He was starting to worry that something was wrong with Leila. Was she doing okay? If anything happened to her, her dad would call him since he had his number. As soon as his shift was over, he would have to figure out what was going on. His stomach felt knotted just thinking about her being injured or sick.

The sound of Shift C gathering their things and heading for the door snapped Ezra back to the present. "Marley from Shift B has a date on Saturday, can anyone cover for him?" Ezra asked as Shift C clocked out, making way for the next shift.

"I'll do it," Dalton volunteered as he ducked out the door.

***

Leila woke up with a stiff neck; she'd cried a few times last night, and Bianca had spent almost an hour talking to her on the phone. Bianca had sensed the tension in Leila's voice when she'd called to cancel their girl's dinner, and she'd followed up with another call before bedtime.

Leila had told her everything about her encounter with Angie. Although Bianca had expressed her doubts about Angie, she'd still encouraged Leila to give herself a few days to pray before talking to Ezra.

Leila had cried a new set of tears after hanging up the phone with her friend. Then she'd silenced her cell phone to ignore Ezra's calls and texts altogether. It hadn't been an easy thing to do since they'd talked every night from the time they'd reunited. The rest of the night she'd tossed and turned, thinking of Ezra and wondering why he'd not been honest with her about Angie.

A pang of jealousy hit her hard at the thought of Ezra's possible relationship with Angie. Things had been great until she'd stopped by the fire station. As much as her mind wandered, she knew it was best to channel her energy into planning her day.

With her mind busy for such a dark hour of the morning, she forced herself out of bed and glanced at her watch. It was still five a.m. The mall didn't open until ten; perhaps shopping would lighten up her mood, she doubted it would, but anything was better than staying in her apartment all day. Too bad Bianca had to work today, but it was probably best because then Leila could drown herself in back-to-school sales without anyone mentioning Ezra's name.

After her morning devotions, which didn't seem as constructive as they would typically be, she forced down two cups of coffee, deep cleaned her already tidy house and jumped into the shower to get her day started.

As she was debating whether to read Ezra's texts or get lost in re-arranging her bookshelf, a soft knock on the door took her by surprise.

She glanced at her watch. It was 7:55, still too early for guests. Nobody ever visited her this early, but then she remembered she'd asked Eduardo to come to fix her faucet. Eduardo was aware of Leila's habit of rising early.

Wasting no time looking through the camera on her door, Leila swung it open, and Ezra stood in front of her, handsome in his navy-blue Fort Rock Fire Department T-shirt. He seemed more exhausted than she remembered him to be. Why did he have to be so good-looking? She wanted to wrap her hands around him and help ease the tension he seemed to have, but now was not the time for that.

***

Ezra's eyes scanned Leila's, and he realized they mirrored his own in exhaustion. He could tell she'd just gotten out of a shower since her hair was damp and he could smell the sweet scent of her conditioner. She was gorgeous in the rugged T-shirt she wore over her black tights. It was hard for him to hold back a smile.

"Hey," Ezra said after an extended silence. He felt disappointed when she didn't smile back. Something was different. He was relieved that she was okay, yet a sense of uneasiness washed over him that things were not okay between them. What had he done wrong?

"Hi." She stood there staring at his face for another moment longer.

"May I come in?"

She stepped aside to let him in, then shut the door behind them.

Now irritated and frustrated, Ezra followed her to the kitchen, and she gestured for him to sit at the dining table with four mismatched chairs. Two black chairs to match the small dining table and a hot-pink and white chair.

She took a seat across from him. Did she have a clue how he felt about her? He was not liking where this was going at all.

"You okay?" he asked, his brows furrowed.

"I'm fine."

Her tone said otherwise.

All the times Ezra had hung out with Leila, and picked her up from her apartment, he'd never been inside. He'd picked her up in front of the door, and when he'd dropped her off, he'd walked her to the same place. Except for the night he'd kissed her, he'd only made it as far as the entrance.

"I will make some coffee," she said dryly.

While Leila made coffee, Ezra's eyes scanned the interior of Leila's apartment. It was small with a modern feel, very organized. There was a bookshelf in the small living room, and the walls had neutral colors with a few nature photos hanging. No surprise, some of them were the pictures Leila had photographed since Ezra recognized the picture with the meadow from their camping trip.

His eyes went to the window, at the magnificent view of Pikes Peak as it loomed in the distance with the colorful sky behind it. He wished he could enjoy it, but somehow nothing seemed enjoyable at the moment. He chose to inhale the blasting vapor from the humidifier in the kitchen that filled the room with the sweet aroma of Leila's oils. It felt relaxing to be in her place, to smell her scent. Regardless of the muggy tension.

She handed him a cup of steaming coffee, and she leaned against the refrigerator.

He wasn't in the mood for coffee, but it was a nice gesture. "Leila, can we talk?" He didn't want to play this game anymore. "What's bothering you, and don't tell me you're fine?" he said as he tried to keep the hurt out of his voice.

"What's bothering me?" She folded her arms angrily across her chest.

"Are you and Angie in a relationship?" She rephrased her question: "Were you and Angie together before you met me?" Her voice rose slightly enough for Ezra to sense the edge in it.

"What do you mean, and why bring up Angie all of a sudden?"

"You know what I mean. Did you give Angie the impression that you were dating or you liked her?" her voice louder. "When we departed from camp, I could tell you had regrets after you kissed me, you barely responded when I said good-bye." She shook her head in disbelief. "Then I run into you at the fundraiser breakfast, with Angie's hand wrapped around you, like you two belong together. What I'm I supposed to think?"

Ezra hadn't seen this side of Leila yet. She'd always had a calm demeanor but got her point across. Now he realized Leila could get mad all right, yet she still looked adorable. He wished she weren't mad at him.

She had a point, however, and he didn't blame her for having doubts about his situation with Angie, given the circumstances of their departure from camp and how she had seen Angie's arm around him. But why of all days did she bring up Angie now? Was she getting scared because of how serious their relationship had become? Not that he could blame her. They'd been doing things together on a regular basis, and Ezra had been fearful when his feelings for Leila rose to another level, but now that he was finally committed to her, she seemed to be holding back. He'd already explained to her about Angie, and she had seemed to understand.

Ezra raked his fingers through his hair. "Do you trust me?"

"I don't have time to play games, Ezra. You're on and off, neither in nor out. Maybe you should first figure out what you want."

He frowned. "What's that supposed to mean?" His tone had a slight edge to it. "I told you already. You're the first woman I've felt the need to pursue. You make me hate my single life." He wanted to add, she was the one woman he hoped to spend the rest of his life with, but he doubted now was the time to say anything of the sort. He didn't want to give her any reason to panic any further.

He pulled himself up and caged her against the refrigerator. He could feel her heart racing. When his gaze met hers, he said, "I want you, Leila, more than anything…" Her eyes softened thank goodness; perhaps he could plant a kiss on her lips to put an end to this conversation. "As for Angie"—he shook his head— "you will have to trust me," his voice low, "and if you don't believe me, I don't see any reason . . ."

"For us to be together?" She finished the sentence for him.

Ezra was very articulate where anything else was concerned except when it came to love. Especially with Leila, he had a very different level of communication now that he felt she was a part of him.

"I didn't mean it to come out that way," he said. The girl seemed too riled up to reason.

She wiggled herself out of his hold and moved farther away.

"I get it, you didn't want a commitment, and here I am, interfering with your life," she said.

Frustrated with his wording, Ezra scrambled for a better phrase. "I love you. That's why this whole thing is driving me crazy. Why are we talking about Angie all of a sudden?" He flexed his jaw. "That's why a single life is perfect for me; relationships have so many complications."

His words came out without thinking, and by the time he realized that his new statement had turned out worse than the first, it was too late to take any of the words back.

Leila turned and looked at him, sorrow seeping into her eyes, with moisture starting to form. She seemed to have so many unspoken words, but none came out of her mouth.

"I didn't mean for it to come out like that," he said. His hands moved to touch her, but she took a step to create more distance between them.

"I'm sorry it turned out this way," Leila said. "I hope you can live your life without any complications."

Ezra scrubbed his hand over his face. "I'm sorry, Leila," he said, his voice shaky. "I don't want it to be like this between us." She moved toward the tiny living room.

Meanwhile, Ezra told himself to stop talking, leave, and perhaps come back later when Leila was not upset anymore.

"Close the door on your way out."

Before he could say anything else, Leila disappeared into another room, slamming the door behind her, which Ezra assumed to be her bedroom.

As much as he wished to follow her, he didn't trust his tongue. On that note, Ezra made his exit and slammed the door behind him. Even as he descended the steps, he felt like he was walking out of Leila's life forever. He didn't like that feeling at all. His emotions were all jumbled up, as fear and confusion hit him like a hurricane. He'd thought she would understand how he felt about her. He didn't know anything about women. Perhaps getting his mind fixed on being single was not such a bad idea after all.

***

It was the second week in September, and Leila's new students were just as sweet as last year's class. She'd gotten into a routine at work—at least she assumed her classroom was more in control than her personal life. When she returned home to face her quiet apartment, she had no idea what to do with herself. It had been just fine being in her modest apartment before Ezra had come into her life; now she was beating herself up for the ordeal she'd created.

She'd thought giving Ezra a break would be a great thing for him to figure out if he wanted to be in a relationship, but since she'd waited too long, she was afraid Ezra was starting to feel comfortable in his single life again. Was he back with Angie? But then why did he send Leila a bouquet of wildflowers on her first day back to work? He'd included a handwritten note in his scribbled writing that she'd so come to love:

I just wanted to wish you a happy first day of school. I didn't mean to hurt you. Please forgive me. I miss your laugh. I love you!

—Ezra.

The note and flowers had left her with heaviness. Even though she'd managed to send a quick text thanking him, she'd wanted to express how much she missed him but figured she wouldn't say anything that would have him flying to see her when he probably needed more time to sort through his feelings.

She missed him so much it hurt. There hadn't been a single day that Ezra hadn't crossed her mind. Several times she'd wondered if she were doing the right thing creating distance between them. As much as she longed for Ezra and wished things would work out between them, she needed him to be sure of being in a long-term relationship. Leila didn't have time for uncertain relationships. She assumed it was best to let Ezra be.

She was meeting with Bianca and Renee for brunch at the Side Cafe in Fort Rock, and then pedicures. Since Leila had canceled Renee's lunch two weeks ago, Renee had kept calling and texting until Leila had responded. Renee had said just because Leila had a conflict with her brother didn't mean they couldn't still be friends.

"I like your new haircut by the way," Leila told Renee as they sat in the corner booth of the small restaurant.

"I love the highlights," Bianca added.

Renee's hand went to her short hair. "Thanks, girls,"

As the waitress served their coffee, the three girls browsed through the menu. They spoke to each other. Renee talked about her current home assignments, and how fast their company was growing. "I have an interview on Monday morning with ABC at the seven thirty home show."

Bianca's jaw dropped.

"Wow, that's amazing." Leila chimed in.

Bianca talked about her vet job and her consideration to join a grief share group, just as the waitress returned to take their orders.

Bianca ordered an omelet, Renee went with a veggie skillet, and Leila just ordered oatmeal. As much as the menu offered a variety of savoring meals, the last thing Leila needed was to overeat since she'd had no desire to work out lately.

"Has Ezra called you ever since he'd sent you the bouquet?" Bianca asked since Leila hadn't said much about herself.

Renee looked intrigued as she ripped open the small container of creamer.

Leila was hesitant to talk about Ezra, especially in front of his sister.

"No." She buried her face in her coffee cup.

"Ezra sent you a bouquet?" Renee's eyes widened. "I'm glad you're finally back together."

Bianca glanced at Leila as if encouraging her to share the details. Leila found herself telling Renee about the sweet note Ezra had sent with the flowers. "He said he missed my laugh and loved me."

Leila felt a lump in her throat, and tapped her fingers to her cup, keeping her gaze down in case a tear decided to escape. Renee must have picked up on her change of emotion.

"Speaking of which"—Renee leaned forward and rested her arms on the table—"I tend not to ignore things when it comes to two people who belong together." She shot a gaze at Leila. "Seriously, what happened between you and my brother? He will not talk to me. I know that he's hurting as much as you are."

Leila lifted her cup of coffee to her mouth and gulped the rest of the warm drink as if she were in a coffee drinking contest.

"Maybe we better not talk about it . . . ," Leila shrugged, as she placed her empty cup to the table, but Renee folded her arms and stared at Leila as if waiting for her to spill it out.

Leila finally told her everything about Angie and confessed that she'd canceled their dinner because she'd needed to be alone after her encounter with Angie.

Renee shook her head, "And you believed her?"

"Well," Leila sighed, "Angie's words held a lot of truth to them."

Renee's brows furrowed. "Do you know how hard it is to find someone you love, and who loves you in return?" She explained how Ezra had been miserable for the last two weeks, and how surly he'd been whenever she'd called him. "I would love to have what you two have," she slapped the table. "Call him."

What kept Leila from calling Ezra was either pride in herself or the fear of what he would say. The fact that she'd dragged this on for two weeks made it harder for her to call. At least Ezra had sent her flowers and a note apologizing. But again, for a guy who didn't want commitment in the first place, Leila didn't feel capable of changing his thoughts.

"I need to give him more time," Leila said.

Renee opened her mouth as if to say something, but then closed it and shook her head instead.

The three of them stared at their cups for a few minutes, until Bianca spoke.

"You're very blessed, Leila, and as your friend, I have to tell you that relationships take work," Bianca told her about how she and her deceased husband had arguments all the time. "Disagreements are healthy in any relationship, that's how John and I grew as a couple." She gave Leila a concentrated gaze. "Ezra loves you, and I know that you love him, too. If you keep pushing him away, using Angie as an excuse, it seems to me you're deciding for him. Don't let the ice princess routine linger on too long; otherwise, it may keep you from having the man of your dreams."

Leila wanted to argue but knew that both her friends were right. Perhaps she would figure out a way to call Ezra sometime next week. It would have to be a weekend when she didn't have to work, in case Ezra was available for them to meet and talk.

She gave a hesitant nod. Deciding not to remain the center of attention, Leila redirected the conversation. She shared about her new devotional app, and both Bianca and Renee finished sharing about their daily routines just in time for the waitress to show up with their food. They prayed, ate, and drove off for their pedicure appointment.

***

Two long, lonely weeks had passed for Ezra, and he figured it was just the beginning of many more lonely weeks in his life. He wondered how he could go back to the days before he'd met Leila, wishing he'd never gone camping the same week as her. He'd lost Leila, yet he'd gotten used to having her a part of his life.

Why did Angie have to come into his life? He regretted not being able to make it clear with Angie sooner that he wasn't interested in her. The fact that Leila had brought up Angie out of the blue continued to be a puzzle he would never solve on his own. He wished he'd asked her, but his temper had taken over when he had the opportunity to talk with her.

With so many unanswered questions roaming through his mind, he'd decided to focus on work for the last two weeks. That was the one thing he was good at.

He'd volunteered for any available shifts to keep busy. The last thing he'd needed was free time to think about Leila. But even with that, he'd been curt with everyone.

He'd gone to visit his parents on Labor Day weekend, one week after he'd walked away from Leila. Thankfully, his brother had to work, and his sister had gone out of town on a business trip. The last thing he needed was to answer to anyone about where his relationship with Leila stood, although his mom, aware of the situation, knew the right words of comfort as she always did. She told him to pray and weigh how much he wanted this relationship, and if it was worth it. Regardless of whether he thought he was right in the matter, taking the blame and asking for forgiveness would go a long way.

At first, Ezra's pride got in the way, but then his mom's words got to him. He needed to let Leila know that he still loved her and that she mattered to him in every single way. He'd sent her flowers and a note, wishing her a happy first day of school.

Leila had sent him a basic text that afternoon thanking him for the note and flowers. What was he supposed to do after that? At least he'd done his part in trying to fight for their relationship. As he rested his head on his pillow staring at the ceiling in the darkest part of the morning, Ezra contemplated what he'd do if Leila never got back into his life.

The vibration on his phone caught him by surprise. Perhaps it was Leila. His heart skipped at the thought. But then he'd done the same thing over the last two weeks each time his phone rang or buzzed, assuming it was Leila calling to let him know, that she wanted him back in her life.

His alarm clock lit the numbers, and it was five a.m. He grabbed his phone from the nightstand, and disappointment darkened his mood at the sight of his brother's name. He loved hearing from his brother, but not when he had Leila clouding his mind.

He took a long breath.

"Do you know what time it is?" Ezra grumbled.

"If that's the way you answer the phone, you will be out of fans in no time." Andrew's voice dripped with sarcastic humor.

Ezra didn't feel up to the cheer and banter.

"Perhaps you should read the proverb that says that a loud and cheerful greeting early in the morning will be taken as a curse. Do you know that I have to get ready for work?" He raked his hair and gave a loud yawn.

"I know you will need a caffeine overdose at the rate you're yawning." Andrew chuckled through the phone, completely ignoring the proverb comment. He said, "Anyway, I will cut right to the chase, little brother."Have you talked to Leila lately?"

Ezra had already had a conversation with his brother the week he'd argued with Leila, but Andrew had told him things would work out since normal couples had fights. He'd called to follow up, but Ezra hadn't returned his calls since he didn't have an update for him yet.

"Is that why you called?"

"If you answer every question with a question, it will take me a while to get my point across."

A heavy silence followed before Ezra answered, "No, why?"

"Because, little brother, you should talk to the girl no matter what happened between you two," Andrew said. "If you take too long, you will both start being comfortable in your familiar single lives."

Ezra knew that wasn't the case for him at all. It would take him longer than two to three years, if not forever, to forget about Leila. As for Andrew always being the expert with relationships, Ezra doubted his brother had ever been in his shoes.

"I already did my part," Ezra said and told Andrew about his note and the flowers.

"That was a great gesture to send flowers, but think about what Leila means to you. How much do you love her, and to what extent would you go to try to have her back in your life?"

Andrew was always the practical one, and confident when it came to relationships—unlike Ezra, who took the cowardly route whenever he had no idea what to do. He gave his best when it came to rescuing people's lives, but his love life was another failed story of his life.

"I . . ." Ezra felt a tightness in his chest and a lump in his throat that he didn't want his brother to recognize through his voice. He cleared his throat and rephrased, "I love her so much," he said, his voice now thick with emotion. "Even if I try to forget about her, I can't picture my future without her in it. The oddest thing is, I find myself smiling when I think of the little things she does when we're together. Like the way she laughs at my dry jokes." Ezra's face creased with a smile at the thought. "She constantly smothers her lips with lip balm, even when her lips are fully moist. The way she tucks a strand of hair behind her ear when she gets nervous." The list went on, but the knot in his throat choked out the words. He lay back on his pillow and remained silent with the phone on his ear.

Andrew remained silent too, and for a moment Ezra thought his brother had hung up.

"Drew, are you still there?"

"Yes, I'm still here. You're passionate about saving lives. Now, do yourself a favor and apply that same dedication in your relationship. I've never heard you this passionate about any woman before."

His brother rattled off several steps he thought Ezra should take to get Leila back. He suggested Ezra show up at her place of work or camp out at her door until she let him inside. Whatever Ezra needed to do to get her attention.

After their long chat, Andrew concluded the conversation with, "That's what I would do if I loved someone as much as you love that girl."

After they hung up, Ezra got himself ready for another long twenty-four-hour shift at work. As head of shift, he usually arrived before anyone else, and he wasn't about to break that habit no matter how broken up he was over Leila.

CHAPTER 20

WHILE PERFORMING a general inspection in the bay, Ezra stood with a clipboard and a pen in his hand. He was taking notes on what might need to be fixed or replaced, or any missing parts from their equipment. The rest of the guys were in their designated areas, Jake wiping the engine in the driveway and Miguel checking the tools for the engine.

"Hey, Leila sent more donuts," Dalton said, his mouth full, as he held a half-eaten chocolate donut in his hand.

Ezra turned his gaze to the probationary officer, who was in charge of starting the saws as protocol for their morning routine, to make sure they were in excellent condition.

Hearing Leila's name reminded Ezra of how he'd messed up things with her.

Until recently, Leila had been having donuts delivered twice a week to their station from a nearby bakery. The guys had been grumbling that he should apologize for whatever he'd done so they could have

431

their donuts. This morning, Ezra had stopped by the bakery and bought some donuts.

Ezra snapped. "Hey, get yourself over here and start the saws."

Dalton blinked rapidly and shoved the rest of his donut in his pocket, then pulled out the six different kinds of saws. He didn't look as confident as all the other guys when it came to machine operation just yet.

"And how do I recheck the belt tension?" Dalton asked, avoiding eye contact with Ezra.

Ezra had already been on edge for the last two weeks, and even after his chat with his brother that morning, his mood was still tense.

"Are you kidding me?" He threw his pen to the ground. "How long will it take you to get familiar with the equipment?" Ezra ranted and gave the young man an earful about how he should be familiar with the equipment by now. The boy's shoulders were tight. He stiffly bent and picked up Ezra's pen and handed it to him.

Ezra sensed the tension as he gained an audience from his captain and the other two guys in the bay. Rarely did Ezra lose his temper at work; he only raised his voice if any of the crew had put their lives in danger, and safety was a factor.

"You're going to spend the next thirty minutes relearning the startup process," he spoke, in a low tone. "I'm sorry," he said and made his way to his office.

He drowned himself in paperwork while his unit finished up with their morning chores. Perhaps he could work on his attitude.

***

The next morning Ezra sat in his office, confused with raging emotions. He stared at the paperwork on his desk, raking his hands through his hair, his eyes darted to the clock on the wall. It was only six a.m. He'd been working on paperwork since five a.m. Thankful for Tuesday morning, he was looking forward to another forty-eight hours off. He hoped it would be long enough to make his peace with Leila, but she had to work, and he had no clue what she would say if he just showed up at her apartment.

"Little Buchanan is here," Jake Larson said, popping his head into the office where Ezra sat entering updates on the computer.

He squeezed his eyes shut wondering why his sister had showed up at his workplace this early in the morning. That couldn't be good. Unsure of the time, Ezra glanced at the clock on the wall again and saw that it was 6:40 a.m. Why his siblings chose to hound him within the same twenty-four-hour shift, he was about to find out.

"Did she say why she was here?"

"I don't know," Jake said and pointed a warning finger to Ezra. "But she doesn't look too happy. You know how your sister can be when she's upset. Anyway, I tried to calm her down a little; I think she's a bit relaxed. It would be best if you two spoke in your office, though..."

Renee stepped in before Jake made his exit.

Jake shot Ezra a look that said Good luck, man and moved out of their way. Ezra turned to face a fuming Renee.

"Hey," Ezra said while his sister paced in his office. "Shouldn't you be at home?" Ezra's eyes went to the clock on the wall. "Or at work?"

"I figured I could catch you before you left for your break." One of Renee's hands went to her waist while the other clung to the shoulder strap on her purse. "But I'm here for a reason."

Ezra figured whatever his sister had to say; perhaps she'd been sent over by their brother, Andrew.

"Are you going to have a seat?" Ezra straightened and leaned back in his chair and motioned for Renee to take the extra chair on the opposite side of the table.

"Aren't you entitled to some happiness?" Renee demanded as anger rose in her tone.

Ezra's eyes widened, "What are you talking about?"

"Why are you not going after her?" she said, throwing her purse on the table.

"Is this about Leila?"

"No, it's about Angie," she said with heavy sarcasm.

Ezra's face creased into a frown as he leaned forward on the desk.

"Is Leila okay? Did Angie do something?"

"She was okay until she left the fire station two weeks ago."

"I don't have the patience for riddles today. If you're trying to make a point, I'm afraid you're going to need to be more specific," Ezra rose from his seat and crossed his arms over his chest. "The last time Leila came over, she was here to pick me up after an afternoon shift."

Renee stared at him a moment, and her angry posture relaxed. "You have no clue what I'm talking about, do you?" She took the chair across from Ezra's desk and gestured him back to the seat. "Turns out Leila stopped by to bring you brownies, the same day we were supposed to meet at my house for dinner." She crossed one leg over the other and explained everything Leila had shared about her encounter with Angie.

Ezra's mind remained stuck in confusion.

Both hands went to his face. No wonder Leila had been so bent out of shape over Angie that day. How could he blame her?

"Come to think of it . . ." His hand tapped on his temple as if reflecting. He then told Renee how Angie had approached him and said she was still available if things with Leila didn't work out.

"Isn't Angie that same girl you'd told me about who's been nagging you to have dinner with her?"

Ezra nodded.

"And that was the last time Angie was here." Ezra had seen Angie that Sunday afternoon, and she'd stayed throughout their night tour.

"Leila must have come when we were called out for the extrication emergency."

After a brief silence, Ezra nodded and said, "I know what I need to do." His future with Leila was at stake, and the sooner he did something, the better chance he would have of fixing the damage he'd done.

"Do you?" Renee asked, her eyes doubtful.

Ezra shook his head. "I'm not sure actually," he said reluctantly. "She's the one who ended things between us."

"You're ridiculous." Renee rose from her seat and took a step closer to her brother. "Who says relationships are easy? All good things take work. As much as she misses you, if you wait for her to come to you, it might be a while. She told me she was waiting for you to figure out what you wanted."

Ezra placed a hand on his sister's shoulder. "If you've ever helped me, now is the time I need you." His eyes pleading, he said, "It's moments like this, you can interfere with my business." He smiled softly.

"I don't need your permission to interfere with your business." She smiled playfully. "God already permitted me when He made me your sister." Curious, she asked, "What's your plan?"

"I want to see Leila, but I'm going to need your help."

After Ezra explained his plan, Renee still looked doubtful but told him she would try. Ezra knew that his sister rarely took no for an answer. And if anyone was going to help him get to Leila, it was going to be her. They departed, and all Ezra had to do was pray and hope that his plan would work.

***

The last twenty-four-hour shift felt like the longest of all Ezra's tours. Not a second went by that he did not think about Leila. After his sister had left him on Tuesday morning, he'd worked hard on his attitude around his colleagues as he waited anxiously for Saturday.

Regardless of how things stood with Leila, it didn't stop him from daydreaming and imagining her in his future. He felt a sudden urge to marry her and be done with the conflicting drama that happened during dating.

A part of him didn't want to scare Leila by not giving her enough time to figure out if he was the man for her, but the other part longed to have her at all costs. He wanted to come home to the woman he adored, to talk to her, relax on the couch after a long day and watch a fun TV show together.

He closed his eyes as he sat on the wooden bench in the locker room. He'd been trying to lace his shoes for several minutes, but his mind was too preoccupied to concentrate on a shoelace. What was Leila doing at the moment? He knew she was awake because she was a morning person. He couldn't wait to tell her what she meant to him and that he was determined to commit to her because he loved her. He had a relationship to fight for, and for the first time in his life, he was confident that Leila was worth every effort he had to give.

He wondered how long people should date before proposing. If there were a way to skip the proposal and marry Leila today, he would do it. He missed her terribly, and according to what his sister told him, it sounded like she missed him too.

"What are your plans today, bro?" Jake asked when he walked into the locker room.

Ignoring Jake's question, Ezra presented a pressing question of his own. "Is it too soon to ask Leila to marry me?"

Jake stayed silent for a few seconds, then sighed. "You're asking the wrong person. Remember I'm divorced?" he said with a questioning look.

"That's why I'm asking the right person." He thought of what Leila had told him when they were camping. "The fastest way to learn anything was to use the experiences of others-taking the good and making it your own while leaving their mistakes behind." He would have to ask Curie next, or Miguel.

Ezra was surprised when Jake responded, "Well, if you are marrying her because you love her and you feel she's the one, then you can ask her today. however, if you are marrying her because you're scared to be alone"—he pulled a shirt from his locker and threw it in his duffle bag—"then you're better off staying single."

In Jake's case, as he'd gradually moved on from his painful divorce, he'd shared with Ezra how he'd rushed into marriage because he'd been vulnerable. He'd just lost his dad and so much was going on.

"Thanks, Larson," Ezra said genuinely.

"You seem to be in your right mind, and I think Leila would be right for you, bro." Jake nodded his head in assurance and added, "She's not the kind of girl looking for a hotshot firefighter. I can tell she loves you for who you are. Go for it." He slapped Ezra's shoulder and made his exit.

Leila had won favor among all Ezra's friends and his family. With the donuts she'd had delivered at the fire station, until two weeks ago, no wonder everyone at work had been aware of Leila's absence over the past two weeks.

Ezra rose and made his exit with great anticipation for what the day held.

***

The crisp sunny morning matched Leila's mood as she opened the blinds and enjoyed the beautiful view of Pikes Peak. She was confident that today was going to be a good day, filled with promise.

After back-to-back phone calls and texts, Bianca and Renee convinced Leila to meet at the campground they'd stayed at during the summer so they could ride together from there to see the fall colors in the high country. Since Leila lived on the opposite side of town, Renee and Bianca were car-pooling and would meet Leila there.

Leila had objected to taking this trip since she'd wanted to call Ezra this weekend, but Renee had told her that Ezra had to work. Perhaps this would give her enough time to think of what she was going to say. She wasn't too keen about the meeting place since she didn't want memories of Ezra haunting her, but Renee had called four days in a row giving her multiple reasons why that was the perfect place for them to meet. The more Leila thought about it, the more she liked the idea of seeing the same scenery during a different season. Her thoughts went to capturing some fall photos.

The familiar elevated blue Jeep caught Leila's attention as she pulled into the campground's main parking lot. She knew Ezra's Jeep inside and out since she'd ridden in it several times. But maybe Renee had borrowed her brother's car since they needed to drive on the back country roads. Was Renee rubbing it in for Leila today? It was hard enough to be back at the place where she'd spent a whole week with Ezra, let alone ride in his Jeep without him in it.

Since no one was in the Jeep, Leila assumed there was only one place the girls could be. She made her way to Site One.

She assumed there were no tenants at Site One since not many people camped in the high elevated places in late September. The weather conditions were unpredictable during this time of the year.

The campground looked beautiful with the golden hues of the maple leaves contrasting with the vivid tones of the evergreens. She couldn't wait to make it to the memorable scenery by the meadow.

As she walked farther along the vast property and made her way to the creek, her eyes were met by the handsome, familiar face of Ezra Buchanan. The same guy who made her heart skip each time she saw him. He was dressed in the same blue Colorado State T-shirt that he'd worn the first day Leila met him at the gas station. He was leaning against the tree, his hand to his neck. Why wasn't he sitting down so that Leila could sneak up behind him? His eyes held a steady gaze toward Leila. Now that her heart was in her throat, she had no idea how she was going to breathe.

Ezra leaned against the tree and watched Leila ascend toward him. Regardless of whether things worked out today, he would have to thank his sister for getting Leila here. If there was one thing Ezra had learned about Leila, it was her dislike of surprises. He hoped she would be okay with seeing him instead of her friends. His pulse raced as Leila neared. Emotions crowded his mind as he pictured an angel in the form of Leila walking toward him. Even though dressed in her stretchy tight pants and a tan sweater with a hot pink owl in the chest, she had her dark hair down; he liked it that way. She was his angel.

He felt vulnerable as the need arose in him to race toward her and sweep her off her feet.

At that moment, his mind pictured his future bride walking down the aisle. The woman he would love as much as Christ loves the church.

When Ezra smiled at her, her face creased into a shy smile as she tucked a loose strand of hair behind her ear. A familiar nervous gesture. It was the same smile that made Ezra lose some of his senses, and the cue he needed to put his thoughts into action.

Ezra took the remaining steps and met Leila, sweeping her off her feet and into a full embrace. He knew they needed to talk, but he didn't care. The talking could wait.

"I missed you so much," he said, his voice hoarse.

He was relieved when Leila responded by holding tight onto him, her head buried in his chest, and Ezra drowned himself in the familiar, earthy scents of her conditioner and luscious oils.

She responded softly, "I missed you too."

Ezra stabilized her feet to the ground and cupped her face to look at her. "I know we need to talk, but can it wait for a few more minutes?"

She nodded, moisture from her eyes slowly falling onto her cheeks. Ezra assumed it was tears of joy because he could feel some of his own through the knot in his throat.

Ezra's emotions were a mixture of assurance and passion. A determination never to let go. He wiped the tears rolling down her cheeks, then kissed her eyes and made his way to her lips, kissing her soundly with raw emotion. He loved her so much it hurt. His fingers dug into her soft black hair as he deepened the kiss, savoring each moment like it was the first day of the rest of their future together.

Leila's feet wobbled, and she lost her balance. Ezra picked her up and carried her to the bench where they'd shared their first kiss in the summertime.

He drew a finger over her parted lips. "You're so beautiful," he said and kissed her softly. Neither was aware of their surroundings; like two teenagers, they were too lost in their own world.

Thankfully, Site One was isolated from all the others, and the site itself looked deserted.

"I love you so much," he murmured against her mouth.

She murmured in response, "I love you too, Ezra."

By the time they were done making out like teenagers, they both needed to catch their breath. They sat a while longer Ezra stretched his long arm around Leila's shoulder. He kept her close, never wanting to let her go again.

They talked about Angie, and both took responsibility for their two-week separation. "If I had been firm with her right from the beginning, perhaps she wouldn't have felt hopeful," Ezra said.

They stared at the scenery, "I can't let you take all the blame. Leila said I think I played a vital role as well. If I'd chosen to talk to you instead of pouting about what Angie had said, we would never have wasted that time away from each other."

Ezra had confronted Angie on Thursday when she'd come to substitute for a guy from Shift B and had asked her what she'd told Leila during her visit, but he didn't get much from her except, "I told her you can't commit to women, and you will dump her as soon as another girl comes along." Ezra knew she'd probably been harsh toward Leila and had said more than that. When he asked her what she wanted from him and why she was still bent out of shape, her response took him by surprise— she'd said she was paying him back for not going out with her. A very immature thing to do, if anybody asked him.

He'd made himself more clear with Angie this time.

"Let's make up for lost time," Ezra said as he rose with his hand still in Leila's.

"I guess this explains why your sister called me for four days consecutively." Leila rose and arched her eyebrow.

Ezra chuckled. Knowing his sister like he did, she was persistent and even more stubborn than Ezra or Andrew.

"That sounds like my sister."

"And I assume you don't have to work this weekend, too?"

"I just got off work this morning."

"I like an Ezra-Leila day even better." Leila leaned into him. "Shouldn't you be sleeping though?"

Being with Leila was way better than sleep.

"I have the rest of my life to sleep. Let's go see some fall colors."

They were off to a place where Leila knew nothing about except for the man taking her.

The rest of the day, Ezra and Leila spent driving to the different parts of the mountain. They rode to various places in Ezra's Jeep. Leila took a few pictures, and she was awed by God's beauty as she remembered the green valley over the summer, which were now a mixture of red, orange, and yellow in the midst of the green pines.

They shared the lunch that Ezra had packed from home, and plantain chips with soda. Ezra had planned out the entire day. About mid-afternoon, they drove to the scenic area where Ezra had been stung by a bee during their camping trip.

A few people were enjoying the view and taking pictures. Leila snapped a few more photos and slid her camera back into her sling bag so she could enjoy the view and the rustling sound of all the golden leaves falling off the trees.

"I've never seen so many vibrant colors before."

"I'm glad I get to see the colors with you." Ezra stood right next to her and gave her a soft kiss on the forehead. "Fall is my second favorite season," he said.

Even though Leila spent most of her days indoors regardless of the season, after this past year and all the exposure that Ezra had given her to the outdoors, she was already looking forward to next summer.

"Summer is my favorite season, and I have you to thank for that." She smiled at him dreamily.

"Turns out that summer is my favorite season, too. For more reasons than just being outdoors." He turned to face her and took her hands in his, stroking the back of her palm with his thumb. "It was a love match at first sight that God used the campground's scenery for us to connect. I fell in love with you instantly, even though I tried to ignore it, but God created more encounters for us to see each other again. I know without a doubt that God has placed you in my life. Even if I have a hard time hearing His voice. I guess what I am saying is . . ." Releasing her hands, he pulled out a black velvet box from his pocket and went down on one knee, and Leila caught her breath.

In his hand, he opened the box that held a glittering round diamond bordered with smaller accent sparkles.

"From that first day at the gas station when I heard your melodic laugh, I knew I wanted to hear it again and again. I want to be a part of your life, and I want to explore the outdoors with you always. Leila Morgan, you are my home. I feel at home whenever I am with you. Will you marry me?"

Her eyes misty, she looked into his stormy gray eyes, and she saw exactly what she was looking for: so much love, words couldn't contain. Instantly, her heart confirmed what she already knew—that Ezra was her home, too. With overwhelming emotions, she swallowed and said, "Yes, yes. With all my heart. I will marry you, Ezra Buchanan!" She shut her eyes, trying to rein in the tears.

"I love you, Ezra," she said as he rose and lifted her left hand, sliding the ring onto her finger. He kissed the finger tenderly then, swept her into his arms, and kissed her longingly and possessively.

The rest of the crowd around them joined in cheers when they finally noticed what was happening. People congratulated them, and one lady offered to take their picture.

Leila smiled up into Ezra's face as the camera flashed. She knew this would be a photo they would treasure forever.

EPILOGUE

IT HAD BEEN one year since Ezra and Leila met on their camping trip, and the seventy-degree weather was perfect for their two o'clock June wedding, at the Hidden Valley Campground. Pastor Jeer, Ezra's pastor, was officiating the wedding, Leila had come to know the kind man over the last three months of their counseling sessions. Confined in a wheel chair after his accident a year ago, hadn't kept him from leading his congregation.

Since Leila hadn't built a connection with her pastor, she'd thought it would be special for Pastor Jeer, and his special relationship to Ezra to be the one to perform the ceremony.

Chris Morgan would be walking his daughter down the aisle. Daisy was the flower girl, and Bianca was Leila's maid of honor. Renee, Andrew, Jake, and Leila's brother, Brian, made up the wedding party. All of Ezra's colleagues from work and church friends were in attendance. Leila had a few of her work colleagues and church friends there as well. Altogether, there were about two hundred people in attendance

The whole campground had was reserved for the weekend, with chairs nicely spread out between the tall aspens and pine trees. The ground was blanketed by pine needles and hot pink flower petals. A beautiful white linen spread in the center to create an aisle for the bride to ascend.

A soft knock sounded on the door of the RV, and Leila didn't hesitate. "Come in," Leila said as she gazed in the fifth wheel's dressing mirror.

Bianca handed Leila a bouquet of wildflowers in purple, white and pink, and then hugged her. "You look gorgeous."

"I already feel teary, Bianca!"

"It's okay to shed some tears of joy. This is your day, let's go."

They left the fifth wheel to meet Chris, who was waiting by the door.

He studied Leila, and asked, "How are you feeling?"

"Nervous!"

He smiled, "Sweetheart, I want you to know that I'm so proud of you, and I have no doubt that Ezra is the kind of man who will love and cherish you always. He's perfect for my adorable daughter." His voice filled with emotion "I have watched the two of you together, and I must say, you are going to make one great team. The love you both feel for each other is so pure and wonderful. You are so beautiful. I love you."

She hugged her father, trying so hard to prevent the tears from coming out.

"I love you too, Dad."

As the bridal march began, Daisy walked up the aisle with her basket of white, pink, and purple wildflower petals, sprinkling the flowers along the path ahead of her, like an angel spreading goodwill and love over the land.

Leila walked with her dad, ascending toward the spread-out camp, taking in the smell of pine and enjoying the view of the meadow. She marched confidently, with her head lifted, and her heart soared as she smiled at the man who waited for her at the other end underneath a tree. Possessed of sun-kissed brown hair and gray eyes, and handsome in his navy-blue suit, white shirt, and a hot pink bow tie to compliment her bouquet, Ezra stood with all the similarly-dressed groomsmen standing by his side, and the bridesmaids in their purple dresses standing in their positions.

It was the first time Leila had seen Ezra dressed in a suit, and he was just perfect.

Ezra was smiling at her, and in his eyes was a light that told her everything she needed to know.

Receiving her with a broad smile and eyes filled with unshed tears, he couldn't feel any reason not to be thankful for the special love he'd found.

Leila's hands stayed in Ezra's as they turned to the pastor as he read 1 Corinthians 13:4–8. "Love is patient; love is kind. It does not envy; it is not proud... "

Thirty minutes later, the pastor turned his gaze to the new couple and said, "I now pronounce you husband and wife." His eyes moved to the groom. "Ezra, you may kiss your bride."

"Mom, close your eyes," Ezra teased, bringing the congregation to an uproar of laughter. His mom, sitting in the front row, stretched her silk scarf toward him as if hitting him with it.

Leila's heart filled with overflowing love as Ezra took her in his arms and brushed his lips against hers.

"May I present to you Mr. and Mrs. Ezra Buchanan," the pastor pronounced.

Leila let out a long breath as Ezra turned to her once again and pulled her into his embrace. Knowing at last that she was his and he was hers.

She tossed the bouquet as they started to march toward the fifth wheel trailer.

Renee screamed in excitement when she caught the bouquet.

An hour later, everybody was enjoying a wide variety of meats catered by the Brazilian steakhouse where Ezra and Leila had had their first real date. Everybody was happy in the great outdoors as they celebrated with the bride and groom at the Hidden Valley Campground's First Site.

If you enjoyed First Site, please consider leaving a review on Amazon or Good Reads. Thanks!

If you enjoyed Ezra and Leila's story, don't miss the next book in

THE BUCHANAN series.

Jake and Renee's bumpy ride. A broken heart is mended.

COMING SOON...

SOMETHING RIGHT

Jake Larson is good at everything...except relationships. When his marriage ends, it leaves the firefighter with doubts he's never experienced before. Now he's determined to protect his crushed heart the only way he knows how: avoid falling in love at all costs. And thanks to his friend Ezra, Jake is more than content to fill the hole in his life with a newfound faith in Christ and the hope for a brighter—if single—future.

Renee Buchanan is one of the best interior designers Colorado has to offer, and she knows it. She's young, skilled, and confident...except when she's around Jake Larson. Every time Jake steps into a room, her carefully crafted professionalism crumbles, and she finds herself lost.

And that's a problem when Jake hires Renee to decorate his fixer-upper of a home. Not only is Jake her brother's best friend, he's also the gentleman of her dreams. And no matter how determined she is to make this the well-designed house of her career, and how thick the walls around Jake's heart are, something new sizzles up between them, something they can't help but be drawn toward.

As they work together to chip away at the walls of both Jake's house and his heart, Jake is faced with a life-changing decision: let himself fall for his best friend's beautiful sister, or stay single but keep his friendship intact. Either way, Jake knows he must let go of his past before he can grab hold of the future...or else risk losing the second chance he desperately needs.

Something Right is a sweet interracial romance between a damaged firefighter and the architect determined to make him whole again.

A NOTE FROM THE AUTHOR

Dear Reader,

Thank you for reading, First Site. The last five summers, my family has had the opportunity to go camping with friends. All our kids have such a great time exploring the outdoors and we have so much fun together at the extensive site at one of the Campgrounds at the National Forest. Although "First Site" does not strictly focus on the camp and the activities we do with other families, it is with those special fond memories in mind that I wrote this story.

Although I am not specific in this story, I pictured the campground as I wrote. The special memories with the friends we camp with are sweet beyond description.

I hope you've enjoyed Ezra and Leila's story as much as I have in writing it.

This is my first attempt at Fiction, and I thoroughly enjoyed it since I live in Colorado and I love spending time outdoors.

This is a fictitious story, and I plan to add two more books to develop some of the characters from First site. The next book in the series is; Something Right.

I hope you can sign up for the newsletter for an update; https://rosefresquez.com/blog/

God bless you,

Rose Fresquez

ABOUT THE AUTHOR

Rose Fresquez is the author of two family devotionals; The Ten Commandments for kids and Signed & Delivered. She's married to her prince charming and is the proud mother of four amazing kids. When she's not busy taking care of her family, she's writing. You can contact or learn more about all her upcoming books at https://rosefresquez.com.

You can also visit her Face book page, https://www.facebook.com/rosefresquezbooks/

Twitter: @fresquezfans

Alternatively, e-mail her at rjfresquez@gmail.com

Sign-up to receive her newsletters at; https://rosefresquez.com/blog/

Made in the USA
San Bernardino, CA
23 November 2018